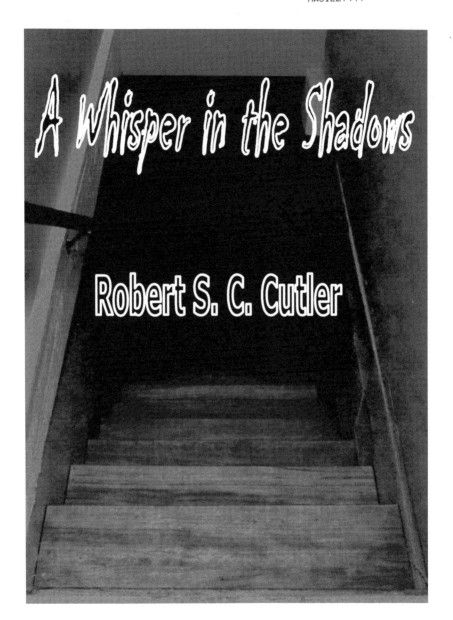

# A Whisper in the Shadows

## Robert S. C. Cutler

*For April,*

*whose love of my stories*

*has inspired me to write.*

# Prologue

## 1964

Norah climbed up into the passenger side of her husband's pickup in search of a fresh pack of Viceroys, but instead found a white, glossy bag on the bench seat where his work gloves usually lay. Confused by her find, she ran her fingers over the embossed gold and black lettering. She had never heard of Andrew's Kansas City Boutique. Neither she nor Gary had been out of the Wichita area within the past two years. The farm, although small, had grown to be too demanding.

Unable to contain her curiosity, Norah opened the bag and removed a sleek, black box with raised gold lettering. "Perfume?" she said out loud. "Why would he have perfume?"

Excited by the surprise of a rare gift, she opened the box and sprayed her wrist. The soft aroma of Jasmine filled the cab of the truck.

The two large barn doors slammed opened, startling Norah back to conscious reality. Frightened of being caught, she jumped out of the truck, taking the perfume with her.

Gary emerged from the barn carrying an old axle from one of his many tractors. He was a large man, well over six-foot tall and weighing two-hundred-thirty pounds. His insulated coveralls and knit cap made him look even more imposing. He tossed the antiquated hunk of metal effortlessly into the bed with a loud clang, bouncing the truck almost off of its back tires.

"Norah?" he called toward the house. "Go 'in to town. Be back after dark… Norah?" He shook his head in disgust from the lack of response.

Norah was hiding in their upstairs bedroom, peering down at her husband just on the other side of the curtains. Feeling she had ruined his surprise, she became distraught with panic and guilt. She watched with great apprehension as Gary first climbed into the cab and then paused when the lingering perfume hit his nostrils. He made a quick search for the white bag, then jumped back out—clearly agitated—scanning the front of the house for his wife.

In haste to make amends, she knocked the bottle of perfume onto the hardwood floor as she turned to run downstairs—shattering the glass and saturating the room with the potent odor. Overwhelmed by the fumes, she opened the bedroom window, letting the cold January air in to clear her head.

"Oh, no!" she said, seeing her husband walking back to the truck. "Gary! Please, wait!"

Rushing to catch her husband, Norah ran dead into him as he stood waiting for her in at the bottom of the stairs. Her slender body bounced off of his large chest, sending her flailing backward.

Gary's face was contorted and reddened by pure rage. He raised a threatening hand, swinging wildly but missed as Norah scurried passed him. "Goddamn, bitch! Can't keep your nose out of my business!"

"Please, Gary. I'm sorry I made you angry. I thought the perfume was for me."

"Why in the hell would I buy you anything? You're nothing but a barren, useless whore!"

Norah's voice quivered. "Why are you talking this way? What did I do? I don't understand!"

"Shut the hell up!" he said, kicking at her and making contact with his heavy work boot. "I should've left you years ago when I had the chance. The only thing you're good for is an occasional lay and to cook my dinner. Neither one has ever been worth the while."

Norah writhed in pain. Her left thigh throbbed and burned. She couldn't believe the hateful words that were flowing so easily out of her husband's mouth.

Gary moved to kick again causing Norah to cower and cover her head. The scent of Jasmine stopped him mid-stride. His eyes narrowed as he sniffed the air. "What did you do?"

"I'm sorry. I broke it on accident. Gary, please..."

"That was a fifty dollar bottle of perfume! Fifty dollars!"

"Who is she, Gary? Please, I've got to know."

"No one you would ever know. She's young, beautiful—nothing like you at all."

He walked out the door, leaving his despondent wife huddled on the floor. His thoughts had already wondered back to the soft, warm body that was waiting for him in Wichita. In his arrogant mind he could easily make his young girlfriend forget about the perfume he had promised.

Before Norah could get up off the floor, the truck's engine roared to life. The back tires fought to gain traction, spitting out gravel in all directions as Gary tore down the long drive to the main road. Hoping to catch him, Norah ran outside, but was too late. His engine faded into the cold night.

A heavy snow started to fall. Norah turned to face the old farmhouse, dejected. The large front porch that had always been a good friend looked dark and uninviting.

**\*\*\*\*\*\*\*\*\*\***

Gary stood outside his girlfriend's apartment, pounding on the door and calling her name. He knew she was home—he could see the light from the television and movement through the curtains. Annoyed that she wasn't answering, he turned to leave, but stopped short when he heard the sound of another man's voice coming from inside. Enraged with jealously, he hit the front door hard with his fist; leaving it ajar and hanging on just one of its three hinges. Clothed in only a camisole and panties, his young girlfriend ran screaming into the back bedroom.

Gary's world flattened out—his vision became sharp—his mind set on one thing: he wanted to find whomever the voice belonged to and tear him apart. The muffled cries of his girlfriend resonated inside his head. He followed them through the cluttered living-room and down the small hallway. Standing sentinel in front of the bedroom door was a young, blonde man trying his best to look imposing. Gary towered over and out weighed the boy by as much as seventy-five pounds.

With one swift kick, the bottom of Gary's right boot made solid contact with the young man's sternum, sending him flying through the closed door. Lying on his back, he struggled to breathe—his narrow chest rising slowly with each breath. Gary pounced on him, driving his large fist into the kid's head and face multiple times until he had stopped breathing all together.

The girl screamed again seeing her insanely jealous boyfriend rise up with his coveralls and face splattered with blood. Attempting to get out of his reach, she scooted back on the bed only to get tangled in the bedspread and sheets.

Gary grabbed hold of her long, brown hair. He pulled her kicking and flailing body close to his—muffling her screams in his powerful grasp. Kissing her hard on the mouth he squeezed with all of his might. Her ribs snapped one by one. The air released slowly from her lungs and out of her blood filled mouth, exciting Gary; giving him cause to squeeze even harder. Feeling the young girl's body relax and become limp, he loosened his grip, allowing her to crumple onto the bed.

The concerned voices of the girl's neighbors startled Gary back to reality. In a rare moment of panic, he tried in vain to cover her lifeless body with the twisted sheet. After reassessing the situation, he came to the conclusion that it was time to leave. He removed his blood-splattered coveralls and knit cap, wadding them beneath his arm. The curtain in the next window moved alerting him that he was being watched. He jumped into the cab of his truck without bothering to clean the accumulated snow off of the windshield and drove off, fishtailing out onto the main road, but not until the neighbor had written down his license plate number.

\*\*\*\*\*\*\*\*\*\*\*

Norah paced back and forth in her kitchen, fretting. It had been three hours since Gary had left. As much as she feared the violence, the thought of losing him and living alone was too much for her to bear.

The fact that he had a girlfriend hurt her deeply. She had suspected him of cheating before, but could never prove it. He would often return home after a long night out only to push her away when she tried to be affectionate.

They had met in California just after she had graduated high school. He was a young, charismatic Marine stationed at Camp

Pendleton and had come to mean the world to her. The loving and attentive couple was soon married and wanting to start a family. After two miscarriages, Gary became disillusioned—upset that his chance of being a father and having a son was slipping away.

Growing distant, he stayed away for days at a time. As the tensions of their failing marriage grew, Gary received orders for Korea. Although he had made it plain to her that he wanted a divorce, Norah waited faithfully, praying each day for his safe return.

The distant sound of the Chevy's engine echoed against the house and barn. Instead of growing louder, it suddenly stopped. Norah raced out on to the front porch—her flannel nightgown flowing in the frigid wind. Searching for her husband, she only found the dark night sky and six-inches of newly fallen snow. She cried out, pleading for him to come home.

Just short of the driveway, Gary struggled to get out of the driver's side door. His truck had slid off the road and was tipped on its side in a ditch. He drudged through the snow replaying the night's events over and again in his mind. He chuckled to himself thinking that his surprise visit had turned out to be more of a surprise for his young girlfriend than had been expected.

Unlike the many times Gary had killed before, tonight there had been major mistakes. The others were planned—not methodically—but planned just the same. Obsessed by the chase, a young girl lost her appeal as soon as the sexual tension faded. Equally obsessed by the exhilaration of watching life as it slowly ebbed away, he would often speed up the process, but not before he was certain he wouldn't be disturbed while disposing of the body. The ground beneath the barn held many secrets.

Norah walked back out onto the front porch hoping to find her husband heading up the walkway. Instead, she discovered his fading footprints in the snow leading to the barn. His work light was also showing through the cracks of the loft door. She called out his name, pleading with him to come into the house.

Gary walked out of the barn carrying a large chain with a hook on both ends. He was heading toward the small utility building housing his two working tractors when he heard Norah calling to him. Dealing with her was the last thing he wanted to do. He tried to focus on the task at hand, but her voice kept cutting through his nerves with each pathetic plea.

He often thought of taking care of Norah in the same manner he had taken care of so many of the other women, but couldn't bring himself to do it. She was different. They had met well before he realized he had the gift—before Korea—before the constant lure of death.

Norah's crying didn't stop, frustrating Gary to the point that he couldn't think straight. Deciding the truck could wait, he threw down the chain and started after her to shut her up one way or another. His brow furled and fists clenched, he half-charged. In fear for her life Norah ran into the house and stumbled up the stairs. Gary easily caught up, knocking her to the floor.

Norah's left knee smacked against the hardwood floor sending a sharp jolt of pain up her thigh. "You, bastard! Leave me alone!"

Gary leaned against the wall chuckling at her language, giving Norah time to get back up. He rushed to her and trapped her against their closed bedroom door. She fumbled for the doorknob and fell backward into the room. Gary grabbed her by the ankle and proceeded to drag her to the top of the stairs and then down, one step at a time—releasing her when they reached the landing. In utter disbelief, Norah watched him saunter into the kitchen to grab a cold beer.

An intense anger welled deep inside of Norah. The strange woman her husband had gone to see must have been responsible for the drastic change in his behavior. She was the reason she was hurting both physically and emotionally.

"Did you go and see her?" Norah's voice was calm and steady, but still showed evidence she was in pain. "Answer me, Gary."

"You're pathetic," Gary said, shaking his head in disgust.

Norah's knee had begun to swell, but she managed to get back on her feet and hobble into the kitchen. Tears were now pooling up in her eyes. "What's wrong with you? What did I do to deserve this?"

"Nothin's wrong with me, babe. I'm perfectly fine," Gary said before he took a swig of his beer. The cool liquid felt good against the back of his throat.

His flip attitude infuriated Norah even more. "What's her name? Where does she live?"

"None of your damn business." he said, thinking it funny that his girlfriend wouldn't be anybody's business ever again.

"I'm going to make it my business, Gary. Now tell me her name!"

Gary laughed. "Or what?" His neck and face had turned red. "What are you going to do about it?"

Norah started to sob. Her entire adult life had been dedicated to taking care of her husband and all of his needs. Even in the rough times she hadn't felt as low as she was feeling now. Gary would often lose his temper early in their marriage—hitting her and going off on a rant for an offense as simple as overcooking his dinner, but he always apologized afterward. She knew he felt guilty, but this time was different—he was different—acting like she had uncovered some dark secret he had been hiding.

"You've changed. I don't even know you anymore." Her voice was low and sober. She made her way deeper into the large country kitchen using the table for support until she reached the sink. Once there, she filled her glass full with water and drank half of it down. "Twenty years of marriage doesn't mean a thing to you, does it?"

Gary leaned against the counter lost in his own thoughts. The face of each one of the girls he had killed flashed through his mind. Their expressions just before death pumped up his adrenalin. He could taste their blood in his mouth—each a distinctive flavor.

Infuriated that Gary was ignoring her, Norah shattered her drinking glass against the backsplash sending droplets of water and shards in all directions. "Pay attention to me, damn it!"

Norah's shrill voice, cut through Gray's subconscious, sending him instantly into a rage. Frightened that she was about to be beaten again, she grabbed a kitchen knife off of the counter and held it up defensively.

"Stay away from me! I swear to God, you better not touch me again!"

Gary's mind flipped over. The fear on Norah's face and the shimmer of the knife's blade excited him. Instead of his wife, he saw prey.

The crazed look in Gary's eyes took Norah off guard. Her body became limp—the knife hung loosely in her hands. She had seen him angry many times before, but never like this. Even his face seemed to have changed. Before she could move he was on her—his powerful arms wrapped tightly around her frail body—his mouth on hers.

Norah felt the first rib snap. Sharp pain radiated through her chest and down both arms. She clenched her hand tight around the handle of the knife as the pain slowly increased. A second and then third rib popped. Her world became a fuzzy, gray haze. Images of her mother picking her up into her arms as a child and then dying in bed flashed before her. Gary looking handsome in his dress blues on the day of their wedding gave her a sense of peace.

A fourth rib breaking caused such immense pain that it shocked her mind as well as her will to live wide awake. She raised the knife in an attempt to fight him off, but was stopped short when his massive hand caught hers in mid-motion. The intense pressure from his grip around her body was relaxed, allowing her to take a deep yet painful breath. Before she could exhale, Gary drove the long blade of the kitchen knife deep just below her ribs. All of the air escaped Norah's lungs with a loud, raspy hiss. He let go, allowing her to fall backward.

The look of bewilderment in her eyes at the onset of death woke Gary out of his crazed state of mind. He screamed her name, realizing what he had just done. He had always loved her, but hadn't realized it until she too lay dead at his feet.

Gary kneeled down to scoop her into his now gentle arms. Blood flowed from the gaping wound and pooled onto the kitchen floor. Instinctively, he dropped her—scooting out of the way.

Out of his mind with grief he ran for the front door, not sure of his next move. How would he explain her death? The police would surely find out it was him when they saw her wounds.

"They don't need to know. No one needs to know," he said to himself.

His mind started to process what had to be done. The only way out was beneath the barn. There she would be out of sight forever—just another disgruntled wife that had run back home to her family. She wouldn't be missed for days.

Gary walked out onto the front porch and took in a chilled breath. The snow accumulation was now well over ten inches. Mid-way to the barn, bright blue lights coming from the direction of the road caught his attention. Fours sets of flashlights appeared around the curve of the driveway accompanied by the booming voices of men ordering Gary to stop where he was. Panic shot through his body. He knew why they were there. He knew what they would find in the house.

Capture not being an option, Gary ran to the barn, falling several times in the deep snow. He closed the large doors, hurriedly nailing them shut with a scrap piece of wood. After placing a ladder in the middle of the barn, he tossed a twenty-foot length of rope over the rafters, tying it snuggly around a stall support and then fashioned a makeshift noose.

The doors buckled inward from the force of the men's bodies slamming against them. Gary slipped the rope around his neck and jumped off of the ladder. The weight from his body easily snapped his neck. He was dead before the police broke through the doors.

# 1

# 2010

Tara James fought her way through the crowd of disgruntled shoppers from the checkout lane to the entrance of the supermarket, and then out into a tangled mess of cars, people, and abandoned shopping carts. The chaotic scene looked more like the final rush of Christmas shopping instead of a mid-November day. She couldn't believe all of the fuss over a possible snowstorm that was promising only six inches at best.

Not in a hurry to get home, she took her time walking to her pick-up with a bag of groceries hanging in each hand. A disgruntled looking woman with a min-van full of kids waited impatiently for Tara to pull out of her spot, so she could claim it for herself. Tara lit a cigarette and checked herself out in the mirror before backing up just to be spiteful.

The trailer park she and Kenny had called home for the past eight years was located a short drive from shopping centers and fast food restaurants on Wichita's southwest side. Their light blue singlewide sat on the furthest lot back, sandwiched between a cinderblock wall and a vacant space that hadn't seen a tenant in over three years.

Tara emptied the contents of her grocery bags, scattering a collection of chips, frozen dinners, and candy onto the kitchen table. She quickly lit up a cigarette, freshening up the stale odor of smoke throughout the trailer. Her tattered denim jacket was tossed on the couch along with a mock leather purse she had acquired at her parent's latest garage sale. She shot the hair band holding back her shoulder length brown hair through the air and watched it land on the bag of cheese puffs and roll to the floor. No sooner had she sat down, the phone rang. "Damn it! Who the hell is that?" she said out loud.

She bolted out of the recliner, grabbed the phone, and glided back into the chair—answering and taking a drag all at the same time. "Yeah?"

"Tara. It's mom. Can you talk, or is he there?"

"Yes, I can talk. And no he's not. Besides it wouldn't matter even if he was."

"Now you know that's not the gods' honest truth, Tara Jean," her mother said.

"I can talk in front of Kenny. He probably could care less about our conversations anyway." Waiting for the next stellar comment from her mother, Tara rolled her eyes and took a long drag.

"Where is he? Out at the bar, or is he fishing again?"

"It's too cold to fish. He's deer hunting."

"I knew he'd be doing something away from you. I just don't know what you see in him anyway. He won't work, and all he does is drink and spend your money."

"What did you call for, Mother?"

"I wanted to invite you over for dinner. Your father and I just bought a side of beef and we're barbequing steaks tonight."

"Isn't it too cold to barbeque?"

"Your father doesn't think so. He still has propane left over from summer and wants to use it all up."

Tara sighed. "Fine. I'll be over in about forty-five minutes. Can I stay the night? I don't like to be alone when Kenny's not home. And if it does snow, I don't want to be stuck at home all day just staring at the walls."

"I guess so, but you'll have to sleep on the davenport. Your father sold the spare bed at our garage sale last weekend."

"What did he do that for? He knew I still used that bed when I stayed over," Tara said.

"He has some harebrained idea that he's going to buy a new computer and turn the spare bedroom into an office. For what purpose only he knows," Betty Jo said. "You'll need to bring a sleeping bag, too. I've been letting the dogs sleep on the afghan since it turned cold. I'll see you in a bit."

The phone went dead, leaving Tara sitting in silence and still holding the cigarette between her lips. "I swear she can be so annoying."

The groceries were thrown hap-hazard in their respective places. Tara filled an overnight bag with *Skittles*, the latest tabloid magazines and a couple of changes of clothes. In her closet, she had to dig the sleeping bag out from underneath two boxes with the name Kayla written in black felt-marker. She paused briefly, studying the name.

Her eyes filled with tears. "No. I'm not going to do it. Just put them back."

She took a deep breath, grabbed the sleeping-bag and walked briskly out of the room, leaving the boxes in the middle of the floor. She threw her belongings into the bed of the pickup and left her home and the trailer park behind. Her parents lived only fifteen minutes away, but thinking about the name on those boxes made it seem more like an hour.

## <u>2</u>

Kenny James was by no means an outdoorsman. He was more or less a cross between a biker and the town drunk. He had never shot at anything in his life, and wasn't about to start this hunting trip. His idea of roughing it was to take a long nap in the front seat of his cousin Jared's Ford Explorer, while Jared and his best friend Todd went off tromping through the woods.

The backseat was littered with empty chip bags and crushed *Old Milwaukee* cans. A half-empty can sat between Kenny's knees while a cigarette, burning precariously close to his skin, was wedged between his pointer and middle finger as he slept.

Jared, rotund and lumbering, emerged from the brush first and well ahead of Todd. Todd was in the middle of one his lengthy stories defaming the reputation of his estranged wife and starring him as the devoted victim. Jared, hearing one version of the story or another on a daily basis, tuned his best friend out.

The SUV was parked at a skewed angle alongside a county road. Through the open passenger side window, Jared spied Kenny asleep with his mouth wide open. He couldn't resist the urge and fired off a shot from his Remington deer rifle, startling Kenny awake; causing him to spill his beer onto the floor and drop the lit cigarette into his lap.

"Jesus! What the hell are guys doing?" Kenny said, squinting into the afternoon sun. His gaunt face, a patch work of bristled hair, complemented his dirty-blond mullet. An old, red flannel shirt hung loosely on his boney frame.

Jared doubled over with laughter, falling hard against the side of the SUV. Todd bolted out of the brush and ran into the middle of the road expecting to see Jared standing over a slain deer.

"Did ya get one? Where is it?"

"Yeah, but I think he's too scrawny and tough to bother with," Jared said, wiping tears from his eyes.

Kenny screamed, batting widely at the still burning cigarette lying in his lap. "Shit, shit, shit!"

Jared cried out in laughter again seeing his cousin twitching about. "What did ya do?"

"I dropt the damn cigarette in my lap!"

"You fell asleep smoking, again? One of these days you're gonna be sorry, cousin."

"I'm sorry, now!" Kenny said, brushing the cigarette and ash out of the open passenger door.

"I'd be more careful with that if I were you," Todd said. "I had an aunt catch her hair on fire when she fell asleep on the couch with a lit cigarette. Scarred her face all up! She never got married or had kids because of it."

"Thank you, Debbie Downer. I think we got the picture," Jared said.

"I was just trying to help."

"You wanna help? Drive us back to the cabin," Jared said, tossing Todd the keys.

Todd took them without question. He placed his rifle in the back alongside of Jared's and opened a fresh beer. Jared grabbed a beer for himself and Kenny, and then proceeded to clear the contents of the backseat out onto the side of the road.

"Let's go, James! I'm fricken starving!" Jared said.

"Hey, did you shoot me some steaks, or are we dining on hotdogs and beer again?" Kenny asked.

His question was answered with a loud belch, followed by a collective "Hotdogs!"

"Ah, man. I want my Bambi burgers! You guys suck!"

Todd took a long swig of his beer and hoisted his short, squat body into the driver's seat. He fumbled with the keys, double started the engine, and stepped down hard on the gas pedal, causing the SUV to fishtail across the road.

"Easy there, champ. I'd like to get back in one piece," Jared said.

Todd ignored his friend's advice and accelerated down the narrow county road. Kenny sat nervously in the front passenger seat, watching the blur of trees fly by.

"Don't miss our turn, Todd. It's just up ahead," Jared said, leisurely motioning out the window.

Todd stared straight ahead, oblivious to what Jared was saying.

"Todd, did ya hear me? Todd!" Frustrated, Jared climbed over the driver's seat and smacked Todd along side of his round head.

"Dude. What'd you do that for?" Todd said, glaring back at Jared.

"Holy shit!" Kenny shouted.

Todd turned back around just in time to see a large doe standing in the middle of the road ten yards ahead. The impact was hard and sudden, sending Kenny flying forward and bouncing off of the windshield, and then smacking his head against the dashboard when Todd slammed on the brakes.

Jared ended up on the floor in-between the front and back seats, cussing and yelling. "You stupid fool! What were you thinking?"

"Oh, man. I think I killed it," Todd said.

Kenny sat dazed shaking his head, trying to focus. His nose and mouth filled with blood. His face became numb.

"Shit, Kenny. You're bleeding all over the place!" Todd said.

Jared struggled back onto the seat caressing his right shoulder. "What the hell, Todd?"

"Sorry, man. She just ran out in front of me. There was nothing I could do."

"You're full of shit!" Kenny said, slurring his words and spraying blood from his mouth. "It was standing in the middle of the goddamn road."

Todd's face became flush with anger. "You calling me a liar? Fuck you, she was standing in the road. I'll kick your scrawny ass!"

"Todd, shut the hell up. If anyone's gonna kick somebody's ass, it's gonna be me," Jared said, smacking the back of Todd's head on his way out of the vehicle.

Like a sulking child that had just been scolded by a parent, Todd climbed out of the SUV with a huff with his head hung down. He sauntered over to the dead deer in the middle of the road with his hands buried deep in the pockets of his hunting jacket.

Jared examined the front of the Ford for damage. "One headlight...the entire front grill...oh, and both fog lights. Nice going, jackass!"

"I told you it wasn't my fault. I didn't see her in time."

"I didn't see her in time," Jared said, mocking Todd while making a face.

"Who cares anyway? Didn't you say that Sadie was getting the Explorer in the divorce?"

"That's right, genius—in good condition—which this is not!"

Kenny opened the driver's side door and vomited onto the road, cursing at Todd. "Stupid, fat-ass!"

"Not in the car!" Jared said as he jogged over to Kenny. "Oh, man...you're face! You smacked it pretty hard! Stay right there."

Jared ran around to the back of the SUV and grabbed a cold beer can that was resting on the bottom of the cooler, beneath the melted ice.

"Here, put this against your nose and mouth. You've gotta get that looked at...Todd, get in the car. I'm taking Kenny to the hospital."

"What for?"

"It looks like he broke his nose."

"What a pussy! He don't need a doctor! I've broken my nose before and never needed to see a doctor. "

"I don't want to see no doctor!" Kenny said.

"You sure?"

"See I told you he don't need a doctor," Todd said.

"Fine. Then we're going home," Jared said, jumping into the driver's seat. "Are ya staying or going, Todd? Because we're leaving with or without you."

"What about the deer?"

"What about it?" Jared's face had become bright red with anger.

"You don't want it to go to waste, do ya?"

"Do you know to field dress a deer?"

"Well, no..."

"Neither do I. Now get in the goddamn car or I'm leaving you here!"

Knowing that Jared wasn't joking around, Todd high-tailed it back to the Explorer and jumped in the back.

## 3

Tara pulled into her parents drive and sat for a moment with the truck's engine running. Dried streaks of tears tracked down her thin cheeks. She wiped her nose with her right sleeve and dried her eyes with her left. Tara's mother, Betty Jo watched her daughter through the screen door, wondering what was wrong this time.

Jumping out of the cab, Tara slammed the truck's dented, driver's side door. The loud metallic sound echoed down the street.

"I wish you wouldn't shut that truck door so hard, Tara. Your father is getting tired of paying to have that broken down thing fixed all of the time," Betty Jo said from the front porch.

"Hello to you, too, Mother," Tara said, grabbing her belongings from the bed of the truck. "Can I bum a cigarette off of you? I think I left my brand new pack on the kitchen table."

"Help yourself. There's an open carton next to the refrigerator. Have you been crying? Your eyes look red and puffy."

"It's nothing. Are Sadie and the kids coming over?"

"No. Little Ami has the stomach flu and all I need is three kids getting sick all over my carpeting," Betty Jo said, taking a long drag off her cigarette. The skin around her mouth wrinkled and sucked in. Smoke poured out of her nostrils, wafting up into the cool evening air.

"Come inside before you catch cold. I don't know why you don't wear a warmer jacket," Betty Jo said.

"You gave it to me."

The small ranch-style home was kept neat with a thin layer of filth, compliments of a fat orange tabby named Harry and two Shiatsus named Max and Mini. The pungent aromas of cigarette smoke and cat urine fought for the attention of Tara's pallet.

Tara's father, Stan squeezed through the sliding glass door carrying a plate of thick steaks and cursing under his breath. His round belly was squeezed tightly into a stained white undershirt that was complemented by a camouflage hunting-jacket. Thin strands of salt and pepper hair lay scattered over his head, matched only in neatness with his two-day old beard.

He stepped square onto the foot of one of the dog's feet sending it yelping into the living room. "Damn Barbeque!" he said with a growl.

"What's wrong, Stan?" Betty Jo asked. A long ash from her cigarette hung precariously over the salad-bowl.

"I ran out of propane. I thought I had enough, but the damn thing just quit working."

"Are the steaks done?"

"No, Betty Jo. They're not done. We need to stick them into the oven until they're finished," he said, dismissing the plate of lightly seared meat on the kitchen counter. He grabbed a can of beer out of the fridge and disappeared into the next room.

Betty Jo stood by the meat with a look of disbelief. "Do you want me to bake them or just put them under the broiler?"

"The broiler, damn it all! Do you want to eat baked steak? I know Tara and I don't!"

Stan sat down in his recliner cursing and trying to dig out the remote from in-between the arm and cushion, blaming the dogs and everyone else for it being stuck there. Tara curled up on the couch with a *People Magazine* and *Skittles*, ignoring her bickering parents. The cat was busy giving himself a bath on Tara's sleeping bag while both dogs sat drooling by the couch waiting for Tara to drop a piece of her candy.

Stan was surfing so fast it was hard to tell what was on any of the channels. The TV rested on the Golf Channel, a favorite of his and a point of anguish for Tara and her mother.

Tara gasped in disgust. "Dad!"

"Go help your mother in the kitchen if you don't want to watch."

"You don't even play golf."

"I don't play football or race Stock cars, either." With that, Stan turned up the sound and reclined all the way back in his chair.

Tara leaped up from the couch causing the dogs and cat to scatter and headed into the kitchen. "Smells good, Mom. When's dinner?"

## 4

Jared sped down the narrow streets of the trailer park toward Kenny and Tara's house, cursing at the alternator idiot light that was flashing on and off. The right headlight was steadily becoming dimmer as were the dashboard lights.

"This is all your fault, Todd! I can't believe your sorry ass hit that fucking deer! What a moron! Look at my car! We'll be lucky just to get home!"

Todd didn't hear a word. He was passed out on the back seat and had been the entire four-hour trip back from Arkansas. Kenny was passed out as well in the front.

Pulling in front of the singlewide, Jared began yelling Kenny's name and shaking his shoulder in an attempt to wake him.

"Come on, Kenny. Wake the hell up! Get out of the car—I've gotta go!" He shook his cousin's shoulders hard again, releasing a rank belch. "Damn, boy! What the hell have you been eating?"

Jumping out of the SUV, Jared jogged over to the passenger's side door and pulled Kenny onto the street. The combination of a hard jolt and the cold November air shocked Kenny awake.

"What the hell, man?" Kenny said, trying to focus.

"Come on, Kenny. Get up! You're home, cousin!"

Jarred pulled him up by his shirt and rolled him onto the front patch of weeds passing for a lawn. Before Kenny realized what had happened, Jared was already headed back down the street.

Kenny crawled up from his knees and staggered into the house. Navigating his way through the kitchen, he found his almost empty fifth of whisky waiting for him on the counter. "Ah, just what the doctor ordered."

The amber liquid burned his split lip on contact causing him to scream out in pain. "What in the hell is wrong with my mouth? What the hell is all over my face?" he said, gently touching his blood encrusted lips and chin. "Tara?"

The bright green box of menthol cigarettes on the kitchen table caught Kenny's eye. He announced he was bumming one off of Tara at the top of his lungs. After lighting it up, he took a deep drag and relaxed. He loved the smell of butane and the taste of a fresh cigarette.

"Tara, where in the hell are you?"

He staggered down the long, skinny hallway and into their bedroom. In the middle of the floor were the two large boxes. Kenny stood over them confused and silent. He sat down on the foot of the bed and took a long drag.

"I thought we agreed we weren't going to do this anymore..."

He opened the box nearest to him and removed a ragged, yellow stuffed rabbit and a pair of white baby shoes. Under a pink quilt was a picture of a skinny seven-year-old girl with uncombed hair, sitting on a brand new bicycle complete with streamers. Her toothless grin was misshapen by a single crack in the glass of the battered picture frame. Kenny stared misty eyed at the image until the welling up of tears blurred his vision. He held the picture close to his chest—tears rolling down his bristly cheeks. "My baby girl. My sweet baby girl."

Lying back with the stuffed animal wedged between his left arm and body, Kenny put the cigarette between his lips and closed his eyes. He was soon asleep.

## 5

A loud banging on the front door followed by a woman's loud, nasally voice echoed through Tara's dreams. She was sound asleep on the couch, buried beneath her sleeping bag and the cat. Her parents had long since retired to the bedroom where the TV drowned out everything including the shrill barks of the dogs and Stan's snoring.

The woman screamed and pounded on the door again. "Tara, wake up! Answer the damn door!"

Across the street, Ed Fulmar was being pushed out of his front door by his concerned wife. Dressed only in his pajamas, robe and slippers, he ventured off of the porch and to the edge of the street.

"Say something, Ed!" his wife said.

"Get back inside, Kathy. Don't you have any sense?"

The woman on the front porch continued her assault on the front door. Her hair was stuffed inside of a worn baseball cap and jutted out in all directions. She was wearing an old olive drab army jacket and a pair of light pink sweat pants.

"Hey, what's all the noise about? It's nearly midnight," Ed said from the safe distance.

"You're not close enough, Ed. She can't hear you," Kathy said.

Ed waved off his wife. He approached closer and then spoke again. Seeing that the loud woman didn't hear him, he walked all the way into the yard and onto the front porch and reached out, tapping her on the shoulder, causing her to jump and shriek.

"Who the hell are you?" she asked defensively, taking a step back.

"I was about to ask you the same thing. Now just what do you think you're doing making all of that racket at this time of night?" he said in a stern and steady voice. "People are trying to sleep."

"I'm trying to wake up Tara. I can't get anyone to answer the door. There's an emergency at her house."

"Emergency? What kind of emergency?"

"Her house is on fire. I've got to wake her up!"

"Fire? I've got a spare house key. I'll be right back."

Ed shuffled back across the street to his anxiously awaiting wife hiding in the crack of the door.

"Well, what did she want?"

"Tara's house is on fire and that woman is trying to wake her up so she can tell her," Ed said, all out of breath. "Where are the keys to the Carter's house?"

"What do you need those for?"

"So I can open the door and wake that girl up. Her house is on fire! Didn't you hear me the first time?"

"Fire or not, I don't think it's polite to just walk into somebody else's house without being invited."

"Quit arguing with me and get the damn keys, Kathy!" Ed's face had grown flush with anger. His wife burrowed through the kitchen junk drawer and produced a ring of keys. Ed snatched them from her hand and darted off back across the street.

As soon as Ed unlocked the door, the anxious woman rushed by searching and calling for Tara. Tara awoke and jolted up.

"What the hell?" she said, trying to make out the figure standing over her. "What are you doing here, Peggy?"

Peggy gushed with excitement. "It's your house, Tara—it's on fire! You've got to get home. I don't know if anything will be left standing!"

"Are you sure?"

"Yes! Now come on, we've got to go!"

Tara grabbed her jacket and followed Peggy out the door. They hopped into Peggy's Impala station-wagon and zipped down the dark country road. Tara sat slumped in the front seat not fully awake. The odor of stale fast food saturated her taste buds. She felt as if she were in a slow moving nightmare, unable to wakeup. Light snow flurries danced off the windshield and through the beam of the headlights. The cold wind blowing off of the plains rocked the station wagon, pushing it slightly into the oncoming lane.

Peggy jabbered on—her voice cutting through the darkness. "I can't believe your house caught fire! You weren't even home. What do you think happened? Don't worry sweetie, I'll get you there in no time."

She gripped the steering wheel tight, her lips slightly curled in anticipation of Tara's reaction to her devastated world. Peggy's imagination raced through scenarios of flames leaping through the air, flashing red and blue lights from rescue vehicles, and firemen escorting Tara to the smoldering ruins of her mobile home. This was the most excitement she had seen in all her twenty-seven years.

**********

Ed Fulmar knocked on the open bedroom door, trying to wake Stan and Betty Jo without startling them too much. He knew Stan had heart problems in the past and wasn't sure how much shock he was able to take.

"Ed, is that you?" Betty Jo asked. Her voice was barely audible above a TV commercial advertising videos of half nude co-eds. "Stan, wake-up. Ed from across the street is in our bedroom."

Ed stood in the doorway trying to split his attention between the screaming college girls and the Carters. "I don't mean to intrude on you folks like this, but there seems to be an emergency."

"Stan, turn off the damn television!" Betty Jo said. "Stan!"

Stan awoke with a snort. Startled, he fumbled for the remote. "What's going on? What are you doing here, Ed?"

"There seems to be an emergency at Tara's home and I..."

"Tara? She's staying with us tonight. How could there be an emergency at her house?" Stan asked.

"That damn Kenny!" Betty Jo said.

"Her house is on fire. A woman came over banging on the door trying to wake Tara up. She and the woman took off to the house. I'm surprised you folks didn't hear all of the commotion."

"It was probably set on purpose by that no good husband of hers just to collect the insurance money!"

"Not now, Betty Jo! Get dressed so we can get on over there," Stan said. "Thanks for all of your help, Ed. It's appreciated," he said as he escorted Ed out of the bedroom and toward the general direction of the front door. "Tell Kathy thanks, also."

Stan turned and walked back to the bedroom commanding Betty Jo to get a move on.

\*\*\*\*\*\*\*\*\*\*

The light flurries subsided as Tara and Peggy approached the trailer park. The station wagon snaked its way through the crowded streets toward Tara and Kenny's home. Peggy was motioned by a police officer standing in the middle of the road to turn her car around. She pointed in the direction of the fire and started moving forward. He slapped the hood of the Impala, directing her once more to turn around. She rolled down her window letting in a mixture of smoke and cold night air. The combination shocked Tara wide awake.

"Her house is on fire. I'm trying to get her home," Peggy said.

"For the last time, turn your vehicle around, Ma'am. This is a restricted area. Unless this is an emergency vehicle, I can't let you through."

"Are you deaf? I said I'm trying to take my friend home. Her house is the one on fire!"

Rotating lights from emergency vehicles bounced of the thick smoke wrapping itself around the array of trailer homes. The heavy smell of smoke annihilated the stale odor of fast food in the station wagon and burnt both of the girl's nostrils. Tara sat up staring out the windshield at the flames leaping over the roofs of neighboring trailers.

The police officer radioed another with the information given to him by Peggy. He looked at Tara, nodded, and walked over to her side of the car and asked her to please come with him.

Peggy tried in vain to complain that she wasn't invited. Hanging out the driver's side window, she yelled accusing Tara of not thanking her, and that maybe she got what she deserved. She slammed her car into reverse and accelerated toward the back street that led to her home.

Tara didn't realize she wasn't wearing shoes until her feet hit the cold pavement. Shivering, she crossed her arms tight. The walk to her home seemed to take an eternity—the smoky streets appeared strange and unfamiliar. Eager spectators stood on their tip-toes, stretching their necks to get a glimpse of destruction at someone else's expense. As she approached she could see her trailer and Kenny's prized Firebird fully engulfed—the heat from the fire dried out her eyes and was hot on her face. Firefighters rushed about spraying the flames with two powerful hoses. Tara watched numbly as her home burnt to the ground.

# 6

Tara was adorned with a blanket, courtesy of the Wichita Fire Department. She stood fifty yards from her smoldering home, shaking like a leaf. Her feet had become numb, making it difficult to walk.

An array of questions flew at her as to what the cause of the fire might have been. *"Were you home? Was there anyone else at home at the time of the fire? Had your home ever experienced a fire before?"* She shook her head to each question. The only thing she could she could think of was holding onto Kenny. He had always made her feel safe, regardless of his short comings.

Twenty minutes into the repeat questioning, Tara heard her father's voice calling to her. She broke down into tears and started in his direction. "Daddy, our house is gone. It's all gone. What are we going to do? All we have is that broken down truck. What am I going to tell Kenny?"

Stan Carter took his daughter into his thick arms, kissed the top of her head, and rocked her the way he did so many times when she was little. Betty Jo stood beside them, gazing at the smoldering ruins of her daughter's home. Her mind raced through the possible causes, always returning back to Kenny.

The crowd dispersed, disappearing altogether when it was apparent that the excitement had come to an end. All but two Wichita Police cars remained, along with a single engine from the fire department. Stan asked one of the officers if he had any more questions for his daughter.

"Not at this time. We have your number, Mr. Carter. We'll be in touch if we need further information," the officer said.

The announcement was distant and almost inaudible at first. Then the radios started to echo the findings in the house.

*"I repeat, we have found human remains inside the far end of the house,"* the voice of a firefighter broadcasted.

Betty Jo gasped, holding her hand to her mouth. "Oh, dear God."

Tara stared blankly in the direction of her home. Visions of who would have been in her house raced through her mind. She kept thinking of Peggy's husband, Randy, and how many times he had broken in. Then her thoughts went back to Kenny, but the boys weren't due back until Sunday afternoon. Maybe he had gotten home early. Jared would never leave early, though; he's too much of a selfish pig.

There was no way of knowing. Even if Kenny had come home after she had gone, he wouldn't have called her parent's looking for her. He would've been more than happy to wait until she returned back home.

Tara started to breathe heavily—uncontrollably. Her body became ridged, except for her legs which buckled.

Betty Jo panicked. "Stan, do something!"

"I think she fainted. I've got her," Stan said, catching his daughter before she hit the pavement.

The officer nearby caught the action and motioned to one of the firefighters still on the scene. They both rushed over to find Tara passed out. Betty Jo stood helplessly by as they administered first aid to her daughter. She stood staring in the direction of the remains of Tara's home with her arms folded tight across her chest—her anger with Kenny growing stronger with each passing moment. "That no good bastard had something to do with this," she said out loud.

"Not now, Betty Jo! There's a time and place for everything and now's not the time or place," Stan said.

Tara sat on the side of the street, her head hanging down between her knees. She stared straight at the ground, not fully aware of her surroundings. The firefighter by her side reassured her she would be okay. She only had a minor panic attack from all of the excitement.

"Ma'am," an officer said. Are you sure your husband wasn't home?"

"Hey, Mike. I don't think you'll be getting too much information from this one tonight. She needs to go home and get some rest," the firefighter said.

"Kenny is on a hunting trip. He's not due back until tomorrow," Tara said, slightly slurring her words.

"It could take a few days to identify the remains. We might need to contact you, so try not to leave the area. Let us know when your husband gets back. We'll need to interview the two of you for the final report." The officer said and then turned around to leave.

Stan reassured Tara that it would all be okay as she climbed in the back of the duel cab. He turned the ignition key illuminating the digital clock which read 2:09 a.m. Tara hadn't realized she had been there almost two hours.

As they drove away, she turned to look out the back window. The heavy smoke had dissipated and the streets were now empty. The emergency vehicles had extinguished their rotating beacons, giving the appearance that life had once more returned back to normal in the trailer park.

# 7

Sadie Anderson stepped onto her soon to be ex in-laws front porch in Wichita's Delano district as her three young children sat fidgeting in the Ford Taurus. Although it was the last place she wanted to be on a Sunday morning, she needed to be there for her sister, Tara.

On her way to church, she had noticed her estranged husband's SUV in the driveway of his parent's home—he and Kenny weren't due back until later that afternoon. It wasn't like Jared to come home early from anything that kept him away from those who needed him most. Sadie knew something was wrong.

Jared's mother opened the front door before Sadie could knock.

"What are you doing here?" the sickly old woman asked. She stood behind the glass storm door staring down Sadie with cold, blue eyes. She was wearing a quilted house-coat, ornamented with coffee and cough syrup stains. Her thin, white hair was matted to one side. Her tongue tried unsuccessfully to wet her thin, chapped lips.

"Diane, I need to know if Kenny..."

Her mother in-law cut her off. "Jared's not home. Call him later," she dismissed, firmly shutting the front door.

Sadie turned away wanting to give up. Worrying the buttons on her coat, she fought with the idea of just going to church and checking back later, but then turned back toward the door. She rang the bell, waited five seconds and rang it again.

The door was opened, this time by Jared's father. He was wearing an opened, dirty brown robe, exposing striped boxers and a t-shirt that barely covered his round and protruding belly.

"Oh, it's the wife."

"John, I need to know if Kenny came home with Jared last night."

He rubbed his almost bald head. "I don't know what she wants. I can't hear a damn thing through this glass door!"

Sadie raised the volume of her voice, certain the neighbors could hear. "I need to know if Jared brought Kenny home last night, or if Kenny's here."

"Jared's not home, he's gone hunting with Kenny." The door closed once more.

Frustrated, Sadie rang the bell repeatedly and pounded on the storm door. Jared's father answered once more, exasperated at the persistence of his daughter in-law. "I told you…"

This time, Sadie did the cutting off. "Go and check your spare-bedroom and wake Jared up, John. I know he's here, because his SUV is parked in the goddamn driveway!"

The old man turned and walked away and returned moments later. "He said to call later. He's sleeping."

Before he could shut the door, Sadie yelled again. "Is Kenny here or did Jared bring Kenny home? Answer the question…please. Tara needs to know!"

"He ain't here. Jared said to mind your own business and stay out of Kenny's and your sister's."

Jared's mother popped her head around the door and scolded. "Why don't you try checking at their house instead of bothering us? Jared dropped the damn fool off there last night."

The Door closed for the last time leaving Sadie on the front porch feeling angry and frustrated.

Determined, she pounded on the door a few more times. "When did he drop him off? John? Dianne? Open the door. I need to know when Kenny got home!"

The glint of broken glass where the Ranger's left headlight used to be caught Sadie's attention. Curious, she walked over to the SUV and examined the smashed in front with tufts of deer hair caught in the broken grill. "You stupid dumb-ass…I guess you finally killed yourself a deer."

Knowing that she needed to let her family know what had happened, she hurried back to the car and her waiting children. The realization that Kenny was most likely home put a knot in her stomach. She wasn't sure if her Tara would be able to handle another tragedy.

Sadie slid into the front seat and checked her eye makeup in the rear-view mirror. Un-manicured fingers attempted to fluff up her short reddish hair. A quick check of the teeth and she was headed back down the street.

"Mommy." her six-year-old son, Joey said from the back seat.

"What is it, Joey?"

"Why do you always do that?"

"Do what, sweetie?"

"Look in the mirror and make all of those funny faces?"

"Don't be rude, Joey," his seven-year-old sister, Erin, said.

"I'm not rude! Mommy, Erin called me rude."

"Knock it off, you two. I'm just making sure I'm beautiful for you three."

"You're pretty, Mommy, not beautiful. You said it wrong," Joey corrected.

"Same thing, stupid," Ami, the oldest said.

"I'm not stupid!"

"That's right," Erin said. "You're rude and stupid!"

Before any more could be said, Sadie put a stop to the arguing. She made a u-turn at the corner and started back up the street. Concerned, Ami alerted her mother to the mistake she had just made. "Mommy, the church is the other way."

"We're not going to church this morning."

"But why?" they collectively asked.

"Because we're going over to Grandma and Grandpa's house instead."

"But we were just there!" Joey said with a frown.

"We don't like it there. Grandma Anderson is mean," Ami said.

"Mean and smelly," Erin said.

"Not that grandma and grandpa...my mommy and daddy."

A collective cheer arose up form the back seat of the Taurus.

# 8

Tara paced back and forth in her parent's kitchen, chain-smoking her mother's cigarettes. She didn't like waiting around and not knowing all of the details. Kenny didn't own a cell phone and Jared wouldn't answer his, so there was no way of getting in touch with them. She just wanted Kenny safe and in her arms.

"Tara, try to calm down. There's nothing you can do until they get back," her mother said from the kitchen table. A worn terry cloth bathrobe with the logo of an extinct Vegas hotel and casino hung loose on her frail body. She took a drag of her cigarette and chased it quickly with a swig of black coffee.

"How can you be so insensitive? I don't even know if Kenny is coming back."

"I'm sure he's just fine. He and that worthless Jared will come waltzing in here clueless as ever, smelling like beer and B.O."

Tara plopped down opposite of her mother and buried her head in her hands. Her tangled and frizzed morning hair flowed in all directions. Her body was numb with worry and she could still taste the smoke from the fire in the back of her throat. The voices of the firefighters claiming that they had found a body echoed through her mind along with visions of Kenny's face. A tear rolled down her right cheek, dropping onto the worn wooden table.

Only wearing blue boxers and black dress socks, Stan wandered through the kitchen in search of a fresh cup of coffee. He glanced over at Tara who now had her head down on the table. "What's wrong now?"

His wife of thirty-five years glared. "Stanley, you must be the most clueless man I have ever known."

Tara glanced up just in time to view her father's back side. "Jesus, Dad, put some clothes on."

"My house. I can wear what ever I damn well please!"

The dogs erupted into frenzy—barking and yipping with their bodies turning in tight circles. Sadie's car pulled into view of the front window. Stan disappeared into the bedroom and re-emerged wearing the matching robe to his wife's.

"He can get dressed for Sadie, but not me?" Tara said.

Sadie and the kids poured through the front door. All three children chanted in unison, "Grandma! Grandma!" Betty Jo opened her arms wide and hugged them all at the same time.

"What about Grandpa?" Stan asked.

"Hi, Grandpa," three little voices giggled.

Tara rolled her eyes and pouted as she watched her nieces and nephew interact with their grandfather "Aren't you supposed to be at church?" she asked with her arms crossed.

"We're going to the later service," Sadie said coldly. "Mom. Can I talk with you in the bedroom?"

"I guess so," Betty Jo said.

Sadie led the way, trying without success to hide the look of concern on her face.

"I stopped off at John and Diane's house on the way to church. Jared's SUV was parked out in front. He came home early and claims he brought Kenny home last night."

Betty Jo sat in silence staring at the floor. Although she loathed Kenny, she couldn't bare to watch Tara go through another loss. "Are you sure?"

"I was just there. When will they be able to identify the remains? Are they going to call?"

Betty Jo shook her head. Tears welled up in her eyes.

Sadie got up, cracked open the door and called for her father. The sound in his daughter's voice warned him not to question. Tara took notice and started to get curious to the goings on in her parent's bedroom. Stan disappeared down the hall, leaving Tara alone with the three children.

"What's wrong?" Stan asked.

"Jared told his parents that he dropped Kenny off at home late last night," Sadie said.

"Well, where is the little bastard?"

"He didn't know. He was less than helpful. Should we let Tara know, or do we wait for the police to tell us who died in that house?"

There was a quick knock at the door. Tara didn't wait to be invited in. "Am I allowed in on this conversation, or should I just return with the other children?"

"We're just trying to help you, Tara," Sadie said. "I wish you could see that."

"Well excuse me, Ms. high and mighty! I think I can take care of myself, thank you!"

Sadie threw her arms in the air and walked out of the bedroom. She sternly told the kids not to take off their jackets, because they weren't staying long. Tara rushed out after her, demanding to know what she and their parents were all talking about.

"Mom, Dad? Will you please help me with this?" Sadie said.

Stan asked both women to come back in the bedroom so they could talk. He couldn't understand why there had to be so much drama. "Just tell your sister what's going on!"

"Why is Mom crying?" Tara asked with her arms still crossed.

"Kenny might have been home last night," Stan said.

"He's not due back until today. They would never leave early," Tara said.

"Jared claims he dropped Kenny off at home last night," Stan said.

Tara's lip quivered and her voice shook. She was on the verge of all out tears. "Everybody knows Jared is a fat-ass liar. You can't trust him."

"He had no reason to lie." Sadie said. "Someone other than me needs to go over to John and Diane's house and try to speak with them. They won't listen."

"I'll get on over there. I've never had a problem with John. He'll let me know what's going on," Stan said while grabbing his pants off of the treadmill.

Tara flopped down on the couch staring at the cartoons on the television. The tears were flowing freely now as images of Kenny floated through her mind. Through the silly voices and silly music, Betty Jo and Sadie could hear Tara's muffled sobs. They both knew they were all in for a long Sunday.

## 9

Monday morning still didn't offer any answers as to the fate of Kenny. Jared and his parents were less than helpful, even to Stan. Everyone knew in the back of their minds that it was Kenny's body that had been found in the ruins of the mobile-home—only Tara was in denial. She was convinced he was hanging at a friend's house, not wanting to come to her parent's home knowing he wasn't welcome. Her plans for the day were to drive around looking for her husband.

Stan barged out the front door on his way to work, wearing a Monday morning scowl. He was glad to get out of the negative atmosphere. If there was a break in the search for Kenny, Betty Jo would call him on his cell phone.

After calling in sick to work, Tara emerged from the bathroom dressed and made up—she didn't want to waste a minute. Her mother tried to talk her into staying home, but Tara ignored her request and left in the same hurried fashion that her father did.

"I'll be back with Kenny!" she said, announcing to the world that everything would be okay. Her old Chevy belched to life, sending her down the road in a cloud of dust and exhaust fumes.

Betty Jo sat at the kitchen table with her newspaper, coffee, and a freshly lit cigarette. The house was strangely quiet after the emotionally charged commotion of the day before. In the midst of Tara's drama, Ami decided that she had the stomach flu after all and demonstrated it on her grandmother's living room rug.

"Little darling," Betty Jo said to herself. "Thank God they only visit."

Bright ads for fresh turkey and all of the fixings reminded Betty Jo that Thanksgiving was just three days away and that she was woefully prepared. It was a tradition for everyone to show up at their house invited or not. A twenty-pound turkey usually provided enough without saddling the Carters with a bunch of leftovers. Stan hated leftover turkey. He refused to touch it, claiming the meat was always dried out, including the dark.

Tara always brought the pies and Sadie brought the green-bean casserole. She would definitely have to cover Tara due to her circumstances, and Sadie would likely be the same case. She just wasn't functioning well during the divorce process.

Betty Jo clipped out a few coupons and started her shopping list. Stan would hit the roof when he saw the grocery bill. She never paid attention to his outbursts though—he had one every year. She also made a list of potential guests. With the absence of both Kenny and Jared, she might be able to get away with a smaller turkey. Although she knew it had to be Kenny in the fire, she included him on the list just incase Tara saw it.

The *Price is Right* blared to life on the TV prompting Betty Jo to abandon her holiday planning and take up residence on the couch. She made it half-way through the hour long show before falling asleep. Sunday's drama had left her exhausted. Between Tara's pacing about and Stan's snoring, she had only managed four full hours of sleep.

The telephone's insistent ringing woke her out of a chaotic dream. The grocery store had run out of yams causing a mob scene at the cash registers. She was cornered with the last remaining can.

"Hello?" she said groggily.

"Betty Jo, this is Wanda," a nasally voice echoed through the receiver. "We just had the strangest visit by the police."

"Wanda, who?" Betty Jo said, still trying to open her eyes.

"Wanda Richardson...from Doctor Stoyer's office."

"Oh, Wanda. I'm sorry; I just woke up from a mid-morning nap. Just a minute, I need to mute the television," Betty Jo said. "What did you need, dear?"

"Well, we just had the police in the office. They served a subpoena to obtain your son in-law's dental x-rays and records," she said in a raspy whisper.

Wide awake, Betty Jo sat on the edge of the couch. "Kenny?"

"They said it was for confidential reasons, but in my experience anytime the police ask for dental records it only means one thing. They're trying to identify someone who had been killed. Did something happen to Kenny, Betty Jo?"

"Tara and Kenny's mobile home burnt down early Sunday morning. Kenny's been missing since," Betty Jo said. "There were human remains found at the site, but we still don't know who it was."

"Oh that's terrible! What a thing to go through after losing her only daughter. Tara must be devastated."

"We're not a hundred percent sure Kenny was killed in the fire. Tara's out searching for him right now. We're all hoping she finds him and that the fire department found someone else—most likely the person who started the fire in the first place.

Please don't say a word to anyone, just incase Tara wanders that way. I don't think she could take that kind of news."

"Don't worry about a thing, Betty Jo. We'll keep things under wraps on our end. You wish that girl of yours all the best. I hope everything turns out all right."

"Will do, Wanda. Have a good Thanksgiving."

"You, too," Wanda said. As soon as she hung up the phone the gossip started to fly.

Now restless, Betty Jo got up and gazed out the front window. The snow that had been promised for the past week turned out to be just a few flurries and a cold driving wind. She knew she should forget about Thanksgiving altogether and should just start planning a funeral instead.

The cold of winter found its way inside the poorly insulated house, giving Betty Jo the chills. The silence of the house and driving wind outside made her feel uneasy. The faint smell of cigarette smoke lingered just above her. For a moment she felt as if someone else was in the room with her. The scent grew more intense, triggering her inner need for another dose of nicotine.

Kenny's face flashed through her mind. The thought of her less than adored son in-law being dead saddened her. She regretted all of the times she berated him in front of Tara for being a leach on her daughter.

The house settled, causing her to jump. She quickly un-muted the television filling the void with a loud air freshener commercial. "Stupid man!" she said out loud.

A fresh cigarette was lit. The smoke encircled Betty Jo's head and wafted up toward the acoustic-ceiling. A tabloid talk show had taken the place of the annoying commercial. The overly dramatic host introduced what appeared to be a line-up of five young males, all sporting tattoos and shaven heads. On the far side of the stage, a young woman posed for the camera and audience while holding a six-month-old baby. The words, "Who's Your Daddy?" flashed on the screen in bold red letters, sending the audience into a frenzy.

"This one, again?" Betty Jo said. "Why do they keep repeating the same old garbage?" She made no move to change the channel.

Her mind drifted from the nonsense on the screen to Tara. Betty Jo knew her daughter would break down at the news of Kenny's death. She knew Sadie and Stan would try to be supportive, but the burden of funeral arrangements and emotional support would fall naturally onto her shoulders. Her husband and eldest daughter talked a good game, but seldom lived up to their promises.

The rattle of Tara's old truck reverberated up the street announcing her arrival. Betty Jo struggled with what to say. The news she received just moments earlier wasn't exactly news, but more like gossip. She didn't know for certain the reason the police had asked for Kenny's dental records. It could have been a hunch on their part. Before Tara reached the door, Betty Jo decided she would say nothing at all.

Tara walked through the front door in a good mood. "Hey, Mom. Wow, my nose is numb. That wind is so cold!"

Betty Jo sat on the couch politely smiling and nodding her head in agreement with whatever her daughter had to say.

"Stacy and Michael wanted me to tell you hi."

"Oh, Stacy is such a sweet girl," Betty Jo commented. "Had they heard from Kenny?"

Tara's facial expression changed. Her eyes lost their shine and the corners of her mouth turned downward. Betty Jo knew she had blown it. She should have let her daughter carry on like nothing was wrong.

"No one has heard from or has seen Kenny, Mother. I think most of them could care less. I guess you were right all of those years."

"I'm so sorry, Tara. I wish there was something I could do for you."

Tara exploded. "If you cared so much, then you wouldn't have been insensitive toward my feelings for Kenny! You, Dad, and Sadie have always been condescending when it came to him. Even after Kayla died, you couldn't find it in your heart to accept or forgive him. If I had somewhere else to go, believe me, Mother, I would go! I would go far away from all of you!

What ever you do, don't mention Jared. It might upset poor Sadie! Sadie and her precious little brats! Let her lose one of them and see how it feels!"

"Tara Jean, how could you say such a thing? You know we all suffered when you lost little Kayla. That was a terrible tragedy. Your father still isn't over it."

Tara stormed into her parent's bedroom. Her wedding picture on the dresser caught her eye. The smile on both hers and Kenny's face brought tears to her eyes. She caressed Kenny's cleanly shaven face with her finger. The picture beside it was that of a little girl in a blue ballerina's dress. Another was the same girl a few years younger.

The tears flowed freely. The deep down hurt and fear that she may never see Kenny again erupted into mournful weeping. She collapsed on the floor and rolled into a ball—her body shaking as she sobbed. Betty Jo walked into the room and erupted into sympathy tears for her daughter.

# 10

Stan grumbled as he marched through the darkened front doorway. The only light in the living room was from the muted television. The six o'clock news anchor was reporting with passion on a mid-day bank robbery in East Wichita. Brilliant graphics popped up on the screen behind his plastered hair.

Stan bellowed from the middle of the living room. "What in the hell is going on? Betty Jo?"

Betty Jo emerged from the darkened hallway shushing her husband. She hurried over and switched the end table light on. "Tara's asleep on our bed, Stanly. She's had a very difficult day."

"Was it Kenny?"

"Was it Kenny, what?"

Stan's face turned bright red with frustration. "Was it Kenny who died in the fire? What in the hell do you think I'm talking about? Come on, Betty Jo!"

Betty Jo shushed her husband again, telling him to follow her into the kitchen. The fluorescent light revealed a clean stove top and counter which equaled no dinner. Stan started to protest and was silenced quickly by a generous offering of pumpkin pie.

"Give me an hour and dinner will be on the table," Betty Jo said, reassuring her pouting husband.

"You didn't answer my question," Stan said in-between bites. "Do you know if it was Kenny they found in the trailer?"

"Not officially," she said while filling a saucepan with tap water.

"Not officially? What is that supposed to mean?"

"Wanda from Dr. Stoyer's office gave me a courtesy call this afternoon. She claimed the police had a warrant or something for Kenny's dental x-rays. She said that usually meant they needed them to identify someone."

"That doesn't prove a damn thing. Sounds like to me that they're grasping at straws. The police have no idea whose body they found."

"Just the same, I didn't dare tell Tara about the phone call. She's in bad enough shape. And if it does turn out to be Kenny's body they found, then I think we should cancel Thanksgiving dinner. I know for certain I won't be in the mood to cook."

Stan liked the idea of canceling Thanksgiving and not spending a bunch of money on food, especially turkey. He just didn't like the reason. Kenny was far from being his favorite person, but he meant the world to his daughter. She had put up with enough heartache over the past two years. She didn't need this.

Stan finished his pie and moved himself to his recliner via the refrigerator and a can of beer. He flipped past the local news, landing on *ESPN* and the pre-pre game show for *Monday Night Football*. He knew in his heart that it had to be Kenny's body that was found in the ruins of his daughter's home. If it were indeed true, the next few days would be hell for everyone concerned. There wouldn't be a decent place to hide. He took great solace in his beer and the remote. It would be a few weeks before he found another peaceful moment.

# 11

Tara dreamt about her youth with Kenny when Kayla was just a baby. The sun was warm and there was a gentle breeze blowing in the park adjacent to the county zoo. Tara watched Kenny fish while holding their little girl on her lap. The young family seemed to be always active—always happy.

*The dream changed location. Tara called to Kayla who was just learning to walk. They were barbequing at her parent's home—Kenny was helping her father grill steaks. Her sister and mother were talking in whispers, which always annoyed Tara. They had their own secrets that were kept just between them. Tara was more like her father. She'd rather talk about the latest college basketball game or NASCAR race. She had no interest in gossip.*

*The sky turned from a brilliant blue to a dark green. The wind picked up blowing debris all over the backyard. Kenny and her father struggled to keep the barbeque from rolling away. Suddenly, Kenny's arm caught fire to the delight of her sister and mother. They both cheered, raising their glasses high in the air while he ran wildly around the lawn trying to put the fire out by blowing on it.*

*Tara tried to get up and help, but was held down by her mother. "Let him burn!"*

*Tara broke free from her grip, but not before Kenny's body became completely engulfed. "Kenny! Kenny!" Tara screamed, waking herself up in the process.*

*The morning sun was blinding. It took a moment for Tara to become re-oriented to her surroundings. Before she could move, she heard the clear and distinctive voice of her daughter.*

*"Mommy. Daddy's here."*

*Shocked wide-awake, Tara bolted out of her parent's bed and ran down the hall into the living room. The next contestant was being called down on the television. She crept into the kitchen and found her mother scrubbing her old non-stick pan from that morning's breakfast. She had her customary cigarette smoldering in the ashtray along side her well seasoned coffee-cup. Tara reached to touch her on the shoulder. Betty Jo turned around revealing a burnt, shriveled face, causing Tara to scream at the top of her lungs.*

"Tara! What in the world?" Stan said. His daughter's scream had caused him to jump and cut his chin while in the middle of shaving. "Betty Jo, get in here, now!"

Tara sat straight up in bed wearing the same clothes she had on from the day before. Her eyes were red and moist from crying in her dreams. The realization that Kenny was still missing crushed her soul.

"What time is it?" Tara asked.

"Just past six. You've had a long, needed rest," Betty Jo said, walking into the bedroom while drying her hands with a dishtowel.

"Did Kenny call?"

Stan exhaled deeply as he attended to his fresh cut. He just wanted to tell the girl her husband was dead and not coming back so they could get the drama moving. He didn't understand the logic behind delaying the inevitable. They all knew he was most likely the person that died in the fire. Nothing else made sense.

"No one called," Betty Jo said. "Why don't you get some coffee and breakfast? We'll try contacting the police this morning. Maybe they've heard some news."

Much to Stan's delight, Tara left the bedroom granting him some privacy—a commodity he knew he would be short on in the coming months. His daughter didn't have the means to recover from losing her home. If his son in-law ever did show up, Stan's personal space would shrink that much more.

"I'll call you at work if we find out anything, Stan," Betty Jo said. "I might need you to come straight home if its bad news."

Stan grunted, signaling he fully understood the seriousness of the situation. He had already made arrangements for the assistant-foreman to handle things until after Thanksgiving and possibly the week after that. He was due some time anyway. It had been over a year since his last vacation.

Betty Jo found Tara curled up on the couch watching the local morning news. She left her alone and started breakfast. After last night's ordeal, she was over saturated with the "Kenny mystery" and welcomed the silence from her daughter. The day had already promised to be difficult with Tara staying home from work again. The subject didn't need to be brought up.

Stan grabbed a piece of bacon and his thermos on the way out the door. He only offered a look of apathy while glancing over at his daughter. Work would offer solace, at least for a few hours. He had promised Betty Jo he would contact the police about the investigation to get her mainly off of his back. He was a stern believer in leaving those who knew better alone so they could do their job. His job was being a foreman at North Sedgwick Rock and Gravel, not a CSI investigator. If the police had found something, they would inform those who needed to know in good time.

# 12

The local news at noon came blaring to life, jolting the semi-conscious Betty Jo out of her world of soap operas. The opening story promised there was a break in the case of the unknown victim in a recent mobile home fire. The name was being withheld until the next of kin could be notified. Her heart sank knowing they would all be on edge until they were told by the police whether it was Kenny's remains in the fire or some other poor soul.

On cue, Tara ran out of the back bedroom asking her mother if she had just seen the story. "That's good, right?"

"What's good?" Betty Jo asked, confused by the question.

"The guy on the news said they knew who the person was they found in my house! Weren't you listening? That means it wasn't Kenny. If it was, the police would've said something by now."

Not wanting to discourage her daughter, Betty Jo nodded her head in agreement. She wanted to believe the police would have notified Tara before the local television stations. She wanted to join in on her daughter's enthusiasm, but something just didn't seem right. The police had promised to be in touch when they heard any news—good or bad. They not only had the Carter's phone number, but their address as well. They would have surely tried to call.

Max and Mini erupted into frenzy, yipping and spinning in circles. Harry, the cat, high tailed it into the master bedroom as he always had when a strange car pulled up to the house. Tara's expression became blank—her complexion washed-out at the sight of the police cruiser. Without giving a second thought, Betty Jo got up to answer the front door, shushing and nudging the little dogs out of her way.

"Please don't answer the door, Mom..." Tara said, pleading in a thin, frail voice. Her eyes had already begun to tear up. Betty Jo didn't hear her daughter over the ear piercing yapping of the dogs.

Two youthful Wichita police officers stood at the front door asking if there was a Tara James at home. It finally dawned on Betty Jo what was taking place. She knew the very reason the police were at her door. She was only able to nod and invite them in.

Tara's world became blurry and her legs felt like rubber. Before her mother could reach her, she had collapsed onto the floor. The officers as well rushed to her aid.

The news that the human remains found in the smoldering ruins of the mobile home were that of Kenny James was never delivered successfully by the young officers as planned. Betty Jo had to ask the question herself. They both answered her in unison and gave contact information for the county coroner's office to make arrangements for the picking up of the remains.

## 13

The severe ice storm in January that crippled most of south central Kansas made it next to impossible for Sadie to sell her house. By mid March, the city of Wichita was still picking up downed tree branches and debris. Her home was not spared the devastation. A large cork screw willow in the backyard was destroyed by over a half an inch of accumulated ice.

Her real estate agent assured Sadie that the market would pick back up and she and her children would be in a new house before the beginning of summer. Living that close to Jared for at least three more months didn't thrill her in the least bit. Sadie was looking for a house far from Wichita. It needed to be a distance that would discourage her children's father from making too many unscheduled and unwelcome visits.

Sadie stretched out on the living room couch with her customary romance novel, while her three children played noisily in the next room. She didn't mind the ruckus knowing their free time was limited on Saturdays. Like clock work, her mother would call around noon to invite them over for dinner, which usually meant burnt hotdogs and hamburgers courtesy of grandpa.

Since Tara had moved in with their parents, Betty Jo had been miserable. She needed some semblance of normalcy so her husband and youngest daughter didn't drive her crazy. Sadie was glad to help, but would dread the weekends for the mere fact it meant spending it with her moping sister.

On few occasions, Sadie would invite her mother over instead. After three or four visits, her father and Tara caught on and started tagging along, leaving Sadie without peace until they all decided to leave.

The phone rang without fail. "Mommy! Grandma's on the phone!" Ami said as loud as she could.

Sad that leisure time was over, Sadie got up and took the phone out of her nine-year-old daughter's hand.

"Hi...a pie? How about a cake instead? The kids don't really like pie...oh, Dad wants an apple pie. I guess I can pick up both. Cookies will do? Okay, see ya there."

Ami hung on every word. With the announcement that there would be of cookies, she did a pirouette, screaming "Cookies, cookies, cookies!" over and over. The other two joined in the chorus complete with dance.

\*\*\*\*\*\*\*\*\*\*

Walking through her parent's front door, Sadie found Tara planted in front of the television watching college basketball with her father—the same place she had left her the week before. Neither acknowledged her arrival.

Sadie's children followed her in chanting "Grandma, Grandma, Grandma! Cookies, cookies, cookies!" resulting in Tara turning up the volume on the TV.

"Can they watch a DVD in your room, Mom?" Sadie asked glancing over at the two slugs in the living room.

"Go ahead, but stay out of Grandpa's coin dish."

The three tore down the hall, each with an oversized chocolate chip cookie in their grasp.

Betty Jo sat down at the kitchen table with a fresh mixed-drink and a cigarette. She exhaled deeply as if she were able to finally relax. Sadie grabbed a pop from the refrigerator, joining her mother at the crumb infested table.

"Did you have any luck with the house this week?" Betty Jo asked, having to yell slightly over the television.

"No. My realtor, Susan, said the buyer's traffic should pickup in the next couple of weeks. I did get to... hold on, Mom. Dad, could you please turn that down a bit? We can't even hear one another talk."

Without a word, Stan turned down the volume. Tara shot Sadie a look, rolled her eyes, and shook her head. Sadie had become accustomed to her sister's rude behavior and paid no attention. A comment would only incite a fight, resulting in Tara sulking more and her father being unbearably grumpy.

"What were you about to say?" Betty said.

"I looked at a beautiful old farmhouse between Garden Plain and Cheney. It needs a little bit of work, but nothing too serious. The owners just put on a new roof and painted the exterior."

"How many bedrooms?"

"Five total: four up and one down."

"Oh that would be perfect. Each child would have their own room," Betty Jo said. "What would you do with the fifth bedroom?"

"I don't know. Maybe use it as a playroom or office. I need someplace better than the kitchen table to work on my lesson plans or grade papers. The house is so big that I got turned around to which way the front door was."

"I know this is a sore subject with you...but have you thought more about what I suggested with Tara? You know, about moving in with you." Betty Jo trailed off, leery of Sadie's reaction

Sadie stared out the kitchen window. She could feel her arms tense up from the stress of being forced to take in her sister.

"Why doesn't she get a place of her own? She has a good job. There are apartments advertising move-in specials all over town. There are quite a few nice ones on the west side of Wichita just minutes from her work. I just don't understand why she's hung on so long here instead of giving herself the gift of privacy."

Betty Jo needed a break from her youngest daughter. She wasn't the cleanest of people and was starting to wear on the weekly grocery bill. The constant sulking didn't help, either. A change needed to be made sooner than later.

"She's not ready to be on her own. It's only been five months since Kenny died. She needs to be around other people. Those places sound nice, but ...she just wouldn't be able to handle being alone."

The guilt trip was working full-force. Just to keep her mother happy, Sadie told her she would consider the possibility. She had already made arrangements to see the house one more time the next day with her mother—bringing Tara along didn't seem like a big deal, and it would get her mother off of her back.

"Would you like to see the house?"

Betty Jo's face lit up. "Oh, that would be wonderful."

"Tara. Tara, turn that down for a minute," Sadie said.

The sound was muted, but Tara still sat staring at the screen.

"Would you like to look at a house tomorrow with mom and me?"

"Why?"

"I wanted your opinion on it."

"I know what you're trying to do. You just want to get me out of the house. You could care less about my opinion on anything. I'm happy just where I am."

"Now, Tara..." Betty Jo said.

"If it will get her off of that damn couch, she's going!" Stan said from his recliner. He turned the volume back up on the basketball game and took a long swig from his beer. Tara pouted and slumped down on the couch. She loathed the idea of going anywhere with her mother, Sadie and the three little brats. She worked too hard all week to be told what to do with her weekends.

# 14

Sunday turned out to be the nicest day of the year thus far. Although cool and breezy, the sky was cloudless and a deep blue. It was a welcome relief from the tornadic weather that had blown through south central Kansas the week before.

Betty Jo and Tara followed Sadie and the kids up the long gravel driveway, stopping under an old walnut tree in the middle of the turn-around. Ami and Erin bolted out of the SUV, followed by their little brother, and headed straight for the tire swing.

A forty-something, stout woman, sporting a million-dollar smile and dressed in a blue blazer, stood on the front porch of the white wood framed farmhouse. "Hello, hello!" she said with great enthusiasm.

Sadie waived back, grinning ear to ear. "It's beautiful out here, isn't it?"

Betty Jo nodded soaking up her surroundings. Tara stood cross armed, looking less than impressed.

The agent excitedly approached with her right hand extended. "This must be your mother and sister. I'm so pleased you could join us. I'm Susan McIntosh, the other half of the McIntosh team. My husband, Jeff, couldn't make it. He's showing another home out in Maize. Betty Jo and Tara, isn't it?"

"Yes. I'm Betty Jo Carter and this is my daughter, Tara."

"James. It's Tara James," Tara said, looking at the ground.

Feeling embarrassed by her sister's behavior, Sadie shot Tara a scowl.

Susan's smile semi-evaporated. "Let's take a look inside," she said, leading the three ladies up onto the porch. "Isn't this a roomy porch? It's so full of possibilities."

"That's where I said I could put a porch-swing," Sadie said, pointing in the far corner.

The group entered the house through the single, freshly painted red front door and onto the newly resurfaced hardwood floors.

"These are the original floors. The owner discovered them under some very worn and outdated carpeting when he bought the house in 2004," Susan said. "The only floor he didn't get around to updating is in the kitchen."

"He became ill, didn't he?" Sadie asked.

"Not in the traditional sense. He had a nervous breakdown, I believe from exhaustion. His brother and sister have taken over the power of attorney and are very motivated to sell."

Tara rolled her eyes. "I'll bet they are. Motivated to make some money."

"Tara!" Betty Jo said.

"Oh, that's all right, Mrs. Carter. Tara actually made a good observation. All proceeds from the sell, however, will go to the owner. He's expected to make a full recovery."

Sadie started to feel sorry that she had invited Tara along. She understood the reasons behind her sister's behavior, but wished she would take her act elsewhere. Today was supposed to be about showing off the house she had found to her mother. In her own opinion, Sadie had very few selfish moments. She would be damned if her moping, starved for attention sister was going to ruin the day.

"The crown molding is beautiful!" Betty Jo said.

Susan gushed back. "All original!"

"Mom. You've got to see the size of this kitchen. It's at least twice the size of yours," Sadie said.

The spacious kitchen had wall to wall painted cabinets and cupboards still in their original condition. The counters were spacious, but warped slightly. The tile floor was separating and yellowed with a dark stain in the middle of the room as well as in front of the double porcelain sink.

Concerned with Betty Jo's worried expression, Susan tried to explain away the kitchen's condition. "This is the only non-updated room in the entire house. For reasons un-known, the owner saved the kitchen for last. He became ill before he could start renovating it."

"That's why the house is appraised slightly lower than market. If I buy the house it will take time, plus quite a bit of money to totally renovate the kitchen. I'll probably keep it the way it is for awhile."

"Our own kitchen makeover took my husband and me at least three years to complete. We made improvements when we could afford them," Susan said. "Why don't we check out the second floor rooms? You'll be amazed at their size."

Sadie and Betty Jo followed Susan up the narrow wooden stairs. Tara lingered behind giving closer inspection to the living room and foyer. Although she would never admit it, she was enjoying the tour of the old farmhouse just as much as her mother. She had overheard most of the conversations between them concerning where she should be living. Before now, she was dead set against moving in with Sadie and her kids. After seeing the home first hand, she had a change of heart.

"Tara, we're up here," Betty Jo said. Tara made her way up the stairs soaking in the view.

"The bathroom has all new fixtures, a fiberglass tub as well as a new tile floor," Susan said, rambling on. "This bedroom has an eastern view of the small barn and the adjacent field."

Tara liked the view out of the large box window. She liked the large room with its pale, yellow walls. In her mind she could see the four poster bed she had always wanted sitting on an oval country rug. She liked the idea of being awakened by a splash of morning sun on a lazy Sunday morning. Something was missing, though. She couldn't put her finger on it, but she knew something was definitely missing.

"Hey!" she said suddenly, causing all three women to jump. "There aren't any closets!"

"That's because the house was built before closets became the norm. They were more of a luxury than a necessity in those days. People would use a large chifferobe to store their clothes," Susan said.

"I like the idea of not having closets. It makes the room seem bigger," Sadie said.

"I have enough saved to buy a new bedroom suite," Tara said without giving it much thought.

"Do you like this room?" Sadie asked.

Tara nodded and walked back over to the window. The children had just jumped off of the tire swing, leaving it twisting on its rope. Likes ducks in a row, they ran single file into the house.

Sadie smiled. "I thought you might. If I'm able to buy this house, I'd really like it if you would come and stay with me and the kids."

Tara wrapped her arms around herself, turned away, and started to cry. Sadie ran over and gave her a big hug. On cue, Ami ran into the room chanting, "They're hugging, 'they're hugging!"

Joey asked at the top of his lungs why girls always had to hug. Betty Jo scooted her three grandchildren out of the room, insisting that they needed to explore the rest of the house. Susan stood uncomfortably in the doorway waiting for Sadie and Tara to dry their eyes.

"I'm sorry, Susan," Sadie said, giggling and sniffling.

"I spoke with the owners this morning. They're more than willing to work with you on the price. We could submit an offer today if you wish. The finalization of the contract would be contingent on selling your current home of course."

"That would be wonderful!"

"Great! As soon as we're finished here, we'll run by my office and write up the offer."

Tara remained in the room for a few more moments before joining the others. She mentally measured it one more time. She knew what bedroom suite she wanted and made plans to put a down payment on it after work on Monday.

Joey and Erin were jumping up and down in the middle of the upstairs landing trying to touch a dangling rope hanging from a trapdoor in the ceiling. A note was taped to the door itself that simply read "Do not open." Betty Jo tried without success to calm the two down. Ami was too busy yelling "Echo" in one of the other three bedrooms to notice her brother and sister were out of control.

"Oh, that's right. The owners said not to open the attic door. The springs for the step ladder are broken and it will come folding out. They said it was too dangerous and they would be over next week to fix it," Susan said. "It's just a room for storage. They told me it was much too small for anything else."

"Did they finish cleaning-up the cellar?" Sadie asked.

"They cleared out all of the debris, if that's what you mean. It won't be useable like modern day basements—there's too much exposed dirt, but you could still use it as a shelter if need be."

With the explanation over, Erin and Joey took off down stairs followed closely by Ami. The adults leisurely made their way back down to the foyer. Tara took off on her own continuing her investigation. The other three women gathered in the living room discussing the unique carvings in the fireplace mantle and molding. The group would spend another good half-hour exploring and asking questions.

# 15

Stan Carter backed the dented, yellow moving truck slowly up to the old farmhouse—Sadie's farmhouse—the Saturday after Memorial Day. Sadie and Tara greeted the movers, a collection of Stan's friends from work, with coffee and doughnuts on the front porch.

The inside of the house sported the unmistakable odor of pine cleaner and bleach, courtesy of extensive cleaning the night before. A blue woven rug, one of many picked out by Tara, covered the dark stain on the floor in the middle of the kitchen. The cupboards and cabinets had new shelf-paper. Kitchen plaques with clever sayings were hung on the drab walls.

The interior of the house echoed with the booming voices of older men shouting commands to one another as they maneuvered the larger pieces of furniture. Sadie had given her father a makeshift blueprint of where she wanted everything placed. He reassured his daughter that if anything wasn't where she wanted it, he would make sure it would get where it belonged even if he had to move it himself.

Sadie watched with excitement as her new home filled up with furniture. The long drawn out battle to settle on the price of her old home left her doubtful if she would ever make it to this point. She was disappointed that she didn't make all of the money her realtor had thought she could, but the realization of her dream to own this house and the nice comfortable distance from Jared made it all worthwhile.

Her mother and father had surprised Sadie with a new chifferobe for each grandchild, which took quite a bit of pressure off of her bank account. She had planned to use cardboard wardrobe boxes until she received the first couple of support checks from Jared.

Susan drove up wearing the same blue blazer she wore everyday. She walked past Stan and the other helpers, bearing a basket-full of fruit, cheese, crackers and wine, greeting them with her flashy, over enthusiastic smile. Sadie met her on the front porch with her own big smile and a hug.

"Welcome to your new home!" Susan said, presenting her latest favorite client with the housewarming gift.

Tara avoided Susan at all cost, often accusing her of being a "phony windbag," which always incited an argument with her sister and mother.

The day that started off with coffee, doughnuts and a full moving truck, ended with pizza, beer, and a house full of boxes and discarded packing paper. Betty Jo showed up two hours early with the kids and the moving truck had to be jumpstarted after Stan had left the headlights on all day.

Sadie closed her eyes and took a deep breath. Today wasn't the day to be upset or angry. She knew the real work lay ahead. She made up her mind she was going to enjoy this moment with her family. God only knew what twists and turns her life would take. After her failed marriage, and the tragedies Tara had to endure, she wasn't taking anything for granted.

# 16

Although Tara had escaped the confines of her parent's home, for the second time in her life, she found herself sleeping once again on an air mattress. She and Sadie had worked hard into the night unpacking the kid's room as well as the downstairs master bedroom; leaving Tara's the only bedroom unfinished and a maze full of un-opened boxes. The furniture store hadn't delivered her new bedroom suite on Saturday as promised; giving her the excuse the delivery truck transporting her bed and chifferobe had experienced mechanical problems and wasn't expected until the first of the week at best.

The floor was surprisingly cold for being on the second floor. Although the temperature had just graced eighty-four in the late afternoon, Tara snuggled under two layers of sleeping bags and still fought to get warm.

Ami and Erin whispering and giggling to didn't help in Tara's pursuit of sleep. She found out quickly that the rooms were not sound proof and they also echoed due to lack of wall-to-wall carpeting.

Little Joey joining in on the fun was about the last straw. Tara waited for Sadie to make an appearance then remembered her sister was safe and probably warm in her sanctuary downstairs. She had no deigns on being the second floor police, so she covered her head and immersed herself in thoughts about the coming day and all of the projects she and Sadie wanted to accomplish before she was forced to go back to work on Monday. Before long, her giggling nieces and nephew were far off in the distance.

\*\*\*\*\*\*\*\*\*\*

*Tara sat alone in the middle of a dark, empty room, cross-leg on a cold, wooden floor. She didn't like the dark. It left her feeling vulnerable and exposed. A slit of light underneath a single door showed the only way out. She could hear faint voices of a man and women talking just on the other side. Their muffled tones made it impossible to understand what they were saying.*

*Something shuffled lightly across the floor to her left. Tara breathed in deeply emitting a high squeak. Her heart pounded, echoing in her chest. Something else bumped against the wall to her right. Tara's body became rigid with fear. She desperately wanted to get up and run for the door, but felt paralyzed—unable to even turn her head.*

*A presence approached from behind—a slight breeze blew past her bare neck—she could feel someone close. A small hand gently rested on her shoulder causing her body to shudder. A thin voice whispered softly in her ear, "Mommy..."*

Tara's scream resonated throughout the entire second-floor giving charge for the children to invade her room.

"Aunt Tara, Aunt Tara! Did you have a bad dream?" Ami asked, shouting more than talking.

Tara sat up embarrassed from all of the attention. Her dream still fuzzy in her head, she tried to recall what she had dreamt about without success.

The commotion her nieces and nephew were making woke up Sadie. "Whatever the reason to be loud was better be a good one, or else it's going to be spankings for everyone!" she said in a gruff voice, stern voice.

Tara ungracefully got up from the air mattress explaining it was her fault.

"I'm so sorry you had a nightmare. It's our first night in our new home. We should all be having happy dreams," Sadie said with a yawn. "Why is it so cold in your room? Lucky! It's like a sweat box in mine. I could hardly get to sleep."

"I'll trade you. You can enjoy my nice comfortable bed," Tara said.

"No thanks," Sadie said, heading back downstairs. "Get to bed you three. If I have to come up here one more time, I will be handing out the spankings!"

Ami, Erin, and Joey all scattered into their rooms. Tara headed down stairs to the kitchen to make a cup of herbal tea. The thought of going back in her room made her feel uncomfortable. Some small fragment of her dream still lingered in the darkness. It had the strange feel of familiarity.

The soothing chamomile tea helped her forget she had a nightmare at all. After a half-cup, she headed back to bed and slept straight through until her nieces and nephew woke her bright and early at seven in the morning.

## <u>17</u>

The daunting tasks of unpacking and setting up the downstairs rooms made Sunday fly by. Before Tara knew it, Monday and a long work week loomed ahead. If she weren't in bed at least by ten, getting up at five-thirty in the morning would be a painful experience.

She threw a piece of left over pizza from Saturday in a baggie, then yogurt and bottle of water into her lunch bag. If she hurried, she could use the last of the day's light to find her work clothes. The lamp-set she had ordered was also on the broken-down delivery truck.

Joey came running down stairs calling to Sadie, "Mommy! Mommy! Ami won't stop it. Make her stop now!"

Erin joined her brother in tattling on their sister. "Don't believe Ami, Mommy. She's a big, fat liar!"

"Watch the name calling, Erin," Sadie said. "What's the matter, Joey?"

"Ami keeps on knocking on my door and then running away."

"I heard her too!" Erin said.

"If your door was open like it should be, then how was Ami knocking on it?"

"Oh, sorry," Joey said, looking down at the floor.

"Both of you go back upstairs and leave those doors open, and send down Ami so I can talk to her, too."

Erin and Joey took off yelling in tandem. "Ami! Mommy wants to talk to you and you're in big trouble!"

Tara watched wearily on the living room couch, thinking that it would have been nice if Kayla were still alive. She was usually the instigator and Ami the follower. The two were always getting into trouble and then being let off easy—much like she and Sadie when they were little.

Ami had become distant for the better part of a year after Kayla had been killed. She had a terrible second-grade year, which almost resulted in Sadie having to leave her back. She didn't become her old-self again until the drama of her parents divorce pushed all three kids together.

"I didn't do it! I swear to God!" Ami said, holding up her right hand.

"I didn't say you did. Just make sure you keep your bedroom door open. I'll be up to check on you guys in a few minutes."

"Can I have another cookie?" Ami asked, grinning and holding her hands up in a mock prayer.

"Take one each up for Erin and Joey."

Ami took off into the kitchen then reappeared with three oversized chocolate-chip cookies in her grasp.

"You're letting them eat in their rooms?" Tara said.

Sadie shrugged her shoulders and smiled. "I'm just trying to keep the mice upstairs."

"Thanks a lot. I need to get out my work clothes before it gets too dark to see in my room," Tara said, jumping up from the couch and grabbing a cookie for herself.

"The satellite people will be out tomorrow to set up the TV. Did you want them to put a box in your room?"

"That would be great. That way I can watch *NASCAR* without being disturbed," she said with a laugh.

"Or the rest of us being annoyed!"

Sadie took advantage of one of the few quiet moments she had to herself and reclined, shutting her eyes. The weekend had been hectic but rewarding. She couldn't believe she was sitting in her own house that she had purchased with her own money, and had the entire summer to enjoy it before she had to be back in the classroom. Without Jared, her future looked bright and promising. She was happy, the kids were happy, and Tara had finally crawled out of the funk she had been in.

## <u>18</u>

The workweek started off with the usual hurry up and get it done speech by Tara's supervisor, which was closely followed by the recent rumor making its way through the various shops and cubicles of Swift Jet. For countless months, stories had circulated about a potential sell of the business-jet maker to some large Asian corporation. Now there was a new twist: twenty-percent layoff across the board—all by seniority. That meant anyone with less than two years with the company was in jeopardy of losing their job. Tara had five.

She tried not to pay attention to the gossip, but this time she had no choice. Her sister's ex-husband, Jared, had just over fifteen months. If he lost his job, Sadie would lose a good chunk of her income, something she couldn't afford just after she had purchased a house.

Tara's lead-man dropped a work-order for twenty sets of terminal strips on her workstation, sending a signal for her to quit daydreaming and get to work. Her supervisor was a play by the rules prick and had written her up once before for being non-productive. She hated her job, but knew she too had a financial obligation to her sister. Although she wasn't on the mortgage, without Tara's monthly contributions Sadie's paycheck would be stretched thin to the point of breaking. She buried herself in her work and blocked out all thought of a layoff.

\*\*\*\*\*\*\*\*\*\*\*

At the end of the shift, Tara saw Jared along with a slew of other second-shift employee's waltz by, carrying an official union news-letter. This activity only took place on certain occasions: either a special union vote or announcements of coming layoffs. The chatter arose to deafening decibels as new rumors took flight in the wire-room.

Three minutes until the end of the shift seemed an unbearable amount of time to suffer the nonsense. Tara stood in line for the clock, sandwiched between two Bitching Betty's whose entire conversation revolved on how terrible their work conditions were, and how they knew that Swift Jet would without a doubt be closing its doors within a year. Mercifully, the three-thirty bell rang freeing the employees from the confines of work. Tara took off, eager to see what all of the commotion was all about.

The print at the top of the official union-flyer was in big, bold font. It simply read *"Notice of Potential Layoffs!"* The body of the letter stated that up to sixty-percent cutbacks were planned over the course of the next twenty-four months. That number was far bigger than the twenty-percent being spread inside the plant. Now Tara was concerned. Even with five years seniority she was still in the lower percentile within her job classification.

A company wide meeting was scheduled for Wednesday, which meant another full day of gossip and carrying on before she heard some factual information. If Tara had enough sick time to take she wouldn't even bother coming in on Tuesday. Unfortunately, as with Kayla's death, she had used all of the time she had saved after Kenny had died.

She ran over the possibilities of being laid-off in her head the entire twenty- minute commute home. By the time she had reached their new house, she was mentally exhausted. Not even a week had gone by and she had to share with Sadie that the income she was counting on to help pay for her new house was in jeopardy.

As she pulled around the drive, she noticed her bedroom window was wide open and the curtains she had painstakingly hung Sunday were being blown about in the volatile Kansas wind.

Sadie was sitting on the front porch sipping on a beer and holding one up for Tara. The girls were screaming, spinning Joey back and forth on the tire swing. Any hope of privacy was just a distant dream. She knew that until the end of summer, her home-life would revolve around Sadie and her kids.

"Hey, you opened my window," Tara said, glancing up once more.

"Uh, I did? I don't remember doing it. Maybe Ami opened it. She was trying really hard to be my helper today."

"Well, maybe next time she could help anywhere but my room. I paid twenty dollars for those curtains. I was hoping that they would last a little bit longer than a day," Tara said as she took the beer from Sadie.

"Don't make me sorry to have given you that beer, Ms. Grumpy. If you're going to be disagreeable, then you can just get back in your truck, drive it around in a circle, get back out, and try again."

"Sorry. I'm in a foul mood. I got this at the end of the day." Tara handed the union-flyer to Sadie. Before she could read it, Erin ran up to give a report on the latest bad word Joey called her.

Sadie took a deep breath. "Ami and Joey! All three of you can go inside now until you can learn to get along." The three shuffled and pouted all the way into the house.

Sadie shook her head and started reading the flyer. "What? Oh my god. What does this mean?"

"I won't know until Wednesday. We're having a company wide meeting to discuss the facts. If I get laid off, then I'll just find another job—two if I need to."

"I know you'll try, but if Jared loses *his* job as well, my child support payments could go down. I can't afford that."

"Won't the state suspend his driver's license if he doesn't pay?"

"Yes, but he can always get a job in fast-food and still qualify under their guidelines, but at a lower monthly rate. He wouldn't even notice the change of jobs in his paycheck. Most of his salary goes to the kids now. He just doesn't care, because he is living solely off of his parents. He claims he's putting the rest away for their college. He couldn't even spell college!"

"Sorry for the bad news," Tara said. "What's for dinner? It smells good."

"Oh yeah! The meatloaf!" Sadie said, hopping off the porch swing.

Just as Tara stood up, a loud bang echoed throughout the house. All three kids came running and screaming out onto the front porch.

"Mommy! Aunt Tara! There's someone upstairs!" Ami said, pointing toward the house. Erin and Joey stood close to her, wide-eyed and nodding their heads.

"I'll go and check," Tara said.

"They're upstairs, Aunt Tara!" Ami said.

Sadie held all three of her children tight in her arms. "Thank you, sis. I'm sure it was just the wind blowing one of the doors shut."

"But we heard foot steps," Erin said. "Didn't we, Ami?"

"Big foot steps!"

"All right, now you're scaring Mommy. Big, brave Aunt Tara will prove you both wrong."

"But I heard it, too," Joey said.

Tara made her way upstairs. All four bedroom doors were closed making the landing and hallway dark even in the middle of the afternoon. The only light came from the small window in the upstairs bathroom. She opened the kid's room first finding nothing but toys on the floors and unmade beds. The windows were closed and the curtains were drawn giving the rooms the same gloomy look as the hallway and landing.

She had a bad feeling when she reached to open her door that the noise they all heard was her boxes falling to the floor, courtesy of three little mice the size of children. Expecting the worst, she turned the knob carefully but found nothing except the wind whipping the curtains in and out of the window.

"Oh, thank you, God. The little darlings didn't break a thing."

Tara stuck her head out the window and yelled down to Sadie and the kids that everything was just fine. The noise they all heard was the wind slamming her bedroom door shut. As soon as she finished her explanation, the door slammed shut again, giving rise to more shrieks and screams from the girls and Joey. She closed the window, putting an end to the drama and then inspected her curtains for damage.

Leaving to rejoin her beer, Tara paused and enjoyed the moment of calm before the kids stampeded back into the house. She found the house had a soothing feel to it. It was if someone gently reached out and caressed your temples the moment you stepped through the front-door. Tara was in love with the house and would do everything possible to ensure she didn't let Sadie down financially.

# 19

Dinner was slightly overdone meatloaf, a bag of frozen corn, and instant mashed potatoes. Tara was thrilled she didn't have to eat barbeque every night of the week anymore. Sadie was thrilled she had more than she and the kids to cook for. For the past few months they had wasted more food than they had eaten.

The three kids worked on finishing up their dinner, all the time eyeing the chocolate pudding cups on the counter. Sadie would place what ever desert was being offered that day strategically in sight, encouraging her children to finish their dinner—vegetables and all. She didn't overload their plates and then claim there were starving children in some exotic country. Instead she gave them equal and moderate portions. If they were hungry for more, then they were free to ask for more. The only rule was that they had to eat what ever they took, or the desert would be saved for the next night. Joey was the biggest offender.

The dinner conversation was light for the kid's sake. Sadie and Tara had agreed to wait until Wednesday to discuss the potential layoff. They would only discuss a contingency plan in the event they found themselves short on money. Neither woman had the capacity to take on more drama. Tara's losses were too fresh in her mind; Sadie's two-year battle at home with Jared had left her emotionally frazzled.

Tara grabbed her third beer of the night and Sadie opened her second. They both retired to the living room to play with the new satellite TV menu.

Flipping through what seemed to be endless channels, Sadie gasped. "It was the satellite guy! You know the guy the installed the dish and boxes? I had him install one in my room as well as yours."

"What on earth are you talking about?" Tara asked.

"That's who opened your window! I blamed poor Ami."

"See, I told you it wasn't me!" Ami said from the kitchen table with a mouth full of pudding.

"Cool, I forgot that I needed to go shopping for a new flat-screen TV this weekend," Tara said. All thoughts of a looming layoff had vanished from her mind. She snuggled into the cushions of the couch, content to let Sadie surf the channels. She hadn't felt this safe and warm in almost three years.

## <u>20</u>

Tara's room was chilly once again, resulting in her sleeping underneath three sleeping-bags instead of two. Exhausted from the layoff drama at work, she fell asleep as soon as her head hit the pillow.

*Her dreams found her back in the darkened room sitting cross-leg on the cold hardwood floor. The voices on the other side of the door sounded clearer, but she still couldn't make out what they were saying.*

*A set of small footsteps approached her from behind. Before she could shudder, she heard a faint but distinct whisper in her left ear. "I can't find Daddy."*

Tara didn't scream this time—she simply woke up, still buried under the sleeping bags. Her cheeks and pillow were wet from her tears. The feeling of helplessness had left her body listless. She was deeply saddened, but didn't know why.

Her alarm clock displayed it was three a.m. which meant she still had a couple of hours of sleep ahead of her. She hated waking up in the middle of the night. She could never make herself fall back to sleep which always resulted in a long and haggard day at work.

She found the strength to crawl from under her covers and noticed the faint scent of jasmine floating just above her head. She stumbled to the door and made her way toward the bathroom. The scent was also present along the dark hallway. There it grew more intense—flowing around her head as she reached for the closed bathroom door.

"Who's in there?" she said in a whisper. "Is that you, Ami? It's Aunt Tara, sweetie. Open the door."

Trying the doorknob, she found it to be locked. She knocked gently against the solid door. The faucet turned on then off again. "Erin...Joey? Are you in there, Sadie?"

The toilet flushed and the lid slammed down. "Finally," she said to herself. The doorknob turned back and forth, but the door remained closed. Tara tried it herself, but without success. Not wanting to fight, she made her way down to Sadie's bedroom.

She shook Sadie's shoulder, rocking her back and forth. "Wake up, Sadie. One of the kids has locked themselves in the bathroom and I have to go."

Sadie turned over and three heads popped up from underneath the covers. "Your perfume really stinks, Aunt Tara," Joey said, half-yelling and jolting his mother awake. The two girls giggled.

"What are you guys doing in my bed?" Sadie asked.

"Everything smells like yucky perfume except for your bedroom, Mama," Ami said in a wide-awake voice.

"I like it," Erin said.

"Then why are you in here with us, you liar?" Ami said.

"Mommy, Ami called me a bad name again!"

Sadie snapped. "All right, all right...shut up all of you...please! What perfume? Who's been into my perfume?"

"Sadie. The bathroom door is locked, and I really have to go!" Tara said, dancing next to the bed.

"Then use mine, for 'Pete's sake'."

Tara reached to open the master bath's door and found it also had been locked. "Oh, come on!"

"I didn't think the lock worked on that door," Sadie said. "Now which one of you has been playing with the locks?" A chorus of 'not me' erupted from all three children.

Tara found the exchange less than amusing. "Now what do I do?"

"I don't know. Go and try the upstairs bathroom again. Maybe the doorknob is stuck."

"I'll try! I'll try!" Joey said, leaping off of his mother's bed and out the door. Tara chased after him.

The bathroom door was wide open with the toilet still running. Ecstatic, she pushed the six-year-old, husky boy out of her way and shut the door in his face.

Joey reopened the door. "We're supposed to knock when the door is closed."

"Good! Now leave me alone!" Tara said. Relieved she had made it without having an accident; she didn't give another thought to the locked door or the strange perfume.

# 21

Sadie had made plans to meet their mother at the Northwest shopping plaza in Wichita, so she could help pick out and buy some new bedding for the kids and some dishtowels for the house. Tara had been suckered into their shopping trap—an activity she usually avoided. The plan was for them all to meet at the newest Mexican restaurant chain for an early dinner. She just wanted to go home, grab a beer, and get to bed early. The next day at work promised to be stressful and emotional for everyone.

Betty Jo waited in the parking lot for Tara to show up, as if her daughter would have gotten lost. She offered a cigarette, warning that the new restaurant was completely smoke free. The two stood semi-silent together. They had little to say after several months of being in each other's space—although, surprisingly to Tara, she had missed her mother and was glad to see her.

"Is Dad coming?" Tara asked in-between drags.

"There's no way in hell he'd eat at a place like this. He can't stand the taste of Mexican food."

"Too bad. I heard they have a great barbequed burrito," Tara said.

Betty Jo rolled her eyes and snickered. Being able to go out with her daughters and grandchildren was a blessing. She had forgotten how lonely she had been before Tara had moved back in. Stan had become more a piece of the furniture than a companion. The majority of the conversation between the two consisted of what was for dinner and how much was spent at the grocery store. Their marriage of thirty-five-years, which had started out with two eighteen-year-old kids in love, had somehow ebbed away into a marriage of convenience.

Tara and Betty Jo joined Sadie and the kids in the lobby. A disgruntled looking girl dressed in a white, green and red ruffled traditional Mexican dress mumbled, "Follow me, please," as she led them to the main dinning-room.

Two tables that had been pushed together to accommodate their larger than average party, was adorned with three sets of crayons and activity menus, along with a complimentary miniature piñata for each child. Large, colorful sombreros hung on the walls alongside flags of Mexico and various trinkets. The aroma of Spanish rice and refried beans dominated their senses, making their mouths water even before they had opened the menus.

"Isn't this nice, Mom?" Sadie asked. "They just opened last month. Carla, the teacher's aid that helped me the last part of the school year, said it was the best Mexican food she had eaten since she lived in California."

"Oh," Betty Jo said, looking around and smiling. "It sure smells good."

The waiter, wearing a shirt with the same frill as the hostess, walked up to the table smiling. "Good afternoon, ladies! I'm Scott. Can I start anyone off with a Piñata's festive icy-margarita?"

"Corona," Tara said, raising her hand without looking up from the menu.

"Waters for me and the kids," Sadie said.

"Water with lemon for me, please," Betty Jo said.

The waiter was off with his order as quickly as he had appeared. A lesser flamboyantly dressed man dropped off two baskets of tortilla chips and salsa. In the background, a recording of La Bamba was being played by a mariachi band. The menus were filled with large, bright pictures of food and over two pages of selections, which for the most part had meat, cheese and a flour tortilla as their main ingredients.

"What are you going to have, Mom?" Sadie asked.

"The number one, I believe. Two tacos should be more than enough for me."

"What about you, Tara?"

"I don't know. Maybe the chicken flautas—I don't want to get anything too heavy. I didn't sleep well last night and I need to get to bed early."

"You're not sleeping well, dear?" Betty Jo asked.

"They still haven't delivered her furniture, Mom," Sadie said.

"That's terrible. Are you sleeping on the couch?"

"Air-mattress on my bedroom floor," Tara said with a mouthful of chips. "The store said they expect their truck to be fixed by Wednesday and that I will be their first delivery. I've also had the same strange dream twice now. I think it also has something to do with me not getting enough sleep."

"Let me guess. You're standing naked in front of a classroom!" Betty Jo said. The word naked made the kids giggle.

Tara also giggled. "No!"

"I'll bet that when you get your new bed, you'll have nothing but nice dreams," Betty Jo said.

"Did you hear anything more at work?" Sadie asked.

"Just more rumors. I'll hear more at the meeting tomorrow."

"Is there something wrong at your job, Tara?" Betty Jo asked.

"There might be a layoff, but I won't know until tomorrow morning when we have our meeting."

"Jared might be affected, Mother, so we are all going to move back in with you."

"Don't give the old woman a heart attack!" Tara said.

"Who are you calling old? I feel better now than I ever did when you two were babies. The only diaper I have to change these days is your father's!"

All three women laughed loudly, earning stares from the people seated around them. The kids paid no attention—they were too engrossed in their coloring.

## 22

Sadie invited her mother back to the house, so she could see it without all of the boxes. Pulling into the drive first, she noticed a box on the porch and a note taped to the middle of the front door. There were deep tire ruts in the gravel which could only mean one thing: Jared had been there. Trying to keep her temper in check, she quietly told the kids to go and play on the tire-swing.

Tara pulled up, followed by Betty Jo. Sadie wanted to read the note before they got out of their cars, fearing Jared had written something demeaning like he was prone to do. The words on the old scrap of notebook paper made her heart sink. *"Thanks for answering the door, bitch!"* was all that was written. She crumpled it and put it into her purse, saddened that her fears were substantiated.

Unlocking the door, she kicked the box on the porch having forgotten it was there. She took the beaten, taped up cardboard box inside and set it on the table. Not waiting for Tara and her mother to come in, Sadie took a knife to the duct tape and opened the box, exposing its contents. Inside were an odd collection of dirty and broken toys that had been clearly left outside in the exact box in which they were sitting. Two ducks with wheels and a pull string, a decapitated action figure, and an assortment of metal dump-trucks and plastic race-cars—none of which had all of their wheels still attached. On top was a note written by Jared's mother. *"Found these out back. Thought the kids might use them."*

"Oh my God, that family has no clue!" she said under her breath.

"What on earth is that?" Tara asked as she entered the kitchen.

"Nothing. Just some old crap from Jared."

"It smells like wet," Tara said, crinkling her nose.

Sadie wasted no time and took the box and its contents out to the trash can. On her way back in, she caught sight of her mother pushing the kids on the tire swing. All four were smiling and laughing. The scene warmed her heart, helping her to remember why she had moved out here in the first place.

When she returned back into the kitchen Tara was leaning against the kitchen counter holding a cold beer out to Sadie and the telephone. "He just called and wants you to call him back."

Sadie's blood boiled. Her arms became tense and her face flush. She took the phone from Tara and dialed Jared's number. "Worthless bastard!" she cursed under her breath. She took a long drink from her beer and waited patiently for the phone to be answered.

"Hello," a sickly voice answered.

"This is Sadie, Diane. Is Jared there?" she asked, trying to be polite.

"It's the wife for you," was her only response.

Jared wasted little time in picking up the phone. "What in the hell is your problem? I drive all the way out there to give the kids something from their grandma and the best you can do is ignore me at the door!"

"First of all, I don't appreciate you leaving profane notes where our children can find them! And you can tell your mother that I didn't appreciate the box of moldy, dirty, broken toys! Tell her to throw out her own trash!"

"If you would have answered the door, I wouldn't have had to leave the note!" Jared said.

"I wasn't home, Jared. We've been out with my mother since noon."

"You're lying. I was out there around two-thirty and could see someone walking around through the front door glass. I thought you would have least said something to me when you opened that upstairs window."

"I don't even know what you're talking about...and the next time you come by, you better call ahead. Home or not, you will not be welcomed unless you do!" she said, clicking the off button on the phone.

Tara stood applauding her sister. "What's he doing home? He should be at work. He'll get fired for attendance before he gets laid off."

"Have you been upstairs, yet?" Sadie asked.

"No...why?"

"Jared claims your bedroom window was open and that I opened it."

"My curtains! It was raining this afternoon!"

Tara took off upstairs. When she reached her room, the pressure from the wind made it difficult to open her door. Inside, the curtains were whipping around and soaked half-way through. There was a small puddle of water on the floor and windowsill. She stormed out of her room and yelled from the upstairs landing. "Sadie!"

Sadie rushed into Tara's room and found her sister inspecting her wet curtains. "Oh, I'm so sorry, Tara. I swear I didn't open the window."

"Then it had to be one of the kids! Please tell them to stay out of my room. I'd hate to see what they might do when I have my things unpacked."

Sadie knew it was time to leave Tara alone. Her mood had swung and it wouldn't be too wise to push her. She headed back down stairs to join her mother and kids outside on the tire-swing. Her day had been too nice for her ex-husband and her sister's temper to ruin it. She would talk to the kids away from their Aunt Tara and put the window opening and the bathroom door locking to rest.

# 23

When Tara arrived at work on Wednesday morning, the management had already begun setting up for the company wide meeting in the cafeteria. The murmur was at fever pitch. She was one of only five people in the wire-room just two-minutes before the start of shift. Her supervisor and lead-man were in the supervisor's office shaking their heads as they peered at the empty workstations. A few stragglers came bustling in, squawking about what they had just heard from the union steward.

Tara, not wanting to be the scapegoat for her co-worker's flagrant disregard of company rules, sat at her workstation—ready for the morning meeting. Unable to see the shop doors from her seat, she could only hear the stampede of late workers as they scurried into the room at the sound of the seven o'clock bell.

Like clockwork, Steve Biles, Tara's supervisor, walked to the center of the wire-shop with a clipboard in his hand. He was dressed for non-success in a pair of faded Dockers and a dress shirt that hadn't seen an iron in at least three washings. A bristled salt and pepper mustache accented his poor attempt at a comb over. His slight potbelly and stooping posture suggested he was pushing sixty instead of forty-five.

He gazed around at his gathered employees and sighed. "As you are all aware, there will be a company wide meeting in the cafeteria today. Since there is not nearly enough room to accommodate the entirety of the employee population in one sitting, there will be three meetings held today: two on first shift; one on second. First shift Manufacturing is scheduled for ten a.m. and the support groups will be at one. Second shift's meeting is scheduled for the start of their shift, so don't expect to give a turnover today.

Management has also asked that you do not eat in the dining room of the cafeteria due to it being used for the meeting, although the cafeteria will be serving a complete menu today."

"Where are we supposed to eat if the dining room is closed, Steve?" the un-appointed spokesperson for the group asked in her best injured union-member voice.

Steve shrugged his shoulders without as much as a glance her way. "Today's morning meeting is not opened for questions. We're already going to lose at least an hour of production because of today's activities. Dave will hand out your work assignments. Please start immediately on them," he said as he headed back to his office.

Not another word was uttered from the group. They all knew it was futile to argue with Steve; he was callused and heartless. If an employee became disgruntled, or didn't see eye to eye with his interpretation of the company rules, then they were free to seek union assistance.

The lead called each employee by name and handed out their work orders for the day. Tara was given ten circuit boards to solder—a job she could perform blindfolded. The job was tedious and time consuming, which meant her day, broken up in the middle by the meeting and lunch, would move by quickly. She immersed herself into the work, shutting out all conversation around her.

***********

The slow precession to the cafeteria started ten-minutes prior to the start of the meeting. Tara took her time. She was in no hurry to find a seat. She usually sat in the back away from her co-workers and anyone else that might try to talk to her. Before the loss of Kayla, she was very social—hanging out with a small group of people at lunch and sometimes after work. She and Kenny would regularly have cookouts or spend the weekend at Cheney Reservoir with Debbie Sheets and her family. She and Debbie had become such close friends, that they were often referred to as "the twins."

After the accident, everything changed. Tara refused all calls and visitors for six weeks—including Debbie. She was so devastated that she wanted just her family to attend the funeral.

Feeling snubbed and hurt, Debbie took it upon herself to spread stories about the real cause of Kayla's death during Tara's leave of absence. She told stories of a dirty home and parental neglect, which led to the seven-year-old girl being hit by a car while riding her bicycle near the entrance of the trailer park. "If she had been a more attentive mother, then that poor little girl would still be alive," Debbie would banter on.

Finding a hostile work environment when she returned, Tara crawled into an emotional cocoon. Even when Kenny had died two-years after Kayla, she only confided to Human Resources and her supervisor to the real reason she was taking another leave of absence. Although the news of Kenny's death had reached its way around the shop, not one word of condolences was offered.

The meeting started out slowly with the introductions of senior management from Wichita, Canada, as well as the heads of the local union. Their faces were grim, causing angst among the disgruntled employees.

"Get a move-on, already!" one burly mechanic said.

"Yeah! We don't give a damn who you are. We just want to know how hard you're going to screw us!" an older and more rotund mechanic said. The crowd erupted with cat-calls and laughter.

"Ladies and gentlemen, please. If I could have a moment of your time, all will be explained to you," the vice-president of Swift Jet said. He was clearly rattled by the mass reaction just two comments received. A bead of sweat rolled down his forehead and dark stains had started to form in the pits of his white dress-shirt.

The next words he was about to utter would most likely cause a commotion he wouldn't be able to contain. The word layoff is both scary and powerful at the same time. He looked at the faces in the crowd and wondered how many lives were about to be thrown into turmoil, and how many foreclosures and bankruptcies would be initiated by a decision made by pure greed.

His stomach churned acid that crept up to his throat. He started to speak and was failed by his nervous, cracking voice. He cleared his throat and let the words flow off of his tongue as if it was just another day on the golf course.

"Folks. Let me put your minds at ease in telling you that the stories of Swift Jet being for sale, or that we plan to move the operations up to Canada are all false. However, due to projected corporate adjustments, the rumors you have recently been hearing about layoffs are true. Starting this Friday, sixty-day notices will be handed out to approximately twenty-percent of the workforce, with an additional twenty-percent to be given their notices within the next six-months.

All layoff selections were made based on seniority and classification. Our current production rate and diminishing backlog has forced us to come up with new solutions in order to stay competitive. Our transition team will continue to evaluate Swift Jet's bottom line, searching for ways to improve the company's future.

For all of our family members we will be losing, you will be greatly missed. Swift Jet is losing some of the best aerospace workers in the industry."

The jeering didn't take long to start. As soon as he was finished speaking, the cafeteria erupted. Swift Jet was a small company with a small workforce, struggling to compete with industry leaders such as Learjet and Cessna. Forty-percent layoffs meant just over six-hundred people were going to lose their jobs.

The upper management types didn't waste time in handing the reigns of the meeting over to the union officials, so they could explain away their fellow union brother's and sister's livelihood.

## 24

Sadie sat with Tara on the front porch rearranging her monthly budget in her head. Dinner had been eaten and the kids were inside watching a DVD. Both women had a collection of beer bottles at their feet. All there was to do tonight was be relaxed and not fret about the future. Sadie knew if their situation became dire, their father would bale them out.

"Well at least I know Jared's good for the money for at least two more months," Sadie said after taking a long drink. "After that, it's off to flipping burgers or mowing lawns."

"You know if he ever figures out that all he has to do is menial jobs to keep up his support payments, he'll never try to get a better job," Tara said.

Ami ran out of the house with the phone in her hand. "Daddy's on the phone, Mommy!" Sadie's face contorted as she took the phone from her daughter.

"What do you need?" she asked with little enthusiasm.

"Don't know if you've heard. I'm due to get laid off this Friday."

"Yeah, so what?"

"So what? You're not getting anymore child support payments is what. If I don't have a job, then you're out of luck!"

"Don't yell at me, Jared. I already know that if you do get your notice on Friday, you will still have your job for sixty-days. That means *two months* from now you won't be employed at Swift Jet any longer. Don't try to pull any nonsense on me. You keep forgetting that Tara works at the same place you do."

"Yeah, but after that..." he said. The frustration had started to build in his voice.

"After that you'll still be legally bound to pay your court ordered support payments, or risk losing your license and getting arrested," Sadie said with a smile.

The line went dead and Sadie hoisted one fist in the air signifying her victory. Tara was laughing so hard, that she started crying.

"Is he really that stupid?"

"Yes! Can you believe I actually married that jerk? What was I thinking?"

"You were only nineteen, Sadie. Back then Jared was cool. I was jealous of you both. You were always holding hands and kissing. You were cute. I didn't have anyone; not until Kenny." She trailed off and tears formed in her eyes again, this time out of sadness.

"I'm sorry, Tara. I've been so caught up in my own dramas that I keep forgetting you just lost him." She took Tara in her arms and started the porch-swing rocking back and forth.

"What am I going to do if I get laid off? I mean when I get laid off. I don't know who I'm trying to kid."

"What's everyone else saying about it?"

"I don't know. I don't speak with any of them."

"Not even Debbie? I thought you two were good friends."

Tara's expression changed. "Not anymore. Not after what she said about me and Kenny when Kayla died."

"That was her saying all of those hateful things?"

Tara nodded and started to cry once more. She stood up and lit a cigarette, kicking over some bottles in the process. Sadie, not being one to stand a mess, picked up as many empty beer bottles as she could carry. She couldn't believe such a beautiful evening could be so full of sadness. The promise of their new home seemed to be constantly overshadowed by life's mishaps and heartaches. Just as she believed she was getting ahead, something came along to push her right back down.

Tara sat herself down on the front steps taking the last sip of her beer. She had stopped crying as soon as she had started. The ability to shut off her emotions was involuntary. The past two years had drained her to the point she hadn't much more to give. She finished her cigarette then joined Sadie in cleaning up their mess.

"You Okay?" Sadie asked.

"Yeah, I'll be fine. I think I'll go to bed early, though."

"Oh, that's right! The store is delivering your bed tomorrow morning. I forgot to tell you," Sadie said.

"Finally! Something to be happy about!" Tara said, shaking her head as she walked into the house. She headed straight upstairs without a hello or goodnight to her nieces and nephew.

With sleep came dreams, but not the nightmares she had been experiencing. Theses dreams were of when she was younger, playing with Kayla and Kenny at a playground full of colorful balloons. The dreams made her so happy that when her alarm clock went off, she started to cry, realizing she had returned back to the harsh and lonely reality of her life.

# 25

Betty Jo drove down the long, gravel driveway of her daughter's new home. She didn't mean to show up unannounced—she just couldn't stand to stay away—not from her family, but from the house. Something about it made her feel safe and welcomed. Its addictive pull had kept her on edge most of Wednesday and throughout the night.

Sadie's SUV wasn't in the driveway or parked in the garage. This didn't deter Betty Jo. It was such a beautiful day that she would be content just to sit on the porch-swing. She rang the doorbell for good measure then, happily, took a seat and started swinging, enjoying the quiet and warm breeze.

The peaceful moment was interrupted by the slamming of a door inside of the house. Betty Jo sat up with a start, scanning the driveway for Sadie. She had dozed off and wasn't sure if the noise was in her dream or not. The house phone rang—it rang only five-times before stopping mid-ring. She thought she heard faint voices, but couldn't be sure if it was only the wind through the trees.

The phone rang two more time and then stopped. Hearing the voices again, Betty Jo got up and took a look through the front door window. The baroque glass was difficult to see through, distorting the view of the foyer and living room.

Glancing down at her watch, she couldn't believe it was already ten in the morning. When Betty Jo looked back up, a silhouette moved past the entrance to the living-room causing her to jump and step back. The rumbling noise from a large truck made her jump again. Sadie and the kids drove up the drive, closely followed by the furniture truck carrying Tara's new bedroom.

Surprised to see her mother standing on the porch, Sadie parked quickly, leaving the kids in the car. "What are you doing here?"

Betty Jo was speechless for a moment. She was still startled by what she saw through the window. She had completely forgotten what she was doing there. "I guess I came over to see you," she said in a weak voice.

"Are you all right? You look a little pale," Sadie said, taking her mother's hand in hers. "You feel cold. Let's go inside so you can sit down and relax."

Just barely through the door, Ami, Erin and Joey brushed by chanting "Grandma, 'Grandma!" The sweet scent of freshly baked cookies filled the house. The familiar odor struck Sadie as odd since she hadn't done any baking since they had moved in. It had the opposite effect on Betty Jo, acting much like a sedative.

"Go and watch the TV, you three. And stay out of the delivery guys way," Sadie said to her kids.

"Is Aunt Tara's bedroom stuff here, Mommy?" Erin asked.

"Yes it is, so we don't want to bother the nice men."

Sadie brought her mother a cold glass of water. She didn't like the way she looked and was getting close to calling the doctor. The delivery driver and his partner knocking at the front door pushed aside the thought. Sadie invited the two workers in and showed them to Tara's room, giving the detailed instructions left by her sister, and then left them to their business.

Upon returning, she was surprised to see her mother sitting up watching cartoons with the kids. "Are you feeling better, Mom?"

"Yes, thank you. I think the drink of water did the trick."

"If you don't mind me asking, what brings you over unannounced?" The word "unannounced" was only spoken in her mind.

"No special reason. I just woke up and decided to come on by. I'm sorry I didn't call you. I meant to before I left."

"Did Tara tell you the not so good news about her job?"

"She didn't have to. I read it in today's paper. What a shame," Betty Jo said, shaking her head. "Is Tara home?"

"No, she's at work."

"Oh, I could have sworn I heard someone in the house. I even think I saw them just before you drove up."

"Saw them? Who did you see?"

"Well I was looking through the front door glass, so it was hard to tell if I saw anyone at all."

"What do you mean?"

"I thought I saw some body walk past the living room toward the kitchen. Maybe it was just the morning shadows."

"Morning shadows, uh? Would you like some coffee? I'm going to make half a pot."

"That would be nice," Betty Jo said.

Sadie wasn't convinced her mother was feeling better. She was rarely this docile unless she had been drinking. Although she would like to deny it, her mother had been known to start drinking as early as eight in the morning, so being slightly tipsy wasn't out of the question.

She left her alone with the kids, making the coffee as promised. Sitting at the kitchen table, she noticed the delivery men leaning against their truck talking and looking up at the house. They were laughing and shaking their heads. The driver saw Sadie through the window and pointed up shrugging his shoulders. She went outside, unable to imagine what the problem was.

"Sorry to disturb you, Ma'am," the driver said. He was a large man, barely fitting in the dark blue coveralls he was forced to wear as a uniform. He reminded her of Jared, but with more hair. "We seemed to have been locked out of the room."

"Locked out? Why didn't you come and get me?" Sadie asked.

The mixture of puzzlement and perturbed look on her face, prompted a nervous response out of the driver's younger and skinnier partner. "She told us to get out. We thought it was you."

Sadie elevated the tone of her voice. "Who told you to get out?"

"The lady that locked the door on us, Ma'am. That's what we've been trying to tell you."

Finished with the nonsensical conversation, Sadie directed both men to follow her up to Tara's bedroom. She opened the door, demonstrating that it wasn't locked. She marched over to the open window, shutting it sternly.

"If you would leave the window closed, then the wind wouldn't cause the door to slam shut," she said as she walked past them.

Both men stared blankly at one another not knowing exactly how to react.

"Did you open the window?" the driver asked his partner. "Cause I didn't."

The younger partner shook his head and proceeded to finish setting up the chifferobe they had brought up previously. Desiring to leave as soon as they were able, the two men kept the conversation to a minimum, working steadily until the job was complete.

**********

Tara walked into the living room shocked to see her mother sleeping on the couch. Sadie and the kids were outside planting a mixture of colorful flowers over by the garage. The only sound in the house was the ticking of the battery operated clock hanging next to the refrigerator. Anxious to see her new furniture, she made her way up the stairs to her room.

Just as she had imagined, her four-poster, solid oak full size bed fit perfectly, leaving plenty of room for the chifferobe and nightstand. The scent of the new furniture made her room smell like a furniture store. Making the bed and unpacking her boxes would take most of the night, even if she employed the services of her sister and mother, so she decided to get right on it after she grabbed a quick beer.

Downstairs, the kids stampeded into the house waking Betty Jo from her cat-nap. Sadie washed her dirt encrusted hands and started dinner. She hadn't expected her mother, so she had to improvise making both hamburger casserole and fried chicken. In the midst of cutting up an onion, her mother wondered into the kitchen looking well rested.

"Can I help?"

"It depends. Are you feeling better?"

"Yes, much better. That little nap of mine really helped. I just can't get over how relaxed I feel when I'm in this house. There must be something in the air."

"Good! You can rinse off those chicken thighs and put them in the frying pan."

"Skin or no skin?"

"No skin. Lately, for some un-known reason, Joey refuses to eat chicken if there is skin on it," Sadie sighed.

"You know I don't like to meddle in your business, but when you girls were little I never let you pick what you wanted to eat. You either ate it or you went hungry."

"Ah yes, those happy childhood memories," Sadie said, half-smiling.

"What happy memories?" Tara asked, walking into the kitchen.

"Eating dinner when we were kids," Sadie said.

Tara scrunched up her face. "God, I hated you and Dad back then for making us choke down liver, spinach, or other nasty food. What did Dad always say?"

"I'm not going there," Sadie said with a laugh.

"Don't worry," Tara said, mimicking her father's voice while pushing out her gut. "It will make a turd!"

Both women laughed until they cried. Betty Jo couldn't help but laugh along, even though she was part of the joke. She just smiled, continuing to remove the skin from the chicken thighs.

"How do you like your furniture?" Sadie asked.

"I love it. I can't wait to get everything unpacked and put it in its place. I was hoping that you and Mom could help."

"I'd love to help. I hadn't a chance to see the room yet," Betty Jo said.

"What's Dad having for dinner, Mom?" Sadie asked.

"He has a selection of leftovers in the fridge to choose from. If he can't find anything in there, then I guess he'll starve," Betty Jo said in a calm voice.

Sadie and Tara snickered at their mother's comment. Dad was always a good one to joke about. He hardly had a sense of humor, often taking the lightest of subjects serious.

Tara grabbed her beer and headed back up to her room to get started. She figured she had a good hour before dinner would be ready. Making her bed up with her new comforter, sheets, and pillows would be first—then her clothes. Her mother would have to help with Kayla's and Kenny's mementoes. Tara still had a difficult time handling them.

## <u>26</u>

Betty Jo finally went home, leaving Sadie and Tara to finish up the bedroom. She had been in a cheerful mood until Stan called to complain about the lack of food in the house. Before Tara could say thank you, Betty Jo was out the door.

"You lived with him for almost eight-months; why is Dad such a jerk lately?" Sadie asked.

"I don't know...I guess he's getting old."

"Well someone should have a talk with him, because he's driving Mom crazy. She's so lonely—I don't think Dad shows her the time of day anymore."

Tara shrugged her shoulders signaling she had had enough conversation about their parents. She had little capacity for personal drama. She continued to stack the folded cardboard boxes against the wall as if Sadie was no longer in the room.

Sensing she had lost her, Sadie brought up a new subject. "Those guys that delivered your furniture did a nice job. They were really careful not to nick the wood when they brought it in the house."

"Yeah, it really looks nice," Tara said, still not looking at Sadie.

"I had a little trouble with them, though. They claimed your door was locked and they couldn't get in."

Tara turned to her sister with a frown. "My bedroom door doesn't have a lock."

"I know. That's what I told them. I had to show them that it was the breeze from the open window holding the door shut. They even claimed I told them to get out."

Tara's face became flush. "My window was open again? What is wrong with you people? How hard is it to not touch my window?"

"Don't get mad at me! The delivery guys opened it! I had to close the window and tell them to leave it alone!"

"Well maybe you should have kept a better eye on them then."

"Well maybe I would have if I didn't have to babysit Mom. I swear she'd been drinking."

"Because she didn't feel well? Contrary to popular belief, Mom doesn't drink all of the time."

"I'm not saying it because I think she has a problem. I'm saying it because of what she told me. She thought she saw someone in the house when she was waiting for me to get home, then tried to tell me it was just the morning sunbeams or something like that."

"Did she actually see someone?" Tara asked in a calmer voice.

"She told me she saw a shadow walk past the living room toward the kitchen when she looked through the front door glass. Between Mom, Jared, and the delivery guys, you would think there was someone besides us living in this house."

The hairs on Tara's arms and neck stood on end. "Well maybe she did see someone."

"Oh, please. I was just kidding. There was no one else in the house when I got home. Mom just saw a reflection from outside. Please don't tell me that the house is haunted," Sadie said.

"Why couldn't it be haunted? It's almost a hundred-years-old, isn't it?"

"Now you're being silly."

"What about the locked bathroom doors?"

"The kids."

"That strange perfume in the middle of the night?"

Sadie rolled her eyes. "The kids again. I just don't believe this house is haunted. I don't even believe in ghosts."

"Don't you remember that black thing that lived in the hallway growing up?" Tara said. "Even Mom saw it."

"You mean the shadow? That was when we were just kids. The shadow only appeared when the moonlight shown through the patio door window. It was just our imaginations."

"What about the toilet flushing and the sink water running in the upstairs bathroom when the door was locked? I thought it was one of your kids until I found them hiding from the perfume in your bed. I can't explain it—can you?"

Sadie frowned. "You never told me that."

"I was too embarrassed. I thought you would laugh at me."

"All I can say is that maybe you were dreaming or sleep-walking. I'm going to check on the kids. They've been a little too quiet the past hour," Sadie said, turning away. "I'm sorry I didn't believe you. I just think there's an explanation for everything."

Downstairs, the music and funny voices from a cartoon echoed through the main floor of the house. The glow from the television screen reflected off of the walls in the darkened living room. Sadie hadn't realized how late it had gotten to be. The clock on the DVD player showed it was already nine in the evening.

She walked into the living room to find Erin and Joey asleep on the couch, while Ami was still wide awake sitting in the recliner and in complete control of the TV remote. Sadie waved at Ami who in turn shushed her for being too loud.

"I'm sorry sweetie. Could you hear us in Aunt Tara's room?"

"No!" she said. "You were too loud in the kitchen. I told you to be quiet, but you wouldn't listen."

"I wasn't..." Sadie stopped. A chill ran down her back. What Tara had said about the house being haunted ran through her mind. She didn't want to say anymore in fear of scaring her daughter.

She walked into the kitchen, peering slowly around the spacious room. She turned on the light and made a closer inspection. Nothing seemed out of place. The feeling of apprehension was replaced by anger. She couldn't believe she had let her sister's superstitious nonsense get to her.

She grabbed a beer, sat down and let out a sigh. Closing her eyes, she tried to blank away the day. This was supposed to be her house where she could relax and enjoy life. Instead, her mother and sister had infiltrated her peace and quiet with their soap operas. She made a pact with herself that she would have a happy day with her children tomorrow. Hopefully, her family would keep their needs and problems far away.

# 27

Tara lay in her new bed, under her new sheets and comforter; the full moon shown through the window, washing her pale yellow walls in a soft, blue light. She was at last completely relaxed. Not even the looming layoff at work bothered her. Although the pained road that had led her to where she was now was at times unbearable, she was able to lift her head up and see a life that promised more than she could have imagined. It wasn't the outside influences driving her forward, but the internal strength she had acquired through so many heartaches.

Her nieces and nephew laughing and yelling just outside her room didn't bother her tonight, but instead helped her to fall asleep. Less than a week in the new house, the familiar sounds of her sister and the kids had already started to comfort her. She had missed the sound of family.

*Her dreams started out light: She was sitting on the living room rug playing a board game with Ami, Erin, and Joey. Ami was taking too long to roll the dice, which upset her younger brother and sister. Sadie looked on from the couch, smiling and shaking her head.*

*The television had cartoons flashing across its screen. The children and Sadie all laughed when it became a live puppet theatre complete with marionettes. Joey, leaping up to see the puppets, kicked the game board, causing its pieces to fly through the air. Ami and Erin became angry with their brother, cursing at him with words Tara had never heard them say before. Concerned by their behavior, she tried to console them by promising she would find all of the missing pieces.*

*Tara crawled all over the floor searching, but only found pennies. They littered the floor from the staircase to the kitchen. She couldn't move without placing a hand or a knee on one the shiny coins. She followed the trail to the kitchen and tried to enter, but some unseen force kept her out—pushing her back toward the living room.*

*Sadie and the kids were now sitting at the kitchen table looking down at Tara whom remained on the floor. They shook their heads in unison when she asked for permission to enter. The light in the kitchen turned off, replaced by a bright light at the top of the stairs. Tara followed it, knowing she would find what she had been searching for there.*

*The stair steps were littered with pennies making it hard for Tara to keep her balance. Her feet slipped on the coins, sending dozens backward down the steps. The landing itself was ankle deep in a sea of coins.*

*A brilliant light shone from beneath her bedroom door, beckoning her to open it. The doorknob was cold to the touch, turning her fingers numb. She pushed the door inward without effort, exposing a dark and empty room with worn and stained carpet that partially covered a dirty hardwood floor. Tattered curtains were being whipped in and out of the open window by the volatile Kansas wind.*

*"So, this is what the room used to look like," she said to herself.*

*The door slammed shut behind her, leaving Tara in almost-total darkness. The brilliant light that had led her into her room was now being emitted beneath the door on the opposite side. The voices in the hallway were back and seemed to be arguing, but were too muffled for her to understand.*

*She sat down in the middle of the floor on the grimy carpet. Footsteps from a child approached from behind. The scent of baby shampoo overwhelmed her senses, sending images to her mind she was too afraid to see. A small hand touched her shoulder—gentle breath blew past her ear. "Mommy... Daddy found us."*

*Tara cried out. She leaped off of the floor and ran for the now opened door washed in light. Instead of running into the hallway, she slammed into the closed door, waking up stunned on her bedroom floor.*

Sadie heard Tara scream and then a loud bang. She made her way upstairs, tripping on and shattering a large jar full of pennies that had been left on the landing. The loud crash jolted Tara fully-awake. She opened her door to find Sadie sprawled out in the hall amongst broken glass and pennies.

"Oh my god! Are you all right?"

"Yes, but the child who left their crap in the middle of the floor isn't going to be!"

Ami emerged from her room to find out what all of the commotion was about. "My penny jar! You broke it!"

"Get back in your room before you cut your feet, Ami," Tara said.

Sadie narrowed her eyes. "Didn't I tell you to leave that penny jar alone?"

"Yes..." Ami said.

"Then why did you take it off of your nightstand again?"

"I didn't—I swear."

"Um! Joey broke Ami's pennies!" Erin said.

"I did not!" Joey said from the safety of his bedroom.

"Get back in your room, Erin!" Sadie said.

"You wouldn't stop messing with them until I said I was going to tell!" Ami said to her brother.

Sadie yelled. "Stop, stop, stop!" All three kids stood in their doorways sniffling. She got off of the floor careful not to step on the broken glass.

"I'm going to put your pennies into a Tupperware in my bedroom until I can get to the bottom of who's telling the truth, Ami" Sadie said. "No one is allowed out of their room until I clean up all of the pennies and glass."

"I'll get a garbage sack," Tara said, skirting the mess on her way downstairs.

Ami spotted a red, plastic ring—the type that would be found in a gumball machine, in the middle of the hallway floor. She gasped and pointed, screaming for her mother to wait. "My ring! My ring!"

"Stay in your room!" Sadie said.

"But I need my ring!"

"No, Ami! I said get in your room! All three of you get to bed now!" Sadie was becoming unraveled.

Tara returned and noticed the plastic ring lying on the floor. When she picked it up, Ami broke down into tears.

"What is it with that ring?" Sadie said.

All Ami could do was cry. She was too upset to speak.

"That's her special ring, Mommy," Erin said. "Kayla gave it to her."

"Is that true?" Tara asked Ami. She looked up at Tara with big, blurry brown eyes and nodded. Tara in turn placed the ring into her eager hand.

"Fine. You can have the ring, but I better have the honest truth tomorrow," Sadie said. She and Tara started separating the glass from the pennies.

"You didn't cut yourself, did you?" Tara asked.

"No, but I did stub my toe on that damn jar!"

Tara tried not to laugh, but couldn't help it. All Sadie was trying to do is come to her rescue and ended up causing more trouble than it was all worth. Tara rubbed the slight bump on her forehead and laughed to herself—embarrassed she had yelled out in her sleep again.

Looking at the floor covered in pennies suddenly brought back her dream. Her body shuddered at the similarities. Her very next thought was of the overwhelming scent of baby shampoo and of Kayla.

"Did you have another nightmare?"

"Yes," Tara said. She tried to hide the fact she had started to cry.

"Did you hurt yourself?" Sadie asked, noticing the tears rolling down her cheeks. "That was a pretty loud thump. I thought you had fallen out of your bed."

Tara sniffled. "Kayla was in my dream…she spoke to me. That's when I screamed and ran into the door."

"I'm so sorry…"

"It wasn't really bad. It was…"

"What?"

"No, you'll think I'm lying."

"Why would I think you were lying?"

"Because I dreamt the floor was covered in pennies," Tara said, keeping her head down.

"If you tell me you think the house is haunted…"

"See! I knew you would react like this! I really did dream the floor was covered in pennies, and I did hear Kayla…" she trailed off. The look of anger on her face had been replaced by a look of shock.

"What?" Sadie asked.

Tara was sitting straight up with tears streaming down her slender cheeks.

"I'm sorry, Tara. I didn't mean to upset you."

Tara smiled. "I'm not sad. I'm happy. She said Daddy found us. He's here, Sadie. Kenny's here!"

Sadie was speechless—frightened that her sister had gone over the edge. She struggled to find the right words to say, so not to upset her any further. The night had already been traumatic enough for her children. She didn't need their aunt losing her mind right in front of them.

Tara cried, placing a hand over her heart. "I know you think I'm crazy, but I can almost feel him. It's like he's been lost, but he's been here the whole time. It took a silly dream to finally realize that neither Kayla nor Kenny ever left. They've been with me every day."

Sadie felt ashamed for thinking her sister was crazy. She felt worse for not being there emotionally for her when she needed her most.

"I'll finish this if you'd like to go and lie back down," Sadie said.

"That's okay. I don't think I could get back to sleep anytime soon. I'll make us some tea, though."

"Sounds good."

Tara carefully maneuvered around Sadie and the few remaining pennies and pieces of broken glass with out another word. Sadie waited until Tara was downstairs and then started to cry.

## <u>28</u>

Sadie awoke with a start upon hearing Tara cursing and slamming the front door. She glanced at the clock, realizing the reason for all of the fuss. Her sister hated to be late for work. Her boss would make it a point to publicly humiliate anyone who walked into the wire-shop late. With any luck—traffic lights willing—she would make it before the seven o'clock bell rang.

Knowing getting back to sleep was out of the question, Sadie got up and made a pot of coffee and threw some raisin bread into the toaster. Hopefully, Tara's tantrum didn't wake up the kids so she could at least relax for a brief moment. Her children were big enough to take care of themselves, but still demanded her attention.

Not seeing the morning newspaper on the kitchen table was disappointing. Tara had been taking a morning walk down the drive while she smoked her first cigarette of the day. Sadie knew her sister must have gotten up late not to at least smoke. She slipped into her tennis shoes and walked out into the warm and sunny morning. The walk down to the road was full of bird song and the fresh smell of summer.

She loved the walk back up to the house as much as she loved the walk to the newspaper box—seeing her beautiful, white farmhouse made all of the sacrifices over the past year worthwhile. Even the two broken down outbuildings looked beautiful in the morning sun. Her father had talked about tearing down the old shed for her, but had said the barn was past his ability. Sadie would have to figure that one out on her own.

Her feeling of complete relaxation vanished in an instant upon seeing the two large barn doors slightly ajar and the padlock hanging open on the clasp. As a safety precaution, Sadie had kept both buildings shut and padlocked. The children were forbidden to play on that side of the house for fear of nails, rusted wire, or broken glass.

She picked up her leisurely pace and headed over to the barn. In the middle of the vast space, an old wooden ladder sat opened beneath the dust and cobweb laden rafters. Puzzled by her find, she looked around but found nothing else out of place. She refolded the ladder and placed it in one of the stalls, and then firmly closed the doors and relocked them—checking the padlock twice.

Thoughts of what Sadie was going to say to her children, this lecture, flew through her mind. Walking back to the house she saw Tara's curtains move. Her peaceful morning had started to turn sour. With her anger building, she marched into the house expecting to find her children scattering out of their aunt's room. Instead, all three were hunkered down in front of the television watching cartoons and eating their morning bowl of cereal.

"Which one of you was just in Aunt Tara's room?" There was no answer. "Ami, were you just in your aunt's room?"

"We were watching cartoons, Mommy." Erin and Joey turned toward their mother and nodded their heads in agreement.

"None of you were just in Aunt Tara's room?"

"You told us not to," Erin said.

"So did Aunt Tara," Joey said.

"Okay, if all of you are so good at following directions, then why did I just find the barn doors open?"

All three children insisted that they didn't play anywhere near the barn or the shed. "You told us not to because we could get hurt," Ami said. "Maybe Aunt Tara was playing in there."

"Aunt Tara doesn't play. She's old!" Joey said, causing his sisters to giggle.

Sadie rubbed her forehead with the tips of her fingers. She was about to give up and go back to her coffee and toast, when a door slammed hard upstairs. All three children's heads turned in a snap in the direction of the noise. Sadie stood frozen with fright. The only logical explanation was Tara's window had been opened again.

Sadie tried to collect her thoughts and calm her temper before she went off on her kids. "If I find an open window, so help me!"

The landing and hallway were dark, which meant all of the doors had been closed. All three children knew this was against the rules. The only door that was allowed to be closed was their Aunt Tara's and the bathroom.

Sadie opened Tara's door expecting to see the window open and the curtains being blown about. Instead, nothing was out of place. The only thing askew was Tara's unmade bed and her pajamas in a heap next to her chifferobe. She closed the door gently, pondering where the noise had come from.

She checked all three of her children's rooms next, as well as the bathroom, but found all of the windows closed. Movement above her head caught her attention. The pull rope for the attic-door was swinging back and forth as is someone had touched it. The taste of fear filled her mouth and the back of her throat became dry. She reached for the rope to stop it from swinging, inadvertently pulling on it and opening the trapdoor.

The collapsible ladder tumbled out. She only managed to partially block it with her forearm—the rest hit her in the face and head. Dazed, she sat hard on the floor with a loud thump. All three kids came running up the stairs to see what all of the commotion was about and found their mother sitting with her hands over her bleeding face.

Panicked, Ami ran and called her grandmother. Through the hysterical crying, Betty Jo was able to establish the need to call 911 and get herself over to the house as quickly as possible.

# 29

Tara drove up to find her mother's car in the driveway along side Susan McIntosh's, Sadie's annoying real estate agent. "Shit! At least it's Friday," she said as she parked next to the garage—not wanting to block the two visitors in—hoping they would leave sooner than later.

Inside she found everyone in the living room, with the exception of Susan, who was in the kitchen on her cell phone. A large white bandage was wrapped around Sadie's forehead along with a butterfly bandage on the bridge of her nose. She was reclined on the couch with the girls and Betty Jo sitting close by. Tara's first thought was that Jared had come over and beat her sister up, but that wouldn't have explained the pleasant company of Susan.

"What happened?"

"Just an accident," Betty Jo said.

"What kind of accident?"

"The attic fell on her!" Ami said.

"The ceiling fell down?"

Susan entered the living room having finished her phone call. With an over pleasant tone, she explained what had happened.

"What little Ami is trying to say, is the attic-door fell open and the ladder unfolded striking your sister. I just got off of the phone with the former owner's brother. He was supposed to have fixed the ladder before we closed on the house. He'll be over in the morning to work on it."

Tara became instantly enraged. "He needs to get his worthless ass over here now before someone else gets hurt!"

"Now, Tara Jean. Don't get Sadie more upset than she already is." Betty Jo said.

"There's no need to get angry. I'll make sure he takes care of the repairs," Susan said.

"Well, Mary Poppins. Is he going to pay my sister's medical deductible?" Tara said.

"Well, I don't know..."

"Are you?"

Betty Jo had had enough. "Please don't do this right now. Your father will make sure Sadie is taken care of. If she needs a lawyer, he'll get one."

Sadie could only listen to the bickering—it hurt too much to talk. She had already thought about what her insurance was going to pay, which wasn't a lot. A lawyer was probably in her future and her father would have to help her out.

"I'll be back by tomorrow to check on you and ensure the work is indeed being done properly," Susan said with tears in her eyes. She took a deep breath and said her goodbyes to Betty Jo and the kids. She was too nervous and flustered to look Tara in the eye.

Wanting to see the condition of the attic-door, Tara went up stairs. "Oh, this is convenient," she said, squeezing past the ladder to get to her room.

Air pressure was forcing her bedroom door closed, which meant her window was opened again. She just wanted to scream.

# 30

Tara sat at the kitchen table with her mother and the kids. She waited until they were eating their coveted pudding before asking the question. She didn't want to step on Sadie's toes, but figured now was a good time while her sister was reclined on the couch wearing an icepack.

"I want you three to help me out. I need to know who's been opening my bedroom window."

Joey raised his hand high, begging to be chosen. His sisters looked at him as if he were crazy.

"Do you have something to say?" Tara asked.

He nodded his head up and down. His lips and chin were smeared with brown pudding. "It wasn't me!"

"Okay. Do you know who did open my window?"

"Ami did it," Erin said, pointing at her sister.

"Nuh uh! It's too heavy to lift!" Ami started to cry, realizing she had just told on herself.

"We tried before you got your new bed, Auntie Tara. All of our windows are stuck," Erin said.

Betty Jo joined in on the conversation. "Stuck? Don't you mean locked?"

"The locks move, but the windows won't," Erin said.

Tara suddenly realized that she had never tried to open her window. She had only closed it. "Come with me., Mom. You three stay right here."

Betty Jo followed Tara up to her bedroom. All of the bedroom doors were closed again. Tara flipped on the hall light so neither she nor her mother ran into the attic-ladder. She walked into her room and caught a slight whiff of cigarette smoke. Betty Jo smelt it also and thought about making a comment about Sadie's strict no smoking in the house policy.

Tara unlocked her window and pushed up on the upper frame in an attempt to open it. It was heavy and bound a quarter of the way up. It took both Betty Jo and Tara pushing up on the window frame to finally get it just half-way open. Both women agreed that there was no way those kids could have ever opened her window even if they all worked together.

They walked back into the hallway and found all of the doors were now opened. "Weren't they all just closed?" Betty Jo said.

Tara nodded—the hairs on her arms and neck stood on end. "Kids...are you up here? Sadie?"

Neither woman wasted time going back down stairs. To their surprise all three kids were still seated at the table and Sadie was still on the couch. They could still smell the cigarette smoke—it was light and seemed to be just above their heads.

"Were any of you just upstairs?" Tara asked. All three shook their head. "What about Mommy?"

"She hasn't moved since you got home," Ami said.

Sadie stirred on the couch, mumbling. "Who's smoking in the house?"

Betty Jo went over to tend to her daughter. "No one, sweetie. You just lie there and relax."

"I thought I smelled smoke."

Betty Jo felt suddenly ill. She kept looking anxiously at her watch, fidgeting with her hands and tapping her feet. She knew her place was right beside her injured daughter, but couldn't help feeling as if she were being pushed out of the house.

Tara took notice of her mother's behavior and just knew that she was going to leave her alone with Sadie in her invalid state. She had no desire of splitting her attention between being a bedside nurse and the three little darling's nanny—there wasn't enough beer in the house.

Betty Jo started to stand up and Tara quickly intervened.

"Mom, where are you going?"

"Well, I thought I'd better be getting home. Your father is probably having a fit because he has nothing to eat again."

"I thought you called him. Didn't you say you were staying the night?"

"I guess I did."

"I can't do this on my own. I can't make sure Sadie's all right at the same time I'm trying to keep the kids away from that stupid attic-ladder. You know they'll try to climb it." Tara kept her voice low so not to give the children any ideas.

Betty Jo sat back down thinking about what Tara had just said. She also knew what she had said, but at this point she didn't really care. She just wanted out of that house. The warm inviting feeling it had the day before had vanished, only to be replaced by an overwhelming feeling of dread.

She stood up once more and headed for the kitchen. Tara felt helpless to stop her. A door upstairs slammed shut causing everyone, including Sadie to jump. Betty Jo started to cry, insisting that she had to leave now and walked out the front door.

The twilight sky was a combination of amber and purple, casting a strange hue across the front-yard. Tara ran after her mother trying to catch her before she got into the car. Just Betty Jo turned over the engine, Stan pulled up with the bed of his truck filled with the pieces to a new swing set.

"What's your mother doing?" Stan said. "Betty Jo, where in the hell are you going? You knew I was coming over."

Betty Jo shut off the engine to her car. She was clearly upset she had been prevented from leaving. She gripped the wheel and stared straight ahead toward the barn and shed.

Tara looked up and noticed her window was partially opened and her curtains were being gently pulled in and out.

"We forgot to close the window, Mom. That's what the noise was. The door slammed because of the open window—that's all."

"What in the hell is going on?" Stan asked.

"I'm not sure. Mom started to act strangely, and then my door slammed shut. I think it scared her."

"Betty Jo. Betty Jo…come on inside. I'll fix you a drink. Betty Jo…" Stan said.

"Mom. Do you need a cigarette?" Tara asked, kneeling beside the driver's side door.

Betty Jo nodded and climbed out of her seat. Her mouth watered at the thought of a good smoke. Her nerves started to feather out at the first whiff of fresh tobacco. Tara invited her over to the porch swing, both with their lit cigarettes in their hands. Stan looked on trying to figure out his wife's strange behavior. He grabbed two overnight bags out of his cab and proceeded into the house.

"Are you staying over too, Dad?"

"Well, I thought it made more sense. I have to be over here tomorrow to baby sit that joker who didn't fix the attic-door, as well as to set up the kid's swing set."

He entered the house to a chorus of "Grandpa, Grandpa!"

Tara swung gently with her mother on the porch. Betty Jo had finally calmed down. The feeling of dread had left, replaced once again by a relaxing peace. The brilliant sky gave way to darkness. Both women enjoyed the softness of the warm summer night and a second cigarette.

# 31

Saturday morning found Sadie still on the couch and Stan snoring away in Sadie's bedroom. Betty Jo had been up a good hour and had already finished off a half-pot of coffee. Although last night's strange occurrences had her on the verge of a breakdown, she took great solace in the peace and quiet of her daughter's home. Something unexplained had touched her—making her feel ill. She couldn't get away from it fast enough. It was if someone had placed a hand over her nose and mouth, torturously loosening and then tightening their grip.

Tara sauntered into the kitchen with her hair stuck out in all directions, wearing old sweatpants and a worn tee-shirt with a faded sports logo on the front. She took two sips of coffee before noticing her mother sitting at the table. "Oh, hi," she said with a yawn.

"Good morning," Betty Jo said in a cheerful tone.

"Seven o'clock and no kids?"

"Shhh...don't jinx us! It's going to be none-stop all day."

"I know. Since Dad is here to take care of the jerk that didn't fix the attic-ladder, I thought I would run into town and shop for a TV."

"Oh, no! You're not going to leave me to chase after the kids *and* your father! And what about poor Sadie?"

"Take the kids back to your house. The peace and quiet would be just what Sadie needs."

"Tara Jean..." Betty Jo said.

Tara always knew she was in for some sort of lecture when her mother started off a sentence with both her first and middle name.

"I am getting quite fed up with the selfish act. For the past few months, it's all been about you and your needs. For a change, maybe you can bring yourself to think about others first."

Tara got up from the table and left before she said something she wouldn't be able to take back. Twenty-eight-years old and she was still being told what to do. She had zero tolerance for personal attacks. As far as she was concerned, she would just stay in her room all day reading while her mother jumped through hoops for her precious grandchildren and their precious mother.

As Tara stared out her window, the former owner's brother drove up in his brand-new, white Ford pick-up. It still had the temporary thirty-day tags. She watched intently as he gathered his tool belt and headed for the front door. Without her father awake, she knew she would have to deal with this guy if Sadie was going to get any satisfaction.

Betty Jo invited him in and offered a cup of coffee which angered Tara even more. She didn't understand how her mother could be so kind to the very person responsible for Sadie's accident. As far as Tara was concerned, the man was useless.

She listened as he clumped up the wooden stairs with his work-boots. She made a quick effort to look presentable before encountering the jerk and telling him where he could get off.

With her fist clenched and her jaw set, Tara opened the door, meeting him face to face. Startled, they both took a step back. He almost tripped over the attic-ladder in the middle of the hall. She was about to say something coy when he smiled at her. Instantly, any thought of abhorrence dissipated.

"Hi. I'm Matt," he said, holding out his hand.

Tara was too embarrassed to take it. Instead, she said the first thing that came to mind. "Are you going to fix it right this time?"

"Yes, ma'am. I'm very sorry you were hurt. We paid a carpenter that was thought to be reliable to fix it before the house sold. He guaranteed his work."

"It was my sister," she said, looking down at the floor. "The stairs hit my sister, not me."

"Oh...please tell your sister that I am very sorry," he said with deepest sincerity and then handed Tara his personal business card. "I didn't catch your name."

"Tara," she said, taking the card and suddenly finding herself flush and unable to speak. She couldn't stop staring at his eyes. They were such a light blue, they seemed to sparkle.

Looking down at her feet she realized what she was wearing and that her teeth and hair hadn't been brushed. Now thoroughly embarrassed, she excused herself back into her room, a prisoner until the man whose face she couldn't get out of her mind was gone.

"This will only take a few minutes, Tara," Matt said from the other side of the door.

Tara didn't dare answer. What she was feeling now, she hadn't felt since Kenny had first asked her out. She was both surprised and angered. She had only been a widow for a few short months. Who did she think she was feeling that way for a strange man? All she wanted to happen now was for this 'Matt' person to hurry up and get out of the house.

Hearing the conversation in the hallway, all three kids popped their heads out of their bedrooms. Matt smiled and waved at them with his screwdriver. Giggles erupted and the three stampeded down the stairs, squealing and chanting at the sight of their grandmother.

Stan emerged from Sadie's bedroom with a scowl. He glanced over at his sleeping daughter on the couch and then Betty Jo, shaking his head and grumbling. "Coffee," was the only word he could manage. Betty Jo pointed in the general direction of the coffee pot and mugs. She didn't dare speak to his majesty before he at least had two cups of caffeine running through his veins.

"Mom?" Sadie said from the couch in a weak voice. "Who's here?"

Betty Jo shushed her grandchildren. "Your father and the children are in the kitchen."

"No. I mean who rang the doorbell?" Sadie said, clearly irritated.

"The man's here to fix the attic-ladder."

"Good," she said, slowly getting up from the couch and heading for her bedroom. Her face around her nose and eyes were slightly swollen. She looked a great deal better than she did the night before.

The loud clomping of work boots down the stairs alerted Stan into action. He approached Matt with the same scowl he had presented his wife just moments earlier. Standing with his coffee mug in his stretched to its limits tee-shirt, black socks, and striped boxers, made him look more comical than imposing. Matt had to contain his amusement.

"Is it fixed this time?" Stan asked with his best growl.

"Yes, sir. I put a latch on the ladder, so it won't fall again. I also tightened up the joint screws."

"I hope you don't expect compensation, because you won't get any."

"No, sir. In fact my brother wanted your daughter to bill him for any medical expenses that her insurance wouldn't cover. Sue McIntosh already spoke with him about the accident. He felt just awful."

"If he feels so strongly about it, then why doesn't he come out and tell her himself?" Stan said.

"He's been ill, Stan," Betty Jo said. "Isn't that right, Mr...?"

"Cramer. It's Matt Cramer, ma'am. And yes, Steven has been ill."

"Just leave his address and I'll make sure Sadie sends him the bill," Stan said.

Matt handed Stan his brother's business card, thanked Betty Jo once more, and then left before Stan could say anything else. He was fairly easygoing, but could only take so much verbal abuse.

Staring up from his truck, he noticed the curtains move in Tara's bedroom window. The reflection off of the glass made it difficult to see, but he knew she was watching him. He made plans to call her in a week—after the accident was not such a fresh a memory.

Tara studied Matt's truck. The name *Cramer Construction Cheney, KS* was painted in bright red letters on the driver side and passenger doors, as well as the tailgate of the truck—along with a local phone number. She looked at the business card with the same information and put it away in her nightstand drawer. She wasn't sure if she would ever call him, but just incase she got up the nerve, it was there.

Even though the attic-ladder had been repaired, Tara still walked cautiously by it on the way down stairs. She found her mother at the table where she had left her and her father at the counter pouring his second mug of coffee—still in his boxers.

"This isn't your house, Dad. Put on some clothes for God's sake! You're going to give your grandchildren issues later in life," Tara said. He just shrugged his shoulders and sat down next to his wife at the kitchen table.

Sadie emerged from her bedroom looking haggard. She also took notice of her father's apparel, asking him sternly to get dressed in her bedroom so she could go back to sleep. Stan got up in a huff, stomping all the way to the bedroom. He came out dressed a few minutes later—announcing he would be out back setting up the swing set if anyone cared. Accustomed to his daily tantrums, Betty Jo never glanced up from the morning paper until he had stormed out the front door.

## 32

Sadie slept the majority of the day away amid her children running in and out of the house and being just plain loud. Her father had spent the day outside setting up the swing set, patiently shooing his grandchildren away. Betty Jo took up residence on the front porch-swing reading a mystery novel and smoking an entire pack of cigarettes. Tara had taken off without a word to anyone, determined to buy a television for her bedroom.

Sadie managed her way into the kitchen to take her pain medication and have something to eat. The bridge of her nose still ached, but the swelling had almost gone away completely. The semi-undisturbed rest helped a great deal. Her parents had been a big help, although she was looking forward to the both of them leaving. She liked it when it was just she, Tara, and the kids.

The view out the living room window was now dominated by a multi-colored swing set complete with a small fort and slide. Her children were running around the structure eager to try it out, while Stan put together the final swing. The project had taken him most of the day to complete.

Erin stopped running and pointed toward Ami's bedroom window with her mouth wide open. Ami also looked up, confused by what she was seeing. The girl's posture and expression made Sadie both alarmed and curious. She got up from the kitchen table and made her way to the living room window.

Stan was looking up at Ami's window as well. He squinted and then took a step back, almost tripping on his tool box. His flush, round face turned white in an instant.

Not wanting to venture outside, Sadie instead tapped on the window gaining Ami's attention.

"Mommy! There's a girl in my room!" she said. The glass muffled her small voice, but Sadie could still understand her.

"What girl?" Sadie asked, shaking her head.

"In my room!" Ami said, fretfully pointing.

Sadie walked to the foot of the stairs and called for Tara. Getting no response, she started up the steps. All of the doors were open with the exception of Ami's. She became annoyed her rule had yet again been ignored.

Though the attic's trap-door and ladder had been repaired, she still avoided it. Hugging the wall, she stepped on something sharp with her bare feet. The same red, plastic ring that Ami had a fit about a couple of nights back lay in the middle of the landing. Sadie thought about throwing it away, and then had a change of heart. She instead picked it up and went into Ami's room, placing it on her nightstand.

Forgetting why she came upstairs, Sadie appeared in the window giving both of her daughters a fright. She got a small laugh out of it until she saw her father sitting down on the grass with his head cradled in his hands.

Sadie panicked and ran downstairs. The words heart attack flashed through her mind. Running out the front door, she alerted her mother, yelling at her to call 911.

Oblivious to their grandfather's health, the girls yelled at Sadie that she scared the life out of them. She shushed them both as she reached her father. "Dad...are you all right?"

Stan nodded and wiped his brow. He was pale and shaking. He glanced once more up at the window, squinting in the late afternoon sun. He didn't want to believe what he saw in his granddaughter's window.

"Stan?" Betty Jo said as she ran around the side of the house. "Are you okay? I called 911."

"Now why on earth did you go and do that for, Betty Jo? I'm just fine."

"Don't yell at Mom. I told her to call."

Stan's chest became tight. He grabbed for his wife's hand, bowing his head in pain. The children, now aware that their grandfather was sick, began to cry.

Five minutes later, the distant wail of sirens carried on the wind; ebbing closer and then fading. Their sound brought some relief to Sadie and Betty Jo. Sadie couldn't believe that she had just lived in her new home for a week and the fire department had already been there twice.

As the big engine roared up the driveway, Sadie ordered her children to stay where they were and not to make a sound or move. All three obeyed by sitting at the far end of the swing set. Betty Jo summoned the firefighters to the backyard and then rejoined her husband who had now become listless.

"This is the same house as yesterday morning," one firefighter said.

"Yep, and there's our patient," the second said, pointing at Sadie.

Sadie stepped out of the way. She crossed her arms tight, gazing at the swing set her father had so lovingly put together, and then toward the sky. Through her tears, movement in Ami's window caught her attention. If she wasn't so upset, she would have sworn she saw someone standing there. She wiped her eyes dry and the figure was gone. The siren from the ambulance jolted her out of her daze.

"I am not paying for an ambulance!" Stan said. The firefighters ignored him and summoned the EMT's over to their patient.

"Mom. Where's Tara?" Sadie asked. Betty Jo shook her head. Not knowing where Tara had gone to infuriated Sadie. Refusing to get a cell phone, there was no way of getting in touch with her.

Betty Jo felt faint and sat herself down in the grass. All three children swarmed to her, holding on tight to her thin arms. Ami started to cry when an oxygen mask was placed over her grandfather's face.

"His pulse isn't good. We shouldn't wait to transport," the EMT said. "Did you want to ride along, ma'am?" she asked Betty Jo.

Betty Jo nodded. Sadie helped her mother up, escorting her over to the ambulance along side her father.

"The kids and I will follow you to the hospital," Sadie said to her mother as she herded the kids into the house. "You guys use the bathroom while Mommy gets ready."

The ambulance left with her father and mother. A few minutes later, Sadie and the kids were following down the road. She left a note for Tara on the front door about what happened to their father and to meet them at the hospital's emergency room. She hoped her sister would get home soon.

# 33

Betty Jo was asleep with her grandchildren on the living-room couch, while Sadie brooded at the kitchen table, trying to think away the throbbing pain between her eyes. She had taken her prescription pain-meds an hour earlier, but they had no effect. The stresses of seeing her father have a heart attack and having to leave him in the hospital was as much as she was able to handle.

Tara's cavalier attitude toward the entire ordeal didn't help matters. The fact that she took time to muscle her new television up to her room instead of coming right away to the hospital, and then leaving before the rest of the family, created a large riff. Sadie had even considered asking her sister to move out in the heat of argument.

The headlights from Tara's truck reflected through the kitchen window. Sadie tensed up in anticipation. She knew they would start fighting as soon as her sister walked through the door.

Tara strolled in sucking on a fountain drink while carrying a sack full of fast-food. Sadie stared her down, inviting an altercation.

"What?" Tara said with her mouth full of taco. "I'm not allowed to eat now? I'm sure you all had dinner when you got home."

Sadie coldly responded. "I don't recall saying anything."

"Just because I wanted to leave the hospital, you have to be high and mighty in my face. The doctor said Dad was going to be fine. We were just waiting to see what room he was going to be in."

"All I wanted to do is wait as a family. I didn't see that being an issue!"

Tara rolled her eyes and gathered up her food. "Since it's obviously bothering you to watch me eat, I'll just eat in my room."

"Enjoy your new television!"

"Oh, I will," Tara said cheerfully. She would have flipped her sister off if she had a free hand.

Betty Jo woke up just in time to see Tara walk by on the way to her room. "Oh good, Tara made it home. Is she coming back down?"

"I hope not," Sadie said.

Betty Jo didn't hear what Sadie said and fell back to sleep. It was only nine-thirty on a Saturday night, but Sadie felt like going to bed herself. The past couple of days had drained her and she still had all of Sunday to deal with Tara.

Getting all three of her children to bed without a scene would be an impossible task. No matter how tired they were, one, usually Erin, found a reason to throw a fit and cry themselves all the way to bed. Sadie didn't have the strength for it tonight.

On cue, Erin went straight to crying as soon as she was removed from the couch. Sadie ignored her pleas to stay up, carrying her seven-year-old up to bed. Ami and Joey followed without a sound. She tucked Erin in first then Joey, leaving Ami for last.

When Sadie walked into her oldest daughter's room she found Ami standing by her nightstand, twirling her red plastic ring between her fingers. "Why aren't you in your bed?" Sadie asked.

"I found my ring. I thought I lost it."

"Actually, I found it out in the hall with my bare foot. This time put it in a safe place."

Ami nodded and placed the ring in a small leather pouch containing polished rocks and marbles. She then leaped into bed and shut her eyes. Sadie felt guilty for even thinking of throwing the ring away knowing how important it was to her daughter. She turned out the light and left the room.

The muffled noise of Tara's new television could hardly be heard out in the hall. Sadie hesitated at her door then thought again. When Tara was in one of her many moods, it was better to just leave her alone until she calmed down.

Sadie covered her sleeping mother with an afghan and turned out the lights. The hulking silhouette of the new swing set through the living room window reminded her of her father and the scare they all had. The girls claiming there was a girl in Ami's room flashed through her mind. It didn't make a lot of sense to her until she remembered she thought she had seen someone also. She decided that it had to be the reflection of the sun or sky off of the glass—nothing else made sense. Things she couldn't explain she set aside for later.

## 34

The television shutting off woke Tara out of a dead sleep. Her dream consisted of doctors telling her if she didn't buy their product she would never feel as well as she could while she searched frantically for a telephone, but only finding empty phone booths.

Trying to adjust her eyes, she squinted in the dark. She searched for the remote and found it on her nightstand next to the empty fast-food bag. A cool breeze startled her—the bedroom window was fully opened—the wind sucked and blew her curtains in and out. She knew she hadn't turned off the television and definitely knew that she hadn't opened her window.

Along with the cool breeze, the scent of jasmine was back. Although faint, it was strong enough to give her a slight headache. The floor creaked by her door and then out in the hall. She turned on her bedside lamp, calling for Sadie. Her words sounded flat as if she were talking in a vacuum.

Gaining courage, Tara walked across her room and opened her bedroom door. Out in the hall the scent of jasmine seemed to be leading her to the landing and down the stairs. The light from the kitchen illuminated the living room, falling on Betty Jo who was asleep on the couch. As Tara set foot on the cold hardwood floor, the kitchen light turned off.

"Sadie?" she said in a whisper, not wanting to disturb her mother.

The floor creaked in the kitchen and then directly in front of her. The jasmine was so strong it choked her to the point of making her cough.

Tara panicked and called for her sister. "Sadie!"

Sadie turned on her bedroom light and threw her door open, startling Tara further. "What's wrong?" she asked, thinking someone was hurt.

The Jasmine dissipated as soon as Sadie appeared. Tara felt embarrassed standing there with both her mother and sister staring at her. She hesitated and then announced she must have been sleepwalking. She apologized and went back upstairs without another word. Still angry with her sister, Sadie let Tara leave without a word.

Upon returning to her room, Tara found her window closed, light off and television on. The remote was laying on the bed along side her pillow. Confused by what had just transpired, she stood in her doorway unsure and afraid to go in. The toilet flushed in the upstairs bathroom and Ami came running out causing Tara to jump.

The room felt unfamiliar—the house unwelcoming. Her thoughts turned to her options for moving out. If her sister truly didn't want her there, then she would gladly leave.

## <u>35</u>

Tara stayed in her room waiting for her mother, Sadie and the kids to leave for the hospital. She was invited to ride along with them, but opted not to. She used an upset stomach for an excuse. The real reason was she had no interest in being around Sadie if she could help it. Her sister's high and mighty attitude while their parents were around got on Tara's last nerve. Tara knew she was in the wrong with the way she acted last night, but would wait to apologize Monday night after her mother had returned home in order to avoid a show.

The SUV's wheels crunching on the rock driveway was a welcome sound. Tara hoped that she had at least three hours to herself before they all returned home. Not planning on leaving for the hospital herself until noon, she laid in bed for another hour watching television.

At ten in the morning, she finally rolled out of bed and strolled downstairs. The sun-washed kitchen brightened her spirits. The smell of fresh raisin bread in the toaster and fresh coffee filled the air. She settled down at the table with the Sunday paper and soaked in the peace and quiet.

Halfway through an article about Swift Jet, the ceiling above Tara's head creaked, followed by what sounded like footsteps. Her bedroom was located just above the kitchen. She froze in mid-sentence—goose bumps rising on her arms. She sat so still, she could hear the kitchen faucet dripping in the sink.

The refrigerator kicking on made her leap out of her chair. Her heart was pounding so hard that it echoed in her head. Just as she sat back down, the phone rang sending her leaping out of her chair once more. She let it ring three times before answering it.

"Hello?" she said.

"Tara. It's Sadie. Are you all right?"

Tara took a deep breath. "Yeah, I'm fine. What do you need?"

"I have Dad's room number. It's 204." She was all business—still angry with her sister.

"Fine. I'll be over in a little bit."

"Mom wants to talk to you," Sadie said, handing the phone to Betty Jo.

"Tara. It's Mom. Your father left his shaving kit in Sadie's bathroom. It has his toothbrush and comb. He would like you to bring it for him when you come to visit."

"All right. I'll be over in about an hour."

Tara hung the phone up on her mother before she could ask for more favors. She sat thinking about what she had heard, and her experience the night before. She was convinced the house was haunted and could care less if Sadie did or not.

She sat in silence for a few moments more listening, and then turned on the television to fill the house with noise. If she couldn't hear it, then it didn't exist—whatever it was.

## <u>36</u>

Betty Jo sat next to Stan's bed holding his hand. He was holding the TV remote with the other, trying to find ESPN without success. She could tell he was becoming aggravated and offered to help.

"If I can't figure this thing out, what makes you think you can?"

"I just don't want you to get upset. Your doctor said no stress."

"Fine," he said, handing the remote to his wife. "I don't understand the reason why I have to stay in this damn place one more night. I feel just fine."

"The insurance will pay for it if that's what you're worried about."

Stan glared and took a deep breath. "All I want to do is go home and sit in my chair and watch my own TV. I can get all the rest I need there."

"Sadie offered to let us stay with her until you get better."

"What part of I just want to go home didn't you get? How am I supposed to rest with her three kids running amuck? Besides, I've seen enough of that house for awhile."

"Seen enough of the house? What does that mean?"

"Nothing…I just don't see the reason to go back. I've built the grandchildren their swing set—they can come over to our house and visit."

"Stanley Frances Carter. I know that look. What else is on your mind?"

Stan's complexion turned pale from the memory of the girl in the window. He didn't want to tell Betty Jo what he saw, but knew it would eat him inside out until he did. That face he knew so well wouldn't leave his mind. He knew the girls saw it too.

"What is it, Stan?"

He took a deep breath and stared at the television set. "I saw something I can't explain. It didn't make sense then and it doesn't make sense now."

Betty Jo frowned. She thought hard about what he could've seen. "I don't understand. What did you see?"

"I'm trying to tell you, Betty Jo. Give me a goddamn chance, already!"

"All right, I'm sorry. Just calm down—you don't want to get sick again."

Stan choked back his tears and collected his thoughts. "I know this is going to sound crazy...I saw Kayla yesterday."

"Kayla? Where?"

"In Ami's window. She was looking down on us from the window."

Betty Jo started to cry. She knew her husband was telling the truth—at least she thought he was. He wasn't the type of person to tell stories or lies. "Did the kids see her?"

"The girls must have. They were pointing up at the window."

"Should we tell Sadie? If her children saw her then..."

"No. If you tell Sadie then Tara might find out. I want to keep this between the two of us," Stan said.

Betty Jo wanted to believe her husband—at the same time she hoped it wasn't true. The thought of her late granddaughter haunting her daughter's new home both saddened and frightened her. She believed adamantly that all children went to heaven without exception. The thought of poor, little Kayla being a ghost was too much to imagine.

Feeling sick to her stomach, Betty Jo left the room. Stan called after her, but received no response. In the midst of wiping the tears from his eyes, Tara walked into the room carrying his shaving kit in one hand and a get well balloon in the other.

"Hey," she said.

"Hey, yourself," he said back, trying hard to hide that he was crying. "Oh good, you brought my shaving kit."

Tara sat down in the chair her mother had been sitting in. The sight of her father connected by wires and tubes to a variety of machines made her feel guilty for not getting there sooner. Beside her on the bedside table sat a big bouquet of flowers with a card that read, "Get well soon, Grandpa!" She felt embarrassed by her less than thoughtful gift.

Stan struggled to regain complete control of his emotions. "You just missed your mother. She'll be back though—I think she just ran to the lady's room. Sadie and the kids aren't due to pick her up for another hour."

"I'm sorry this happened to you. I feel bad for not being home," Tara said—her own eyes had welled up with tears prompting Stan to become emotional all over again. He choked back hard and got lucky with his channel surfing by landing on the Golf Channel. Tara's huff, displaying her dislike of his selection, caused them both to laugh.

Betty Jo walked into the room still wiping the tears from her eyes amidst her husband and daughter carrying on. "Oh good, you found your channel," she said, clapping and smiling. Her display made them both laugh harder. "Did you remember your father's shaving kit?"

Stan held it up for her to see. Through all of the laughing, he still couldn't get Kayla's face out of his mind. Tara sitting next to him didn't help, either. As he settled back down, a feeling of helplessness flowed over him. Betty Jo didn't feel any better. Just the thought of Kayla would take her to the verge of tears.

Tara could tell something was going on between her parents. Although they had been together for more than four decades, they didn't display a lot of emotion when interacting. She had a bad feeling it had to do with how serious her father actually was.

"What did the doctors say, Dad?" Tara asked with sternness in her voice.

"I have to stay one more night in this shit-hole."

"He just needs to rest," Betty Jo said. "They said it was just a mild heart attack and he has an appointment Tuesday with the Cardiologist."

"They don't know a damn thing! All I want to do is go home. How can they expect me to watch anything on this little TV?"

Tara didn't believe them. "Are you sure they said it was mild? It seems pretty serious to me."

"I'm so thankful it wasn't more serious," Betty Jo said, nodding her head at Stan.

"Don't worry about me, sweetheart. I'm a tough old bear. It will take more than this nonsense to hold me down."

"All right," Tara said with reserve as she stood up. She still didn't believe either of them—something else was going on. "I'm gonna get going so you can have more private time with Dad," she said to her mother. She kissed her father on the forehead and walked out into the hallway.

"No more discussions about what I said," Stan said. He looked away from his wife in the direction of the window.

"No more," Betty Jo said. She had tears rolling down her cheeks. They both cried in silence—each reliving their own personal memories of their granddaughter.

## 37

Tara pulled into the driveway around eight in the evening. She had a two-liter bottle of pop and a sub-sandwich from the little carryout restaurant in town. Sadie heard the truck door slam and immediately tensed up. The evening was going smoothly without her sister on the scene.

Betty Jo was fighting sleep while watching a DVD with the kids that she had just bought them that afternoon. Sadie hoped Tara would head straight upstairs and not disturb them in the middle of their movie.

Tara walked into the kitchen glancing at the television to see what they all were watching. After pouring some pop, she paused at the entryway to the living room and worked up the courage to say something to Sadie. Her sister responded by only raising her eyebrows. Tara motioned that she wanted to talk. Reluctantly, Sadie got up and followed Tara up to her room.

"I wish you wouldn't eat up here," Sadie said.

Tara took a deep breath trying to contain her anger from yet another attack by her sister. "I didn't ask you up here to fight."

"I don't want to fight, either. When you eat in your room it stinks up the whole upstairs."

"Fine. I'll eat in the kitchen. I just wanted to tell you that I was sorry for yesterday." Her eyes became moist and her voice started to quiver.

Tears streamed down Sadie's cheeks. "I'm sorry, too. It's been so hard the past few days. We've just been in the house for a week and already we've had the fire department over here twice, you and Jared might get laid off, and I can't get mom to go home!"

"She won't leave?" Tara said.

"She said she didn't feel safe without Dad in the house."

"What about their pets? Who's taking care of them?"

"Ed and Kathy from across the street have been feeding them," Sadie said, wiping her nose with the back of her hand.

"Dad said he was going home tomorrow...oh no! What's Mom going to do? She won't be able to smoke in the house," Tara said.

"She doesn't smoke in the house while she's here. She'll have to go out on the porch."

Tara shook her head. "She's just being polite. She's smoked in that house for over thirty-years. You know Mom; she's not about to let anybody tell her what to do in her own house. And Dad will just let her do it, because he doesn't think he's really sick."

"I know this sounds terrible, but as long as she gets the hell out of my house, I don't care what she does in hers," Sadie said. Tara laughed. "Amen!"

"I don't want to fight with you anymore. You, Mom, Dad, and the kids are all I've got," Tara said. "I was so lonely today that I visited Kenny and Kayla's graves."

"Is this the first time you went alone?"

Unable to talk, Tara just nodded and cried. Sadie took her in her arms and cried herself and then snorted causing them both to laugh so hard they could be heard in the living room. The two walked back down to the kitchen sniffing and wiping their eyes.

Betty Jo was asleep on the couch with her head back and mouth wide opened. Tara commented on how attractive their mother looked sending the two sisters into hysterics. Erin, annoyed by the interruption, shushed them both.

## <u>38</u>

Monday saw the release of Stan from the hospital, Betty Jo going back home, and another dull day for Tara at Swift Jet. After the official announcement of forthcoming layoffs, the rumor mill had nowhere to go—dissipating as fast as it materialized. Tara didn't mind; the less non-sense at work the better. She just wanted to earn her paycheck and drink beer at the end of the day.

Ami, Erin, and Joey played on their new swing set the entire day. Sadie was spared another visit to the hospital when her mother insisted on picking up her father. She took complete advantage of the temporary peace by taking a nap in the lounge chair while her children played.

The evening was as uneventful. The five ate a big meal of meatloaf, mashed potatoes and corn. The children ate so much, only Erin asked for a desert—which she failed to finish. Tara waddled out to the front porch with a beer and a new pack of cigarettes. She loved the scent of fresh tobacco, inhaling deeply when she took off the plastic wrapper. Sadie joined her on the porch-swing with a beer of her own. They both sat in silence listening to the crickets and June bugs.

The two were not surprised to find all three kids asleep in front of the television when they finally strolled in at nine. Tara helped her sister with escorting the sleepy-eyed children to their beds, and then excused herself for the night. She was more than ready for bed—not even bothering to turn on her new TV. Sleep found her quickly—floating her back to the dark dream.

*The room felt cold as winter. The floor was gritty and smelling of mildew. A light from beneath the door shown brightly, causing Tara to look away.*

*A woman's voice called out, answered by what Tara thought to be a man. His voice was deep—resonating off the walls in the hallway. She just couldn't make out the words with the exception of one: Bastard.*

*The sound of the woman calling the man a bastard struck Tara as funny. She started laughing to herself repeating the word over and over. A child pleaded in the darkness for Tara to be quiet. The hairs on the back of her neck stood on end.*

*"Who's there?" she asked in a whisper.*

*Something moved to her right and approached closer. The sent of baby shampoo wafted past her Tara's nose—her body trembled and she was close to losing control of her bladder.*

*The child whispered back. "Don't say another word, Mommy. If they hear you, they'll find you."*

*"Kayla?"*

*"Mommy, shhh..."*

*The little girl's face materialized inches from Tara's. She scooted backward, screaming in terror. The door burst opened flooding the room with a blinding light. Two dark figures approached, reaching out with long, black fingers.*

Tara screamed again, waking up in her room with both the light and television on. "What in the hell?" she said, jumping out of bed and barely making it to the bathroom before she had an accident. She struggled to remember if she had fallen asleep with the TV on. She knew she had turned out the light. Her only explanation was that she must have been sleepwalking again.

Knowing there was no getting back to sleep, Tara opted for an early breakfast. A cigarette sounded pretty good, too. In the pantry she found two unopened packages of cookies: chocolate chip and sandwich with extra goo in the middle. She also found her favorite Earl Grey tea.

"All right! Sadie went shopping!" she said out loud. She placed a mug with water into the microwave, hit beverage, and the oven hummed to life.

Tearing open both packages, she placed a chocolate chip cookie into her mouth. Through the loud crunching she thought she heard someone walking across the kitchen floor and stopping just behind her.

"Oh, you caught me," she said with a giggle. "Don't worry; I'm only going to have one or two. You want some tea? It will just take a sec."

"Why are you here?" she heard a woman say from behind her. The voice was dry and faint—the now familiar scent of Jasmine hung lightly in the air.

Confused by the question, Tara replied. "I couldn't sleep?" She turned to talk to her sister, but no one was there. "Sadie? Where'd you go?"

Tara turned back toward the sink and caught the reflection of a slender woman with long, blonde hair in the window and screamed, dropping the cookies onto the kitchen floor. By instinct, she turned around finding no one there again. She ran to her sister's bedroom and shook Sadie awake.

"What's wrong? Are the kids okay?"

"There's someone in the house!" Tara said.

Sadie sat up in bed. "What?"

"I saw her in the kitchen. She was standing right behind me."

Sadie scrunched her face and looked at her sister. "She? Are you sure?"

"She said something to me—I thought it was you."

The microwave buzzed, signaling Tara's hot water was ready. Both women sat in silence—holding on to one another tight—listening hard.

"Where's the phone?" Sadie asked.

"I saw it on the kitchen table."

"Shit!"

The microwave door creaked open—the mug crashed to the floor. Tara gasped, placing her hand over her mouth. Fearing for her children, Sadie bravely peered out her bedroom door. The coffee mug was in full view. It was broken into several small pieces. Water was spread over the dull, yellow tile floor and under the kitchen table. The microwave door was wide open, half hanging over the edge of the counter.

"Do you see anybody?" Tara whispered.

Sadie responded, with an irritated tone. "No!"

The kitchen seemed to be deserted. The only sound was coming from the battery operated clock on the wall. They peeked further around the corner finding no one.

"Did you open the side door?" Sadie asked. Tara shook her head.

Sadie crossed the living room and walked slowly into the kitchen. As she reached for the doorknob, the door flew violently inward. The kitchen lights went out leaving the two sisters in total darkness. Tara screamed when two bodies ran passed her and through the open door and knocking Sadie to the ground.

"Are you okay?" Tara asked, her voice trembling.

Every light in the house was suddenly illuminated, blinding them both. Sadie closed the door and turned the deadbolt.

"Mommy? Where are you?" a chorus of voices queried.

"Aunt Tara. Why are all the lights on?" asked Ami. The three children walked into the kitchen rubbing their eyes.

"Stay out of the kitchen. There's broken glass on the floor," Sadie said, shooing them out.

"Go sit on the couch, guys," Tara said.

One by one, the lights in the house turned back off. Spooked, all three children looked around. Sadie and Tara stood still, waiting for the next surprise.

"Should we call the police?" asked Tara.

"Yeah," Sadie said, grabbing the phone. Make sure the front door is still locked just in case they try to come back.

Tara checked the front door which was still dead bolted and chained. She joined the children on the couch and turned on the TV for comfort.

A few minutes later, Sadie stormed into the living room scowling and tossing the telephone onto the coffee table. "Ass holes!"

"Did you get a hold of anyone?"

Sadie articulated her answer. "Yes...I...did!"

"What did they say?"

"They are undermanned this morning due to illness and won't be able to come out until later this evening."

"What does that mean for us?"

"That means the police won't be out here until later this evening. Didn't you just hear me? Whoever broke in might still be out there and we have no hope in calling the police if they are!"

Tara sat teary eyed holding Erin and Joey tight. "I'm sorry. I'm just as frightened as you are."

"Did a burglar break into the house, Mommy?" asked Ami.

"I think so."

"Maybe it was the girl in the window," Erin said.

"What girl?" asked Joey.

"The girl in Ami's window. She looked like..."

Ami glared, trying to shut her little sister up before she said the name. "There was no girl in my window!" She had seen her also, but didn't want to admit it was her cousin, Kayla.

"Yeah, huh! Grandpa saw her, too!"

Sadie realized what her children were talking about. She remembered them all looking toward Ami's window and then seeing something move herself.

"I need you two to stop. All you saw was a reflection in the glass," Sadie said.

"And it looked just like Kayla!" Erin announced.

Ami gasped at her sister. "Dummy! You're not supposed to say her name in front of Aunt Tara!"

Tara felt suddenly numb hearing her daughter's name. The face in her dream flashed in her mind. She could see it so clearly. She knew it was Kayla—she knew it was her voice.

"Are you all right?" Sadie asked. Tara's eyes were moist with tears.

"She's crying, Mommy," Joey said.

"I'm so sorry, Tara. Guys, why don't you get into my bed and snuggle down." After a brief protest by Erin, all three children obeyed.

"It's not Erin's fault. She doesn't understand," Tara said.

"I wish I could help you. I just don't know what to say."

"I dreamt about her. That's why I'm up so early. It frightened me so much, I woke up panicking. I almost wet the goddamn bed! Maybe I was still dreaming in the kitchen."

"That definitely wasn't a dream. There was somebody in the house."

"I don't know. I smelled that strange perfume again, just before I saw the woman."

"Please don't go there. All we need is for the kids to over hear us and think we have ghosts in the house."

"But there's no other explanation," Tara said.

"Yes there is. Someone broke into the house and we surprised them. That's it, case closed." Sadie threw up her hands and walked into the kitchen to attend to the broken mug and water on the floor.

"I know what I saw. None of it makes sense. And what about the lights? It's like we had an electrical overload!" Tara said, following her sister into the kitchen.

"Maybe there was a power surge."

"At the same time whoever or whatever it was ran out the door? Come on, that doesn't make any sense."

Sadie stooped on her hands and knees picking up the pieces of mug thinking about what Tara was saying. *She* knew what had just happened didn't make any sense, but neither did the explanation that her house was haunted. She had never believed in ghosts and wasn't about to start now.

"When the police come over this evening, I'll ask them about the power surge. I'm sure they'll have other complaints about it, or a report from the utilities company. Until then, let's not mention haunting or ghosts. I don't want to frighten the kids anymore than they are now. It's bad enough they think somebody broke into the house."

Tara agreed and knelt on the floor to help her sister clean up the mess. When Sadie made up her mind there was no getting through no matter how rational the argument. It was easier to just let it go. Tara knew what she had seen, heard, and smelled.

## 39

Tara drove down west Maple straight after work to visit one of her old friends. She hadn't spoken to Lindsey for at least two-years since she and her boyfriend had moved out of the trailer-park. She also hadn't liked the way she flirted with Kenny. Lindsey was very touchy-feely—something Tara was not.

Turning onto a side street, Tara spotted Lindsey's dingy white bungalow sandwiched between two brick homes. The small lawn was mostly weeds—the front porch was filled with worn furniture and cardboard boxes in different stages of decay. Lindsey's old Escort Wagon was parked in the narrow driveway. Butterflies fluttered around in Tara's stomach. She felt strange about coming by uninvited, as well as nervous about seeing her old friend.

"Tara? Oh my god, is that you? What are you doing here?" Lindsey came bubbling out of the house. Her dark brown hair was long with a perm. She was barely squeezed into her faded blue jeans and her belly was pouring slightly over her waist just below her low-cut blouse.

"Same old Lindsey," Tara thought to herself.

"Wow, you look good," Lindsey said while giving Tara a hug. "I'm so sorry about Kenny."

"Thanks. It's been really hard without him."

"Come inside. There's someone I want you to meet!"

Tara followed Lindsey past the trash heap and eclectic collection of furniture. Inside was a little cleaner, though it bore the distinct aromas of dirty diapers and incense. A blue-eyed baby with orange remnants of carrots on her face peered at her from a bright yellow playpen. A collection of colorful baby toys were in a pile close by.

"This is Nickie."

"Oh, my gosh...I didn't know! She's a sweetie," Tara said, picking up the ten-month-old. "Hi, Nickie." She bounced the baby gently in her arms. "She's so light! I'm used to my nieces and nephew. Of course they're a lot older. She's got Randy's eyes."

"Not Randy's," Lindsey said with a smile.

"Oh, I'm sorry..."

"That's okay. You didn't know. Her daddy's name is Chris."

"Are you married, or do you guys live together...?"

Lindsey laughed. "Only in the form of a child-support check once a month."

The baby had started to fuss, so Tara handed her over to her mother. The furniture was adorned with pictures of the baby and Lindsey's family, but none with the father. Tara didn't ask why—she felt as if she had intruded enough.

"So what brings you by?" Lindsey asked, leading Tara into the kitchen. This was by far the neatest area of the house. It was so clean that it didn't seem to fit in.

"Well..." Tara had become suddenly nervous. "Something happened last night that I can't really explain and I thought you might be able to help. I think my house was broken into..."

"I haven't seen Randy or Michael in at least a year. I haven't even done stuff like that since I was in high school."

Tara gasped. "I didn't mean that! I hope you don't think I would come all the way over here to accuse you of breaking into my house."

Lindsey's face became flush. She stood holding her baby mortified and speechless in her own kitchen.

Tara fought for the words to say. "I feel like such an idiot. I think someone broke in—well Sadie does—and anyway...it's hard to explain. Are you still into all of that paranormal stuff? You know Ouija boards and Tarot cards?"

"Not since before Nickie was born. Why?"

Tara looked away. "I think the house we just moved into is haunted."

"Wow, are you sure?"

"Pretty sure."

"Like haunted how? Have you seen anything?"

"And heard and smelled."

"No shit?"

"A couple of times I've woken up in the middle of the night to the smell of this awful perfume...like some old woman would wear."

"What about Sadie?"

Tara's eyes welled up with tears. "She thinks I'm just imagining things. I don't know...maybe I am."

"You should hold a séance."

"I was hoping that maybe you could do one."

Lindsey shook her head. "Me? I kind of remember the basics, but…I do know someone who still practices. I can give you her number. Do you remember Arianna Jensen?"

"Sure," Tara said, wiping a tear from her eye. "She knows about all of that stuff?"

"She's the one who taught me," Lindsey said as she wrote down Arianna's cell phone number. "Where did you move to?"

"Out between Garden Plain and Cheney. Sadie bought an old farmhouse just south of Kellogg."

"Wow. It must be really quiet out there."

Tara smiled. "Only when the kids are in bed. Why don't you come by? Sadie would love to see the baby."

"Yea, that would be great! I need a break from this place. Since I had Nickie, I never get out anymore. I only see my mom a couple of days a week, and she usually comes here."

"I get home from work around this time. Is tomorrow too soon?"

"No, that sounds great."

"Just don't say anything about the house being haunted in front of Sadie or the kids. She'll have a major shit-fit!"

Lindsey laughed. "No problem. If I remember right, she's always been a bit rigid. Here's Arianna's number. If you call after eight you'll probably catch her."

Tara took the piece of paper from Lindsey who had also written her number down as well. "Is this your home or cell phone?"

"Yes," Lindsey smiled. "I can't afford a home-phone or cell-phone, so I bought a pay as you go phone instead. My mom buys me minutes every month whether I need them or not."

Lindsey handed Tara a blank sheet of paper. "Write down your number and address for tomorrow. Do I need to bring anything?"

"Just Nickie."

# 40

The distinct odor of Spaghetti O's hit Tara hard as she walked through the front door. The kids were arguing about who tripped who by the swing set. Sadie was busily stirring the red and brown delicacy on the stove top. The daily bribe of dessert was missing from the counter. Tara figured it wasn't needed due to the overwhelming approval of tonight's dinner. Tara and Sadie loved Spaghetti O's, too.

Tara held off on her usual "get home from work beer", opting for a tall glass of milk to compliment her dinner. Sadie raised an eyebrow at Tara's beverage selection.

"Hitting the hard stuff, are we?"

"After dinner," Tara said, scouring through the morning paper.

"Aunt Tara! Aunt Tara!" Joey tugged on her sleeve. "Did you know robbers were in our house?" Visions of masked men flew through his mind.

"She was there, stupid!" Ami said.

"If you don't want to go to bed early, Ami, than you better apologize to your brother," Sadie said without looking up from her pot.

"But, Aunt Tara was..."

"Now!"

"Sorry," she pouted.

Erin sat back watching and listening to the exchange. She knew better than to get involved. She was already on the verge of missing desert for tripping Joey earlier in the day.

Tara ignored the whole routine. She was too engrossed in the latest article about Swift Jet. The headline read *"More financial woes for leading businesses jet maker."* She was surprised the article didn't stir up any new rumors at work.

"Guess what the police said when I called to see if they were coming over?" Sadie asked her disconnected sister.

"They might be by tomorrow?" Tara said without looking up.

"Yeah! How did you know? And then they said that they might not be able to come by at all—and if I wanted to, I could come down to the station and file a report there!" she said as she slopped the saucy concoction into four bowls, placing them in front of her anxiously awaiting children and Tara. Instead of a bowl, she ate directly out of the pot. Now it was Tara's turn to raise her eyebrows.

Erin protested. "You're not supposed to do that, Mommy!"

"When you're the mommy, then you can make all the rules," Tara said. "What do you expect, Sadie? We moved to a town full of Barney's!"

"Just make sure all of the doors are locked before we go to bed."

"Oh, you'll never guess who I saw today," Tara said.

No one came to mind, so Sadie played by the rules and asked her who.

"Lindsey Slade."

"Who's that?"

"From the trailer park. Remember her boyfriend, Randy?"

"Lindsey and Randy," Sadie repeated to herself. "Oh, yeah. Wasn't he in and out of jail? And she was always stoned and liked to play with those fortune-teller cards."

Hearing Sadie describe Lindsey sarcastically angered Tara. Now she was embarrassed to tell her that Lindsey was coming over the next night. She thought momentarily about calling and canceling.

"Is that who you're talking about? Where did you see her?"

"She lives on Maple by the university. I drove over there after work. I invited her and her ten- month-old daughter over tomorrow night. She's changed quite a bit. She isn't with Randy anymore and I don't think she's into fortune-telling, either," Tara said with a slight attitude. "And before you ask, she seemed pretty sober to me."

"Sorry. You asked me if I remembered her and that was what I remembered!"

"Well, she'll be here shortly after I get home from work." Tara took her bowl to the sink, grabbed a beer from the fridge, and walked out the front door without another word. With a fresh cigarette in her mouth, she was able to relax.

She didn't want to fight with her sister. Sometimes it was just unavoidable. Deep down, she knew Sadie didn't mean to be a jerk about other people—especially people Tara knew.

Sadie joined Tara outside with a beer of her own. "I wasn't trying to make you mad. I'm sorry I have such unflattering memories of the girl. I probably won't even recognize her. I think it will be fun to see her baby. Mine are so big—I can't even try to imagine what it feels like to hold a real baby again."

"She's changed a lot...her personality that is. She still looks as incredible as she did when I last saw her, even with a baby. She's real lonely, though. The father isn't in the picture and she only sees her mother twice a week. Other than that, it's just her and the baby."

"It will be fun for the kids to see a baby, too. Except for church, they've never really been around one."

Erin came running out the front door, "Mommy. Me and Joey want to watch cartoons, but Ami has the TV on the Animal Channel again!"

Sadie rolled her eyes and got up with a huff, "I'll be right back."

"Don't hurry," Tara thought to herself. She liked the peace a quiet.

An argument ensued inside. She took the last drink of her beer and was irritated that she hadn't thought to bring out two. Not wanting to get up, she weighed the pros and cons of having just one.

She finished her cigarette and discovered she was just too thirsty to wait. Reluctantly, she dragged her tired body off of the porch swing and into the very loud house. She kept telling herself over and over that it was better than living with her parents.

<u>41</u>

Tara lied about being tired and left Sadie by herself in the living room. She wasn't in the mood for an old movie from the forties, or her sister's ramblings about their parent's future. Tara needed Tara time which meant two more beers and her own television to watch. Halfway through her second beer, she fell asleep on top of her bed, still wearing her work clothes.

*A driving, freezing wind shocked her wide-awake. Her window was open again. In the dark she fumbled for the lamp, knocking it over, and sending it crashing to the floor.*

*A woman's voice echoed in the darkness just outside the window. She was weeping for somebody—pleading for them to stop. The booming, low voice of a man yelled back. His tone was dismissive.*

*Wanting to know who was fighting, Tara went to the window. Unsure of the number of steps from the bed, she stubbed her big toe on the baseboard. Writhing in pain, she gripped the window ledge hard and cursed.*

*A faint light in the barn caught her attention. A single set of footprints in the deep snow led directly to the double doors. A large shadowy figure stood in the entrance to the barn. The figure didn't bother her as much as the fact there was snow on the ground in the middle of June.*

*A light from inside the house reflected off of the snowy driveway. The shadow of a woman paced back and forth, accompanied by mournful crying. Tara leaned further out the window, straining to see who was on the porch.*

*The light touch of a child's hand on Tara's arm made her jump, causing her to hit her head on the window frame. The shadow stopped pacing—the cries fell silent.*

*"Mommy," a little voice whispered in Tara's ear. "Daddy's afraid. Now that they know you're here, he won't stop hiding."*

*Tara's heart pounded in her chest. She recognized the voice in her ear. Her lower lip began to tremble.*

*"Tell him to come out, Mommy…please."*

*Tara's attention was split suddenly by the realization she was being watched. The dark figure in the doorway of the barn was staring up at her. The snow crunched beneath his feet as he approached. The shadow of the woman disappeared from view—the front door opened and then shut. Footsteps crossed the living room floor and tapped lightly against the wooden stairs as someone ascended.*

*"Open your eyes, Mommy, before they find you!" Tara didn't understand—her eyes were already open.*

*The footsteps in the snow were now just beneath her window. The loud clumping of boots on the porch steps sent shivers down her spine. The front door was thrown open and then slammed shut. A man's demanding and angry voice called up the stairs. Tara couldn't make out what he was saying and didn't want to know.*

*The small voice pleaded again for Tara to open her eyes before it was too late. Both of her wrists were held tight. She was forced down to her knees and came face to face with the vision of her dead, little girl.*

*"Kayla?" she cried. Oh my God, it is you." Tears filled her eyes and streamed down her face until the vision became a blur.*

*The doorknob turned violently back and forth. Tara could see movement in the light shinning from beneath the door. Kayla tugged on her arms trying desperately to get her mother to listen.*

*The door was forced open, flooding the room with light. Two shadowy figures approached. In a frantic attempt to gain her attention, Kayla screamed—pleading again for her mother to open her eyes.*

*Tara returned her gaze back to her daughter's vision and gasped in horror. The little girl's face had turned from a soft and beautiful silhouette to the shriveled and sullen face of her daughter in the grave.*

*Tara closed her eyes and screamed.*

She sat straight up in bed, the noise from a loud and obnoxious television commercial blared in her ears. Her jeans and bedding were saturated. At first she thought she had wet the bed, but quickly realized she had spilled the rest of her beer.

With the nightmare still fresh in her mind, a deep sadness descended upon her heart. She could still feel her little girl's hands around her wrists—hear her sweet little voice in her ears. Tara began to sob.

Glancing at the clock through tear filled eyes, she noticed it was just past three a.m. and she was up for good...again. Remembering last night's fun, she opted to stay in her room until it was time to get ready for work. She grabbed the box of tissues off of her nightstand and flipped through the channels until she found an info-commercial she liked. The television and bedroom light kept her company and feeling secure.

# 42

Sadie didn't hear Tara leave for work. She woke up at nine, an hour before she had promised her mother that she and the kids would come by and visit. Stan had been home from the hospital a total of two-days and was already driving Betty Jo nuts.

The kids had been up for an hour and had managed to spill cereal all over the counter and kitchen floor, along with splatters of milk on the kitchen table. Sadie emerged from the bedroom with her hair sticking up in every direction, looking more like a crazy-woman than the loving, caring mother she actually was. She directed Ami, whom she always relied on to be her helper, to get dressed for Grandma and Grandpa's and help her brother and sister pick out the appropriate clothing.

Sadie made quick work of the cereal mess and got dressed herself. She hated the thought of leaving her comfortable home for what she imagined would be the hostile, hospital like atmosphere of her parent's home. Her mother was bound to be full of stories of hate and discontent—her father a list of miseries, if he were talking at all. Sadie's stomach became tight at the thought of spending the entire day with them. She started thinking of excuses to leave early.

Joey, running past the kitchen and out the front door, startled Sadie. She had never known her son to move fast for anything but dessert. She ran to the door curious to see what he was up to. As she stepped out onto the front porch, the sight gave her pause. Joey was standing just a few feet from the barn with his head cocked toward the pathway that led to the side entrance. She called to him but received no answer.

Joey heard the man's voice—quiet, yet stern. It beckoned him to come closer. "I have a football—come and see."

A dark, hulking figure moved in the shadows, motioning for Joey to follow. "Daddy?" Joey queried.

Sadie's attention switched from her son to the un-latched padlock and the two big barn doors slightly ajar. She knew she had closed both doors and locked them the week before.

Joey's quick movement brought Sadie's attention back to him. He disappeared around the side of the barn yelling what

Sadie thought was "Daddy." Before she could reach him, he was already in the barn.

Without giving it much thought, she ran in after him, stopping just inside. Particles of dust danced on the sunbeams piercing through the filthy pane glass windows. Cobwebs adorned each rafter and stall. Even though there was a small cross breeze, the air inside the immense space was stale. Her heart leaped finding the old wooden ladder set up once again in the middle of the barn.

Joey's hand touched Sadie's arm. "Mommy?"

Sadie shrieked and jumped back. "Shit, shit, shit!" she yelled, holding her hands over her chest. "Don't ever do that!"

Joey started to cry. "I'm sorry, Mommy."

Sadie scooped him into her arms. She was hardly able to lift him. "Its okay, sweetie. I'm not mad. You just scared me. What on earth are you doing in here?"

"I thought I saw Daddy," he said with his bottom lip stuck out.

"Daddy? Where?" Her tone was steady and flat.

"I thought he came in here. Maybe he's outside."

Sadie put Joey back on his own two feet and walked him out of the barn with his hand firmly grasped in hers. The open padlock hanging on the clasp to the side door caught her eye.

"Daddy!" Joey called.

Sadie put her finger to her lips in an effort to quiet her son down. She couldn't fathom why Jared would have driven all the way out here this time in the morning. Waking up at noon was early for him.

"I don't see the Taurus," she said out loud.

"Maybe he walked."

Sadie tried hard not to laugh. Jared got winded walking from the refrigerator to the couch and back. She couldn't even imagine his holiness walking up the drive to fetch the mail.

"Oh, we live too far away for Daddy to walk. Are you sure you saw him?"

Joey stood by his mother's side squinting in the bright morning sunlight, thinking. The figure was big like his daddy, but different. "He didn't sound like Daddy," he said, looking straight ahead. "His voice was deeper."

A chill ran down Sadie's back. A feeling of apprehension filled her gut. She had been ready to dismiss Joey seeing his father as just her son's imagination running wild. Hearing him describe a man's voice made her think differently.

"What did he say?" she asked. Her lips trembled slightly.

"He had a football."

Her first thought was that it must be whoever broke in the other night—probably local teenagers with nothing else to do but cause trouble. That would explain the locks. Thinking about that night and the ineptness of the local police infuriated her. Fear was now replaced with out-right anger.

"You little creeps better stay away from my kids! I'm going inside right now and calling the police, so you better leave if you know what's good for you!"

Her voice echoed against the house and barn, carrying across the fields of wheat adjacent to her property. She felt stupid for yelling at what was probably no one.

"Go inside and get ready," she gently told Joey. "Grandma's waiting for us." He ran to the house without arguing or looking back. She scanned the barn and the adjacent area just incase someone was actually lurking about.

All three kids bounding out of the house—equipped with backpacks and a juice box—snapped Sadie out of her daze. She hurried inside to get her purse and keys and was back out before Erin had a chance to start complaining about the door not being unlocked.

"Get in and buckle up, guys," she said as she started the SUV's gas guzzling engine.

Still not convinced that no one was lurking about, she drove to the backside of the barn finding nothing but debris, overgrown grass and brush. If somebody did try to sneak through the back they would easily be stopped by the collection of old barbed wire fencing and scrap wood littering the field.

Just as she started back forward, Erin started bouncing in her seat pointing out the window toward the house. "Mommy, look! Mommy!"

Sadie pushed forcefully on the brakes. All three kids lurched forward in their booster seats. "What now?"

Ami saw what her sister was all excited about. "It's Aunt Tara's window, again!"

"What about it?"

"Look, its open!" Ami said.

Erin pouted, complaining that she wanted to tell about the window.

Sadie rolled her eyes. Exhaling, she stated that the window was their Aunt Tara's problem and she would have to deal with it when she got home from work.

"Yeah, let her deal with it," Joey said.

"Don't talk like that, Joey. You sound just like Daddy," Ami said.

Sadie agreed and ordered all three kids to not make a peep until they arrived at their grandparent's house. The peace and quiet lasted until someone touched someone else, calling them a name for good measure. Sadie tuned them all out and headed down the road in deep thought, secretly wishing the school-year would start in June instead of August.

# 43

Stan was camped out in front of the TV as expected. The end table by his chair had a collection of prescription drug bottles and old wadded up tissues. Betty Jo was out on the back patio smoking. The doctor had insisted that Stan was no longer around cigarette smoke. Sadie noticed immediately the difference in air quality in her parent's small home. The only offensive odor now was coming from the pets.

The kids made a bee-line for their grandfather. Stan struggled to sit up in his chair, giving them each a big hug. Sadie warned them all not to be too rough. Betty Jo walked into the house announcing she had expected everyone an hour earlier.

"Sorry, Mom—I overslept. Believe it or not, Tara was actually quiet when she left for work this morning. Is Dad doing better?"

"He seems to be," she sighed. "He bit off my head this morning for making his toast too dark. I told him he could make his own damn toast if he didn't like the way that I made it."

"That's a big surprise."

"Your father's been nothing but grouchy and spiteful since I brought him back home."

"He must have cabin-fever being stuck inside all day. You know he lives to be outside in that nasty, dirty gravel. When does he go back to work?"

"The doctor said next week should be fine. She wasn't as concerned, because it was only a minor heart attack."

"Did she say what caused it?"

"It could have been any number of things. I think it was being in the hot sun all day, myself."

"Have you ever noticed any teenagers hanging around the property, you know, like in the fields surrounding the house when you've come by?" Sadie said.

"No...I can't really say I have."

"I think Joey saw someone. No, I pretty sure he did—a man. He thought it was Jared at first, and then he wasn't sure."

"Maybe it was a neighbor," Betty Jo said.

"Maybe. I thought it might have been kids...the same ones that broke into our house the other night."

"Broke into your house?"

"Oh, that's right. You and Dad don't know. You've been so busy dealing with him; I haven't had a chance to tell you."

"Did you call the police?"

"Yes and they are worthless!"

"Did they take anything?" Betty Jo asked. She was now on the edge of her seat.

"No. All they did is break a coffee mug and knock into us when they ran out the side kitchen door. It made me think of something a kid would do on a dare."

"Well, you know how teenage boys are at that age."

"I don't think they were all boys. Tara said she saw the reflection of a woman in the kitchen window—probably a girl."

"Oh, just like your father saw..." Betty Jo clammed up—her eyes became moist, causing her to look away.

"Are you all right, Mom?"

Betty Jo didn't answer. Instead she got up from the table and proceeded to fix herself a rum and coke, adding two shots of rum instead of one. Taking a deep breath, she drank a quarter of the cocktail down.

"What did Dad see?"

Betty Jo stood still at the kitchen sink. She stared straight ahead through the window. Tears filled her eyes and descended down her thin, weathered face. Choking back more tears, she took a long drink, this time consuming at least a third of the glass.

"Mom?"

Her temper short, Betty Jo answered with a weak and raspy voice. "I don't want to discuss it."

"I don't understand."

"Damn it to hell, Sadie. I said I don't want to discuss it! Why isn't that good enough for you?"

"Because he's my father and I care a great deal for him," Sadie answered with tears in her own eyes. "I know he saw something. Erin told me he did."

Betty Jo took another long drink. Her mind had already started to unravel. Her body relaxed giving the impression she was about to give into her daughter's demanding questions.

"Whatever Dad thought he saw was probably just the sun reflecting off of Ami's window. That's all it was. I saw it too."

"It wasn't the sun. I know your father better than anyone. What he saw wasn't the sun," Betty Jo said, downing the last of her drink. She poured herself some more soda without the rum and sat back down.

"Maybe she was on his mind. The combination of building that swing set by himself, along with the heat probably made Dad dizzy."

"Sadie, don't." Betty Jo started to cry. She buried her face deep into her hands.

Sadie grasped her mother's frail hands gently in hers. "What Dad thinks he saw is impossible. Ghosts aren't real. Kayla is gone—she's with God in heaven. I told Ami and Erin the same thing. It was just all their imagination and nothing else."

Betty Jo lifted up her head. Her eyes were red and swollen from crying. "I want so much to believe that."

Ami came skipping into the kitchen acting as envoy for her siblings and grandfather. "Can we each have a cookie, please?"

"They're on the counter, sweetie," Sadie said, pointing toward the bag of cookies.

Ami noticed that her grandmother was crying. Concerned, she walked over to the counter listening hard to what was being said. When she heard Kayla's name mentioned by her mother, she knew exactly what they were talking about.

"Ami," Sadie called to her daughter. "Did you get what you needed?"

Ami nodded and walked quietly out of the kitchen. She looked over at her misty eyed grandmother until she passed. Sadie knew by her daughter's expression that it was time to change the conversation.

## <u>44</u>

Pulling into the driveway, Sadie was surprised to see a battered, green Escort wagon parked in front of the house behind Tara's pickup. All she needed after today's visit with her parents was to entertain.

"Is that Aunt Tara's friend's car, Mommy?" Ami asked half a sleep.

"Oh, that's right. I think it is."

"The one with a baby?" Erin asked excitably.

"I'm not a baby!" Joey protested in the back seat.

"Not you, Joey!" Ami said.

"All right, all ready. No more from any of you. Get yourself in the house and put your things away. Then you can see Aunt Tara's friend and her baby."

The open barn door reminded Sadie of how her day had started out. The chance that would-be burglars had opened it crossed her mind again, and then she remembered the owner's brother coming over to fix the attic-stairs. If he still had the key it would all make sense. He probably went into the barn to get something he had left behind.

The house was full of giggles and squealing—the foyer was littered with the children's various belongings they had brought with them to their grandparents. All three kids were on the floor playing with Lindsey's baby.

"Hey, you guys. I said put your things away first. Be sure to wash your hands, too. You've all been messing with those nasty dogs of Grandma's."

"How are Mom and Dad?" Tara grinned.

"Just as we thought," Sadie grinned back.

"Do you remember Lindsey?"

"Yes, I do now," she said, gently shaking Lindsey's hand. "And who's this little sweetie?"

Lindsey picked up her daughter and presented her proudly to Sadie, "This is Nickie."

Sadie took her into her arms. "She's so little! Oh how I miss my babies. They were so cuddly when they were her age."

"You have a beautiful house. It's so warm, that it almost embraces you!"

Not knowing quite how to respond, Sadie simply said thank you. She handed the baby back to Lindsey announcing she needed to get dinner started. "I hope you all like Hamburger Helper."

"Sounds good to me," Tara said.

Sadie got to work on the dinner and then remembered the barn. "Tara. Could you come here, please?"

"Uh oh, I'm in trouble!" Tara said. Lindsey giggled and the girls burst into laughter. She walked into the kitchen finding Sadie at the stove.

"Did you by chance unlock the barn doors?"

"No, why?"

"Well I found both the padlock to the big doors and the one to the side door unlocked and hanging on the latches this morning. That old ladder was set up again, too."

"That's strange. Well I know it wasn't me. I have no interest in going anywhere near that nasty, dirty place."

"I thought it might have been our intruders and then remembered that guy was just here to fix the attic-stairs. Would you mind calling him to see if it was him and if he still has the keys to the locks? Either way I'm planning on changing them. I'm just curious to see if it was him."

"Yeah, sure. I have his business card up in my room."

"Oh! I almost forgot. Your window was left opened again this morning. The kids made a point of showing me as we were leaving for Mom and Dad's."

Tara stopped mid-step. "Are you sure? It wasn't opened when I got home. The first thing I did with Lindsey was show her my room."

"Maybe not," Sadie frowned. "I guess I was more tired than I thought this morning."

Tara ran upstairs and was back quickly. She handed her sister both the phone and business card.

"Could you call instead? I have nothing nice to say to those jerks," she said, handing both items right back.

Tara's face became flush at the thought of calling. She studied the name on the business card, remembering with great detail the color of Matt's eyes. "I'll call tomorrow after work."

"Why not now? I'd like to know who's been screwing around. Joey claims he saw someone this morning on the side of the barn and that they said something to him. I don't know whether to believe him or not, but I don't want to take any chances. It will only take a minute—please."

"He saw someone? Who would be walking around here?"

"I have no clue. At first, I thought it was the creeps that broke in the other night. Joey thought it was Jared. I looked around and didn't see a thing. Do you think it was that fixit guy?"

"No…he didn't seem the type," Tara said.

"Maybe he needed something out of the barn and was too stupid…sorry…too embarrassed to come to the door."

Tara thought for a moment and then walked over to the far side of the large kitchen and dialed. She glanced over her shoulder to check if Sadie was listening.

"Hello?" a man's voice answered on the other end. "Hello?"

"Is this Matt Cramer?" Tara asked timidly.

"Yes it is. Who's this?" He was all business.

"Tara James. You were over last weekend to fix our attic-stairs."

"Oh yeah, Tara—you're the sister. How's it going? Is there a problem with the stairs?" His tone was now relaxed.

"Not so far. They haven't fallen down and hit somebody yet if that's what you mean." She started to feel more comfortable. "I actually have another question."

"Go ahead, shoot away."

Sadie turned and urged Tara to ask the question.

"Did you happen to stop by this morning? My sister found the barn doors unlocked and opened and thought, maybe, that you needed something you had left behind."

"No, can't say I did. I would always call before coming by. Besides, I wouldn't have had a reason to go in there."

Tara held the phone away from her and covered the receiver. "He said he wasn't here."

Sadie crossed her arms and shook her head. "What about the keys?" she prompted.

"Oh, do you still happen to have the keys to the padlocks?"

"Funny you should call. I found a box full of old keys as well as odds and ends with your address on it while cleaning out my brother's truck. They could be one of those. I could swing by and drop it off for you."

"He's got a box full of old keys and things for the house," Tara informed her sister. "He wants to drop it by."

"Fine. When will he be here?" Sadie asked.

"That would be just fine. When will you be by?"

"How about I pick you up for dinner at seven on Friday?"

Tara froze. She swore he had just asked her out, but was too stunned to respond.

"Or would six-thirty be a better time?"

"Six-thirty would be fine," she said, barely able to speak.

"Great! I hope you like *Velours Noir*. See you then," he said, ending the conversation.

The line went dead. Tara stood in the corner still holding the phone to her ear. She couldn't believe she just said yes to a date with a man she didn't know, just a few months after her husband had died.

"You know what that means don't you?" Sadie said as she placed the hamburger into the skillet to brown. "That means those bastards that broke into the house also got into the barn. When's he bringing by that stuff? Tara?"

Turning around, Sadie found her sister still with the phone in her hand wearing a slight grin. "What's wrong with you? Is he going to drop that stuff by or not?"

Tara couldn't help but show her complete excitement. She giggled and squealed, doing a slight dance as she slid the phone across the table.

"What in the world is wrong with you?" Sadie laughed.

"Holly shit! You won't believe me!"

"Believe what, for God's sake? What's wrong with you?"

"He asked me out Friday night."

"Who did? The guy who fixed the stairs?"

"He's taking me to Velours Noir! I can't believe it. What do I do?"

"You're eating at one of the nicest restaurants in Wichita. Order what you want!"

Lindsey walked into the kitchen amidst Tara's celebration. "What's going on? Sounds like the party's in here."

"Tara just got asked out on her first real date in years," Sadie said.

"That's fantastic. What's his name?"

"Matt," Tara giggled. "Oh no, it isn't too soon since I lost Kenny, is it?"

"No way, Sis. I caught a glimpse of him when he left. Very cute," Sadie said.

"Don't worry about it. Just have fun," Lindsey said. "Is he taking you anywhere good?"

"Velours Noir."

"Wow! He must be nice to be taking you there—and rich!"

"Rich is nice," Sadie said.

"Not to break up the celebration, but do you mind watching Nickie for me while I use the little girls room?"

"Sure," Tara said. "She's such a cutie."

"You can use mine, Lindsey," Sadie said.

"Mommy," Ami said from the living room. "She can't use your bathroom, because Erin's in there."

"The one I share with the kids is up the stairs and then straight ahead," Tara said.

"Thank you," said Lindsey, as she quickly ran up the steps.

As soon as she closed the bathroom door, the doorknob started to turn back and forth. Lindsey felt a little embarrassed about having to tell Sadie's kids to please wait until she was finished. A child's footsteps retreating made her feel as if her pleas for privacy worked.

While washing her hands, the footsteps returned. The doorknob was once again jiggled back and forth. She thought to herself that this was what she had to look forward to when Nickie got older. "Just a minute, please. I'll be right out."

Upon opening the door, Lindsey found nobody waiting. The hallway was quiet and dim. The only sounds she could hear were her baby playing with Sadie's kids.

The linen closet door between Erin and Ami's rooms swung open a quarter of the way, making a loud creek in the process. Startled, Lindsey jumped and gasped. Looking toward the closet, she could see the shadowy outline of a child crouched inside.

"I see you!" she said. The door was pulled shut. "Come on out now. I don't think your momma would like you playing in there."

The door remained still even as Lindsey approached. She tried to coax the mischievous child out once more, but without success. She reached slowly for the doorknob, and then pulled it quickly open, saying "Gotcha" in a playful voice. The closet was empty except for a few folded bath towels, bed sheets, and extra toilet tissue.

Lindsey tried to catch her breath. She was certain she had seen a child hiding in the closet. She knew the door had moved back and forth. With the hairs on her arms and the back of her neck standing on end, she felt suddenly frightened. Someone was watching her.

She hurried down the stairs and back into the family room where Tara and the girls were still playing with her daughter. Joey was reclined on the couch watching cartoons while fidgeting with a toy race car. Sadie was stirring in the ingredients of the Hamburger Helper.

Tara looked up at her pale friend, stating that she looked like she had just seen a ghost. Lindsey's only response was a slight shudder and a small tear rolling down her smooth, rounded cheek. Knowing something was wrong; Tara got up off of the floor and took Lindsey into the foyer, while keeping the children in her sight.

"What's the matter?"

"Have you called Arianna, yet?"

"Arianna?"

"You know, Arianna Jensen? I gave you her number."

"No, not yet"

"You need to call her now. You were right, Tara. This house is haunted. I'm not sure what I just saw up there, but I'm certain I never want to again."

Tara became frightened herself. She wasn't sure what her friend had seen, and didn't really want to know.

"I know your upset, but I need you to try and calm down before we go back into the living room. All we need is for the kids to see you crying. They'll alert the media, and then we'll never hear the end of it from Sadie."

Lindsey laughed at the thought of the kids sounding the alarm and Sadie coming unhinged. "Okay. I'm all right now."

"Erin's out of my sister's bathroom. You can pull yourself together in there." Lindsey agreed and quietly made her way to Sadie's bedroom.

Tara bounded into the living room announcing that dinner smelled wonderful, and that she was so hungry she could eat three little children up in one bite. Ami and Erin squealed causing the baby to screech.

# 45

Sadie stood on the front porch watching Tara swing her truck around and Lindsey pull away. She privately wondered what might have happened to change Tara's sweet and happy friend into someone who was obviously upset.

"Ready for a beer?" Tara asked as she climbed out of the cab.

"Only if you tell me what's going on with your friend," Sadie said.

"What do you mean?"

"Well, for one, she hardly had anything to eat, and…"

"Maybe she was just being polite."

"Did I say something to offend her?"

"I mean, she's not used to being around a lot of people. We probably wore her out."

"Did the baby get hurt?"

"She's always been emotional."

Sadie grabbed hold of Tara's arm. "I know you're hiding something from me—I can tell. Did the baby get hurt?"

"No."

"Then what's going on?"

"Fine. After I get the beers." Tara felt like she was fifteen and confessing to her mother about her role in steeling grocery store carts with her boyfriend, Josh. She hated that her sister had such an effect on her. "You can let go, now."

"Oh, sorry."

Tension traveled up Sadie's arms and to her neck. She could feel a headache forming behind her right eye. She hated it when Tara acted like one of her kids. "Just tell me the damn truth, "she said to herself.

Staring off across her yard, movement by the barn caught her eye. She could have sworn the large barn doors had just swung outward. Remembering she hadn't locked them back up, she stormed across the drive cursing under her breath.

"Pain in the ass! Maybe I could hire Tara's new boyfriend to tear the damn thing down."

As she reached out to push the doors shut, something large stirred past a stall near the back of the barn. Sadie held her breath—not entirely sure she wasn't imagining things. With shaky hands, she closed the rusty lock and pulled on it several times to ensure it was indeed locked. Feeling uneasy, she hurried back to the safety of the front porch.

"Do you feel okay? You look really pale," Tara asked, handing Sadie her beer.

Sadie took a long drink and sat down, leaning her head back against the porch swing. "I'm fine," she lied. She didn't dare tell Tara what had just happened—she would never hear the end of it.

"Are you sure…"

"Yeah, I'm fine," she snapped.

Tara backed off. "All right."

"So, what's up with Lindsey?"

"I'm not going to discuss it with you. You'll only get pissed off."

"Did one of the kids do something? Did I?"

"No, nothing like that…she…"

Sadie started to raise her voice. "She what?"

"What are you so upset about?"

"Damn it, Tara! Just tell me!"

"Okay. Jesus Christ, calm down!"

Sadie raised her eyebrows prompting Tara. Tara bit her lower lip and shook her head knowing how Sadie was going to react to what she was about to say. "Lindsey saw something upstairs that frightened her."

Sadie lowered her head and scowled. "Tara…"

"See? That's why I didn't want to say anything, but you kept pushing."

"For the last time, the house is not haunted."

"How do you know? Just because you haven't seen anything doesn't mean its not there."

"Now you're sounding like Mom," Sadie said.

"And you sound just like Dad!"

"Aunt Tara?" Ami said, bounding out the front door.

"What is it, sweetie?"

"Your TV's really loud. Can you turn it down? We can't hear our show."

"My TV's not on…"

"We'll go take a look," Sadie said.

The stairwell was filled with the sounds of canned laughter and the eerie glow from the television in Tara's room. Both women ascended with caution, flipping on the hall light for security. Each bedroom door was shut with the exception of Tara's.

Tara walked into her room and shut the television off. "I wish the kids would really stay out of my room."

"I'm sorry. They all know better."

"Well I guess this means it was Ami," Tara said, holding the small, red plastic ring up for Sadie to see.

Sadie had turned completely around facing Ami's room. She was staring across the hall at the narrow opening of the now open door. Someone was staring back. Tara called to her without success. The familiar scent of cigarette-smoke hung lightly in the air.

"Hey. It smells like..." Tara stopped in mid-sentence. After adjusting to the light, she also saw someone staring through the narrow opening. "Sadie?" she whispered.

Sadie didn't respond. She was paralyzed with fear. Both women stood in the middle of the hall in some type of standoff. Neither one dared to move.

Breaking the silence, Ami bounded up the stairs and rushed into her bedroom. Both women shrieked, scaring the nine-year-old girl into tears. Sadie ran to her daughter and scooped her in to her trembling arms. Tara followed close behind, searching the corners of the bedroom for a possible intruder.

"Did you see where they went?" Sadie asked as quietly as she could, trying hard not to frighten Ami anymore than she already had.

Tara shook her head. She had the dreadful feeling they had just seen what Lindsey had earlier. "Can we go downstairs, now?"

Without a word, Sadie headed down with Ami. Not wanting to be the last one in the hallway, Tara followed close behind.

Erin and Joey, engrossed in their cartoons, were oblivious to the world. Sadie reassured Ami that everything was fine and she had just surprised her and her aunt. She rejoined her brother and sister, becoming instantly mesmerized by the bright colors of the television.

Desperate for a cigarette, but too frightened to be outside alone, Tara opened the side kitchen door and stepped just outside. The smell of fresh cigarette smoke drew a scowl from Sadie.

"Lindsey's has a friend that conducts séances."

"Tara..."

"She said that this woman knows what she's doing."

"No way in hell. I'm not letting some weird psychic person in my house!"

"I met her before and she seemed normal to me."

"No, Tara. That's my final answer."

"I know you just saw the same thing I did. You can't just sit there and tell me you don't think your house is haunted," Tara said, blowing cigarette smoke out of her nose and mouth.

"Quit saying that! For the last time, it's not haunted!"

"Aren't you worried about the kids sleeping up there tonight? What ever we saw in Ami's bedroom is probably still there. There's no way in hell I'm sleeping up there. Lindsey saw it too. That's why she was acting so strange."

"I don't know. I don't want some strange woman scaring the kids with ghost stories."

"Have Mom watch them."

"No. It's just too weird for me."

Tara threw the butt of her cigarette out onto the driveway earning another scowl from Sadie. "So, are we all sleeping downstairs tonight?"

Sadie watched her children sitting innocently on the couch. They were oblivious to what had just happened. Even Ami didn't seem to know.

An upstairs bedroom door slamming shut broke the silence. Both Sadie and Tara leaped and the children screamed in unison.

"Mommy!" Erin said. "Did you here that? Is someone upstairs?" she asked with wide eyes. Joey was close by her side.

Ami waltzed in rolling her eyes. "Its just Aunt Tara's window again, dummy. The door always slams when it's open."

"Sit back down, guys," Sadie said. She was clearly on her last nerve. "Go ahead and call her, Tara. I don't know what else to do."

Tara searched the kitchen for her purse and then remembered she had left it upstairs. "It's in my bedroom," she said, almost laughing. "I'll get it later."

Sadie started to cry.

# <u>46</u>

Needing to get ready for bed, Tara found the courage to go up to her room. Feeling as if she were being watched, she collected her clothes and purse, and made a dash down the stairs, running all the way into the kitchen. She dug Arianna's number out of the cluttered chasm of her purse and dialed before she lost her nerve.

"Who are you and how did you get this number?" Arianna answered abruptly.

"Um, this is Lindsey's friend, Tara."

"Lindsey's friend? Did you say Sara?"

"No. My name is Tara. Lindsey recommended you."

"For what?"

Tara felt silly for calling her. She knew Lindsey wouldn't mislead her, so she took a deep breath and answered. "She said that you conduct séances."

"Oh, she did?"

"You still do, don't you?"

"Not for awhile since I started working legit," Arianna laughed. "I had to take a job at a health food store to keep up with the bills. My boyfriend took off on me, sticking me with a load of debt."

"Oh, I'm sorry to hear that. Would you know of anyone else? You know...someone who conducts séances? We're kind of desperate."

"I think you misunderstood me. I can still do it—I just haven't had the time lately."

Tara perked up. "So, will you?"

"Sure—especially if Lindsey recommended me. Just name the day and time...except for Monday through Friday ten to five."

"This Saturday?"

"I'm filling in for someone at work. Can I be there after eight?"

Tara breathed a sigh of relief. "Yeah, that would be great. Do I need to do anything special?"

"Yes. Boil some bat wings and frog's eyes."

Tara stood silent, not sure whether to take Arianna as serious.

"I'm kidding with you!" Arianna laughed. "Just a little witch humor. I do need to know why you're in need of a séance, though. Did someone just die? Are you trying to reach a dead relative? Do you think your house is haunted?"

"Yes...the last one."

"Haunted house," Arianna mumbled as she wrote down the information. "I also need your address, so I can do a little research on the house, and so I can find my way there."

"4150 South 329th Street. Will there be a fee?" Tara cringed, waiting for the answer.

"I usually charge one–fifty," Arianna thought out-loud. "But since you're Lindsey's friend, I'll only charge one-twenty-five."

The price was very much within Tara's budget, so she didn't barter. "That's very generous of you. Will you be bringing Lindsey with you?"

"Sure. I'll see what she's up to that night. I've got your number on caller ID, so I'll call you if I have any questions."

"Thank you so much. You don't know how much this means to me."

"No problem. I'll see ya Saturday."

Relieved that Arianna had agreed to the séance, Tara joined Sadie and the kids in the living-room. She snuggled down into the recliner and turned on the last of the evening news. She was asleep within minutes.

## 47

*Tara awoke to Sadie calling for her in the distance. The air in the house was biting cold—Tara's breath floated in front of her in a fine, lucent mist. Every light in the house was off except for the stairwell. The laughter of children echoed all around her as she cautiously made her way up the stairs. As she reached the landing, a strong breeze flowed out of her bedroom, followed by dancing flurries of snow.*

*Tara ran into her room to close the window, but stopped abruptly at the side of her bed. Beneath the covers, a large body shaped mound moved slowly up and down as if breathing. Angry that someone was in her bed, she pulled back the covers, revealing the skeletal remains of four small children. Terrified, she ran from her room, screaming for Sadie.*

A bright flash of lightning, followed by a large crash of thunder, woke Tara out of her dream. She sat straight up in the recliner just as Sadie ran out of her room to attend to the weather radio. *The National Weather Service* was reporting a severe thunderstorm twenty-five miles due west of downtown Wichita—which meant they were right in the middle of it.

"Don't worry. No tornados yet—just a lot of noise and wind," Sadie said.

"Good! I really don't want to go into that nasty cellar."

"Do you want some coffee or tea?" Sadie asked.

"What time is it?"

"Just after one." Sadie jumped as another crash of thunder shook the house.

"Make it herbal. After the dream I just had, it's going to be hard to get back to sleep."

Two more flashes of lightning illuminated the darkened windows. They were followed closely by thunder, but further away. The storm had already begun to move out of the area, bringing a sense of relief to both women.

The house became eerily quiet, bringing with it a different sense of un-rest. What they had both experienced the night before was still fresh in their minds. Sadie was genuinely confused—Tara was just plain frightened. Neither would as much as glance toward the stairs.

"I see you got your clothes," Sadie observed. "When did you go upstairs?"

"When you guys were asleep on the couch—before I lost my nerve."

"Did you see anything?" Sadie asked, completely embarrassed about admitting her house might be haunted.

"No, but all of the doors were open. I'm sure when we came back downstairs all but Ami's and mine were closed."

Sadie agreed. She sat down at the table with her arms crossed tight, looking past Tara—lost in her thoughts. Being a prisoner in her own home didn't sit well with her. She had never believed in ghosts—not even as a little girl. She was too sensible. Tara and her mother always seemed to be conjuring up one mystery or another when they were younger—Sadie was always looking for the logic behind the hype. Even in church she would pick apart the pastor's message, ensuring he was preaching from the Bible and not his own personal made-up beliefs.

"I called the medium Lindsey recommended. She'll be here after eight on Saturday night," Tara said, breaking Sadie out of her trance.

"This Saturday night? What about the kids? I really didn't want them exposed to that kind of thing."

"Have Mom watch them,"

"Mom's too busy taking care of Dad. Next time, let me take care of my own kid's childcare. I don't know why you felt free to make a decision like that without asking me first."

"You were asleep! I thought you wanted to do this! You were as freaked out as I was! If you don't want to be part of the séance, then maybe you should go over to Mom and Dad's with the kids!"

"I never said that! I just don't like it when people insert themselves in my children's business. I'm their mother, not you."

"That's right! I'm nobody's mother—not anymore." Tara's voice trembled with anger.

"I didn't mean..."

Tara cut her sister off before she could offer up one of her patented apologies. "Save it for someone who'll believe your bullshit. I'm not buying it. If you're not interested in finding out what in the hell is going on in your own house, then don't expect me to hang around. I can't even sleep in my own goddamn bedroom tonight!"

"I don't know what you want me to say. I'm not going to allow you or anyone else to tell me what to do with my own kids. That woman's not coming over when they're here!"

"I'm sorry I stepped on your mommy toes. If you would get your head out of your ass long enough to listen to what I'm saying, then maybe you would have heard that I'm not sticking around if this problem isn't resolved. Don't you care that your children aren't sleeping in their own beds tonight? You saw the same thing that I saw, Sadie. You should want to take care of it as soon as possible."

A bright flash of lighting followed by the low roar of distant thunder stopped the argument momentarily. Both women took a deep breath and stared away from one another.

"Fine. I'll see what I can do about babysitting on Saturday," Sadie gave in slightly. "This so called medium better not be a hack. I don't know what else we can do, short of having the house blessed by a priest."

Tara didn't answer. She walked silently over to the couch, covered up with an afghan, and turned away from Sadie. She was too upset to continue the heated conversation with her sister. Not even tea would calm her nerves.

Sadie sat for a moment and then got up herself, leaving her freshly made tea on the kitchen table. Her fight with Tara had made her tense, but she would rather lie awake in her bed than sit in the kitchen staring at her sister on the couch. She didn't like the idea of being alone, either. What ever she had seen upstairs was still too fresh in her mind.

# 48

Not liking the idea of she and the kids being home all day with what ever seemed to be occupying the upstairs, Sadie loaded up the kids in the SUV and headed to her parent's house. Betty Jo was thrilled to see them and greeted all four with a big hug. Stan was in his usual spot watching a re-run of a recent Golf tournament. He offered a grunt and then disappeared into the master bedroom.

"Is he feeling all right?"

"Yes. He's just as miserable as always," Betty Jo said.

"We went to the store, Grandma!" Joey announced, holding up a green army man connected to a plastic parachute.

"I'm thirsty," Ami said.

Erin jumped up and down, raising her hand. "Me, too."

"You know where the glasses are," Betty Jo said.

"Don't spill water everywhere, you three," Sadie said as she followed her mother into the kitchen. An ashtray full of cigarette butts in the center of the table caught her attention. She fought the urge to say something to her mother but lost the fight.

"I thought you weren't supposed to be smoking in the house."

Betty Jo shrugged her shoulders as if it were no big deal.

"Didn't Dad's doctor say he shouldn't be around cigarette smoke?"

"Yes...but your father doesn't mind."

"It's not about him minding, Mom. It's about his health."

"Did you come over to visit me or lecture me?" Betty Jo asked, lighting up just for spite.

"Now that you've put it that way...I would really appreciate it if you would refrain from smoking in the house while the kids are over. I know it's your house, but I feel rather strongly about it."

Knowing her daughter was like a machine when she found a soapbox to stand upon; Betty Jo put the cigarette out, smiled, and turned her attention toward her grandchildren.

"I don't want you to be mad at me, Mom."

"I'm not mad—I understand perfectly. Would you like some iced tea?"

"Sure, that sounds nice," Sadie trailed off, thinking about how she was going to ask her mother if she would be able to watch the kids on Saturday night. "Mom," she hesitated.

Betty Jo poured some rum into her glass full of cola before answering. She needed the extra courage to deal with the simplest of things these days. The past few months had taken their toll on her nerves. "Yes?"

"I feel stupid for asking you this after my lecture," Sadie hesitated once more. "Would you mind if the kids stayed over with you and Dad Saturday night?" She tensed up waiting for the answer.

"I guess that would be all right. I know your father won't mind. Do they need to be brought to church?"

"No, that won't be necessary. We haven't been to church since Christmas," Sadie laughed. "Thank you, Mom."

"Oh, that's okay. You don't have to thank me. We enjoy having them over."

"I'll drop them by just after dinner...around six."

Stan interrupted the conversation by making a rare appearance in the kitchen. Since the heart attack, he had put off drinking beer in favor of iced tea. He stood in front of Betty Jo shaking his empty glass. Betty Jo promptly obeyed by filling his glass with some fresh brew.

"Hi, Dad," Sadie said. He only offered another grunt, leaving to join his grandchildren who had overtaken the television with their cartoons.

"That's the most he's said all day," Betty Jo laughed.

"You need to get out of this house, Mom. Would you like to go shopping with me tomorrow? That is, if Dad is able to be left alone."

"Oh, that would be wonderful. I could swing by in the morning..."

"No!" Sadie abruptly cut her mother off before she could think. "I mean, I wouldn't want you to drive all that way just to have to turn around and drive back the other direction."

"Oh, it's no trouble. I'll be there by ten."

Before Sadie could argue back, Betty Jo was in the living room announcing their shopping plans with her grandchildren.

The kids gave a collective cheer in response—Stan celebrated in silence to himself. He needed a break as much as Betty Jo did.

## <u>49</u>

Tara pulled up to the driveway fuming. Sadie's SUV was nowhere in sight, which meant she was going to be alone in the house. She sat in her truck staring at the front door, digging up the courage to go inside. Afraid she would see something, she didn't dare look up at her bedroom window. The need to use the bathroom, and an overwhelming thirst for a beer, pushed her to finally leave the safety of the truck.

The closed blinds and curtains gave the house a dark and lonely feel. The faint scent of chocolate chip cookies hung in the air—with it, the distinctive odor of cigarette smoke.

Tara made quick work of turning on the TV for ambient noise and comfort. She felt that if she couldn't hear any strange noises upstairs, then they didn't exist.

Throwing her purse onto the kitchen table, she accidentally knocked over the cheep, plastic napkin caddy, scattering a colorful assortment of paper napkins onto the floor. She told herself that she would pick it all up after she cracked open her first beer.

The first swig traveled up her nose. She choked on the rest, spitting it out at the sight of the now straightened caddy full of napkins. Her purse was hanging neatly on the coat rack on the opposite side of the room.

The ceiling above her head creaked. Someone was walking around in her room. She felt as if she were in a vacuum, hardly able to breathe. Beads of sweat formed on her forehead and beer dribbled off of her chin.

The footsteps continued across her room and into the hallway. From the kitchen Tara could see the upstairs landing. A shadow passed by heading into Ami's bedroom. She emitted a small whimper from the back of her throat and turned to unlock the side door, but found it already unlocked and ajar. Unable to stop her momentum, she stumbled down the steps, landing head first on to the flagstone walkway. The nearly full bottle of beer shattered, spraying Tara in the face and hair.

Sadie pulled up just in time to see Tara spill out of the house. She threw the SUV in park and ran over to assist her sister. All three children followed after their mother.

"What was that all about?"

Seeing she had an audience, Tara kept her answer simple and nondescript. "I tripped, that's all. I'll talk to you after I clear my head."

**********

Tara lay on the couch with a homemade icepack on her forehead. She was angry with herself that only one day before her first date in years she had a big bruise on her face. Thankfully, her jeans took all of the damage, saving her knees and allowing her to at least wear a dress.

The kids were all outside playing, leaving her alone with Sadie who waited patiently for the rest of the story. Tara felt a little better, but was still fuzzy on all of the details.

"So...," Sadie prompted. "What happened?"

Tara hesitated for a moment. "Let me tell you, that what ever we saw last night is definitely still up there."

"You went upstairs alone?"

"Hell no! I'm not that brave. I heard it above the kitchen, in my room, and saw it walk across the hall into Ami's."

"You saw it? What did it look like?"

Tara hesitated before she answered. She wasn't actually sure what it looked like. "All I saw was a dark shadow, like Mom and I saw all of the time when we were little...but smaller. It's hard to explain."

"You said the shadow was like the one in our old house?"

"Not really. What I saw as a kid was more stationary, like maybe the shadow from a tree outside. This thing was moving. Oh, and it smelled like somebody was baking cookies and smoking a cigarette when I walked in the house."

"Just like the other day..."

"Something else happened. At least I think it did. You see my purse hanging on that old coat rack?" Tara said, pointing toward the kitchen.

Sadie couldn't actually see the purse from where she was standing, but nodded her head just the same. "What about it?"

"When have I ever hung up my purse?"

"You don't. You usually just throw it on the table."

"That's what I did when I got home!" Tara said, sitting up with her eyes wide open. "I threw it on the table and knocked the napkin holder along with all of the napkins onto the floor!"

Sadie glanced over at the kitchen table and noticed nothing out of place except a single, blue napkin lying underneath. "Are you sure you knocked everything off of the table?"

"Yes! I threw my purse on the table, knocked all of the crap off, grabbed a beer, turned back around, found my purse had been hung on the coat rack and the holder and napkins had been neatly returned...all on their own!"

Sadie's stomach sank. "How is this séance stuff going to help?"

"I don't know."

"Then why are we bothering with…"

"Because I know if we don't try something, it will just get worse. Look at my hands...they're still shaking."

"This person does know what she is doing...right?"

"Lindsey says she does."

"I'm dropping the kids off at Mom and Dad's at around six on Saturday. When is she coming again?"

"Eight."

"Good. I'll make sure I'm home in plenty of time."

# 50

As soon as she arrived home from work, Arianna got busy surfing the internet for any possible information on the farmhouse. News was generally slow in that part of Kansas, so the search proved to be quick and simple. To her surprise, the query returned several headlined stories concerning the home in the mid-sixties.

*"Murder-Suicide in the Heart Land,"* the first headline stated, followed by, *"Victim and Assailant identified." A local woman, identified only by the last name of Stouts, was found dead in her kitchen, lying in a puddle of her own blood.*

"Holly shit!" Arianna gasped. She read further down the page, skipping through countless articles of speculation, until she reached the murder victim's bio.

*"Norah Stouts, housewife, age 35. Originally Norah Jamison of San Clemente, California, married to Gary Stouts of Garden Plain, Kansas. Mr. and Mrs. Stouts were both found dead at their residence on the evening of January 17th."*

Curious about the husband, Arianna searched further. There was only one story pertaining to him, simply stating that he had been found dead, hanging by the neck in the barn—victim of an apparent suicide. *"Mr. Stouts, a decorated Marine and veteran of the Korean War, is still the main suspect in a double murder near Lincoln and South Oliver in Wichita."*

Arianna sat for a few moments staring at their pictures, especially Gary Stouts. She was oddly drawn to him. Her eyes locked onto to his—her breath became shallow—goose bumps rose on her bare arms causing her to shiver.

"What a creep," she said to herself, snapping out of her trance.

She printed the information and clicked out of the web page. A knot formed in the pit of her stomach and with it, a feeling of dread thinking of Gary Stouts, the house, and what Saturday night might bring.

## <u>51</u>

Tara woke up on the couch twenty minutes into her alarm. The very thought of going upstairs alone was enough to make her hit the snooze and cover her head with the blanket. The thought of being written-up for being late got her moving in the right direction. She turned on every light possible—hesitating before going up the stairs. Each door had been left opened, including the linen closet.

Well into her shower, she heard the distinctive squeak of the hinges on her bedroom door. Her first thought was that it was only her imagination. After turning off the shower, she thought differently. She could hear the muffled sounds of her television through the common wall of the bathroom and her bedroom.

Toweling off, she opened the bathroom door and popped her head out into the hallway. As soon as the cool air hit her face, the noise from the television stopped. She dismissed it as just her imagination.

Not wanting to linger too long upstairs, she got dressed as fast as she was able, nearly running out of her bedroom. When she reached the top of the stairs she noticed that entire downstairs was dark. Even the front porch light that shone through the baroque glass was out.

Caught in-between fear and annoyance, she made her way down the darkened steps and fumbled for the light switch in the foyer. Able to see again, she proceeded to turn on every light in the living room and kitchen.

"What are you doing?" Sadie asked from the couch.

Tara gasped and jumped back. She stood wide eyed staring at her sister submerged in a blanket. "Shit! Don't do that to me!"

"Sorry. I didn't mean to scare you. What's with all the lights?"

Tara's face became flush from embarrassment. She felt like an idiot standing there in front of her sister searching for a good excuse. "I was about to make some coffee," was all she could get out.

"Oh, good. Could you make a whole pot?"

Tara looked at the clock to make sure she had time. She had over thirty-minutes to spare, so breakfast sounded pretty good to her, also. "You want some eggs and toast?"

"I'll make the coffee and breakfast if you go and get the paper," said Sadie.

"Fine, but don't be too slow. I have to leave by six-twenty-five."

The morning was unusually cool for June. The sun had just started to illuminate the eastern sky—washing it in pink and yellow. Tara took in a deep breath of fresh air followed by a long drag. Walking back up the driveway, her thoughts turned to tonight's date with Matt. She hoped she wasn't making a mistake. A tinge of guilt hit the pit of her stomach. She started to worry again that it was too soon after Kenny's death when the newspaper headline caught her attention.

*"Swift Jet to close its doors. Layoffs scheduled for today."*

Tara's heart sank. Her stomach became more upset than it had been. The thought of calling off work had suddenly become inviting. She walked hastily back to the house so she could read the entire article in the light.

"Eggs will be done in just a minute," Sadie called from the kitchen.

Tara ignored her and sat on the couch to read in private. To her bemusement, the headline was the only shocking part of the article. It was full of the same old business she had been hearing over the past few weeks. The only bit of useful information was the fact that notices could be handed out as early as today, but the no official number had been given.

"The goddamn paper is just as bad as my company when it comes to honesty!" Tara said as she tossed the paper onto the table.

Sadie placed a fresh cup of coffee along with a plate of buttered toast and scrambled eggs in front of Tara. She stared with her mouth opened at the headline. "Oh, no!"

"Don't believe it," Tara said, already chewing on her toast. "There might be notices handed out today. No one's sure except for the company and the union."

"Call me from work if you hear anything."

"With what? My pretend cell phone?" Tara laughed.

"Oh, yeah. Never mind. I'm sure Jared will be more than gracious in letting me know if he's lost his job. The jerk is probably counting on it so he doesn't have to work as hard."

"Don't forget, I have that date tonight, so don't make too much for dinner."

Sadie smiled. "Oh, I haven't forgotten. Do you need me to pick up a boutonnière?"

"No thank you, smart-ass. I'm gonna get going. Maybe I'll overhear some legitimate gossip before the bell."

Tara scooted back from the table and picked her purse off of the coat rack, thinking about how it ended up there. "Thanks for breakfast," she said, while taking a last sip of coffee. She was headed for the front door before Sadie could respond.

# 52

Forgetting her mother was coming over; Sadie fell back asleep on the couch, only to be awakened by the doorbell ringing and the obnoxious music of one of her children's favorite cartoons blaring through the television speakers. She shooed Joey off of her legs and made her way wearily to the front door. As promised, her mother had come over at ten, ready to go shopping.

"Good morning, sleepy head!" Betty Jo said with a big grin. Sadie couldn't tell if her mother was happy to see them, or if she was just elated to be away from her father.

Sadie yawned. "Sorry...I fell back to sleep. Tara woke me up this morning getting ready for work."

"Hi, Grandma," the children gave a collective greeting. Not one of them budged from in front of the television.

"They're not dressed, either," Betty Jo said. "I guess I should have come by later."

"Give us forty-five minutes, Mom, and we'll be ready," Sadie said. "Go and get dressed, guys. We're going out with Grandma."

Betty Jo watched with curiosity as her grandchildren grabbed their clothes from behind the couch and got dressed. Ami directed her younger brother and sister to go brush their teeth. Instead of going upstairs to use the bathroom, they both made a bee line to the kitchen sink, while Ami picked up their pajamas and folded them neatly on the couch.

"Is there something going on I should know about, Ami?"

Ami shrugged her shoulders and shook her head.

"Shouldn't you three be getting dressed and brushing your teeth upstairs?"

"Mommy told us that were not allowed to go upstairs right now and we're not allowed to ask why."

"Grandma! Grandma!" Erin shouted from the kitchen. Joey still had toothpaste all over his mouth.

"You look disgusting, Joey. Go and wipe your mouth," Ami said.

Erin shouted again. "I know why we can't go upstairs, Grandma!"

"Shut up, Erin! You're going to get us in trouble!"

"In trouble with whom?" Betty Jo asked.

Joey ran back into the living room with a clean face. "We can't go up there because it's haunted, Grandma!"

"Joey! You weren't supposed to say anything!" Ami said.

"Haunted? What do you mean haunted?"

"There's a ghost that lives in Aunt Tara's room and the hallway. I overheard Mommy and Aunt Tara talking about it," Erin said. Ami was close to tears. She knew her mother would be angry with all of them for telling.

Betty Jo's thought's turned to what Stan had seen in Ami's window. She knew if she thought about it much longer she would start crying herself.

"I think that will be enough talk of ghosts for now. We don't want to upset your mother." Walking into the kitchen, she excused herself and poured a tall glass of water.

Footsteps above the kitchen startled Betty Jo. She followed the sound with her eyes until Tara's bedroom door opened with a squeak. She walked back into the living room, looking in the direction of the stairs. She thought she saw someone walk across the hallway toward Ami's room but couldn't be certain.

Sadie walked out of her bedroom drying her hair with a towel. "What are you looking at, Mom?"

"Oh, nothing." Betty Jo couldn't help but stare—waiting to catch a glimpse of something. "Are you ready, dear," she asked turning toward Sadie. "I guess not."

"Give me ten more minutes and we'll be out the door," Sadie said while inspecting her children's progress.

Betty Jo returned to the kitchen and took some ibuprofen. What had promised to be a pleasant day had started to be more stressful than a day home with Stan.

\*\*\*\*\*\*\*\*\*\*

Halfway to the mall, Joey couldn't help himself from blurting out what he had told his Grandmother. An argument erupted in the backseat, resulting in Ami pinching her little brother on the arm. All of the crying and screaming nearly caused Sadie to loose control of the SUV.

"Whoa, you three! Knock it off, already," Sadie hollered.

Betty Jo sat quietly in the front seat trying to block out the commotion. The ibuprofen hadn't touched her headache which was getting worse the longer she was in the vehicle with her grandchildren.

Erin proudly told on her sister and repeated what Joey had said. Infuriated that her mother knew about the supposed ghost, Sadie grounded all three for being trouble-makers. The last thing she needed was a slew of questions. She had visions of her mother and Tara holding their own secret séance like they had when they were children.

Five-minutes later, Sadie pulled into the mall parking lot. Betty Jo still hadn't uttered a word, giving Sadie a sense something was bothering her mother.

"What store would you like to go into first, Mom?"

"Well...hmm," Betty Jo paused. "I didn't know we would be coming here. I assumed we were going to the larger mall on the east side of town."

"I'm sorry, Mom. I don't recall ever mentioning where I was planning on going," Sadie said. The back of her neck became red—she could feel the blood rush to her arms.

Betty Jo sat in the passenger seat looking straight ahead. Her facial expression clearly displayed her dissatisfaction with their shopping destination. Her headache now moved behind her left eye.

"Since we're here now, which store would you like to go into first?" Sadie said.

"If you really want my honest opinion, Sadie. I'd much rather go to the larger mall on the east side."

"They have the same stores in this mall! What does it matter?" Sadie's face had become fully flush. The anger welled up inside until she snapped. "Fine!" she shouted, throwing the SUV in drive, barreling out of the parking lot, and heading back toward the highway.

All three kids started to cry. Betty Jo sat in silence, also tearing up. The angry emotion Sadie was feeling changed into guilt upon realizing she had made her mother and children upset.

"I'm sorry that I snapped. We've all had a rough night."

"Well obviously, if you're all having to sleep downstairs," Betty Jo said.

"Oh, yes...that."

"Is there something you're not telling me?"

Sadie hesitated with her answer. The last thing she wanted to do was to discuss ghosts with her mother. "I...it's hard to explain. I really don't want to discuss it in front of the kids."

Betty Jo let it go. She sat staring ahead—unresponsive, with a tight, fidgeting grip on her purse. She had changed her mind about wanting to go shopping with Sadie, but felt she had no other choice.

Seeing she wasn't going to get anywhere with her mother, Sadie continued east down Kellogg Road without saying another word.

# 53

Tara waited anxiously in her bedroom for Matt to arrive. The need for privacy and space to get ready overruled the fear she had of being upstairs alone. She turned the television on for company—burying her thoughts in what to wear and what shade of lipstick to use. She had bought two sundresses the weekend before she had moved in with Sadie, but wasn't sure about either. Frustrated, she yelled for her sister to come and help.

Sadie hesitated for a moment before ascending up the stairs. "What?" she said, exasperated at the bedroom door.

"Which one?" Tara asked, holding both dresses up for inspection.

"I thought you decided on the floral one?"

"I know, but..."

Sadie laughed and shook her head. "You'll look great in either. Just put one on. He'll be here in a few minutes."

The realization that her first date in years was about to show up sent Tara into a mini panic-attack. The fact that she had dreaded tonight, more than she had looked forward to it, was something she had kept to herself. She prayed that Matt would do most of the talking.

"I better get back down there with Mom. I left her on the couch with an ice pack on her head."

"She's still here? She better not stick her nose into my business tonight."

"I doubt that she'll even get off of the couch. She's pretty frazzled after today."

"I still can't believe you told her that we had a ghost in the house. You know how she gets."

"It wasn't me—I swear! The kids blurted it out. Ami, with her radar, must have overheard us talking...again. When we got to the East Mall, Mom just broke down crying."

"That's because you yelled at her."

"Well, yeah..." Sadie felt embarrassed. "That, and then she started to rant about Dad seeing things and how she knows it has to be true, and how we need to get the kids out of the house because it wasn't a healthy environment."

"She's really changed since Dad had his heart attack…and I know Dad thought he saw Kayla in Ami's window. I also know you've all been trying to keep it from me."

Sadie was speechless. She was afraid Tara would start crying just before her big date, or worse, call the whole thing off.

"Don't worry. I'm not going to call off the date," Tara said as if she had just read Sadie's mind. "I'm not that upset. I figure that Dad misses Kayla as much as the rest of us do, and Mom is just sad for Dad."

"I'm sorry I tried to keep it from you."

The doorbell rang sending Tara back into her panic mode. "Shit… he's here!"

"Don't worry; you'll be just fine."

Tara stared in disbelief at the woman standing in front of the full-length mirror. The sulking blue-collar worker, whose usual attire consisted of an oversized tee-shirt and faded blue jeans, was gone. In their place was a still youthful twenty-eight-year-old girl. Her hair had been curled and pulled back showing off her double pierced ears. She dabbed on a little perfume, and then forced a smile thinking she would scare him for sure.

The front door was shut firmly, rattling Tara's window. She took a deep breath and walked out the door, returning to take one more look. Satisfied, she walked gracefully down the stairs and into the waiting gauntlet consisting of her mother, sister, nieces and nephew, and finally Matt.

"Hi," Matt said. He looked overwhelmed by the audience. "Here's the box of odds and ends I promised." He handed the box to Tara who then handed it over to Sadie.

"I'm ready if you are," Tara said, anxious to get out from under the microscope.

Matt smiled and told the crowd goodnight. Both he and Tara breathed a sigh of relief when the front door was closed behind them. He held the passenger side door of the same new truck Tara had seen from her bedroom window. She climbed in and breathed in deeply in an attempt to calm her nerves.

As soon as Tara and Matt drove away, Betty Jo decided that it was time for her to leave as well.

"You're leaving? Are you sure you're okay to drive?"

"I'll be all right," Betty Jo said, never glancing Sadie's way. "I just wanted to stay long enough to see Tara off." The slight scent of cigarette smoke lingered just above her head, making her mouth water. She took a cigarette out of her purse and lit it before she had walked out the door, infuriating Sadie.

"Mom..." Sadie started and then hesitated. She felt that she had already brow beat her mother enough for one day. "The kids and I will see you tomorrow night at six."

"That will be fine," Betty Jo said. She got into her car, not bothering with the seatbelt, and drove away.

"What's wrong with Grandma?" Ami asked.

"Grandma just has a headache...that's all." Sadie sighed as she watched Betty Jo's car disappear around the corner of the drive. "Come on, let's get inside."

## <u>54</u>

The drive to the restaurant was very pleasant for Tara. Matt did most of the talking, discussing everything from work, to how crowded and built-up Wichita had become over the past ten years. She could tell he was nervous which put her more at ease. The only subject he hadn't breeched was that of prior relationships and she was glad for it. She wasn't ready to be that personal. It would take quite a few more dates for Tara to open up.

The parking lot was packed, but unlike so many of the chain restaurants, this restaurant required a reservation. Tara waited for Matt to open her door. As they walked through the front doors, she felt as if she was in a vacuum—she could only hear herself breathing. Every face was a blur with the exception of Matt's.

The couple was seated in a far corner table just big enough for the two of them. Tara noticed one detail immediately—no children. Then she looked at the prices on the menu and discovered why. She looked up at Matt and smiled, deciding she would order on the lower side and blame it on her not being that hungry.

"Don't worry about the prices, Tara. Next time we'll do drive-thru to balance my wallet," he said with a smile.

Tara laughed nervously at his comment; she needed a beer to calm her nerves. Trying not to draw attention, she scanned the dining room to see what the other customers were drinking. Below replicas of French Impressionist paintings, each table had either water or wine. Nonchalantly, she picked up the wine list thinking it was the cocktail menu.

"Would you like a glass of wine?" Matt asked.

Tara's face became flush. "No thank you," she said, putting the menu back down on the table.

"I'm more of a beer drinker myself," he said.

Tara perked up. For a while she thought she had gone on a date with Mr. Straight and narrow. "What do you drink?"

"Whatever's on sale that week," he laughed.

"Oh, that's my favorite brand, too."

"If you would like, after dinner we could go over to that big pool hall off of Kellogg and grab a beer or two."

"Or three or four," Tara laughed again. Feeling more at ease, she decided to take Matt's advice and not focus on the price, instead ordering the prime rib.

\*\*\*\*\*\*\*\*\*\*

The conversation was light, but relaxed as Matt and Tara drove west from the east side of town. The taste of prime rib still in her mouth, Tara longed for a cigarette and a cold beer, or even a piece of gum. She wasn't sure how long she could keep up the good girl routine and not break down and light one up.

As promised, Matt pulled into the parking lot of the pool hall. The couple grabbed a free table in the corner away from the crowd and settled down to a game. Tara let Matt order a beer for her. It felt odd to be doted on, but she didn't mind. She was thoroughly enjoying her first actual date as an adult.

When Matt pulled a pack of cigarettes out of his shirt pocket, Tara gasped. He saw the look on her face and thought that she was offended that he smoked. "Oh, sorry. You don't smoke, do you?"

"Yeah! I'm just waiting for you to offer me one!"

They both laughed at how much they had in common already. Tara almost snorted beer out of her nose causing Matt to laugh even harder.

After her third beer, Tara became bold. "So why didn't your brother finish the kitchen? If I was in the house restoration business, that would have been the first room I gutted."

Matt's face became flush. He had held himself to just one beer—taking small sips so he could keep his head.

"Remember? He got sick and couldn't finish it. He couldn't work at all, so we had to sell your house and one other in Cheney to keep up with the bills."

"He had a nervous breakdown, right?"

"I guess you can call it that. More like hallucinations."

"Hallucinations? Hallucinations of what?"

Matt thought Tara was extremely persistent, especially when she drank. He liked her more when she was sober. "It will just worry you if I tell you."

"Oh, you can't worry me," she said while placing two more quarters into the slot on the side of the pool table. She finished off her beer and announced it was his break and time for another round.

"And it's your rack," he smiled, ignoring her request for another beer.

"Well? What did he see?"

"Um…it was actually a combination of different things. He claims that whenever he was in the kitchen, the floor above his head creaked and the upstairs doors continuously opened and slammed on their own." He paused, readying himself to break the rack. "After a few days, he also noticed the distinct scents of perfume and cookies baking."

Matt didn't notice Tara had turned pale. He was too preoccupied with taking his next shot. What she was hearing validated what she and Sadie had seen.

"Oh…and the one thing that sealed the deal for him was that woman in the kitchen."

Tara's throat had become dry. "What woman?"

"He claims that there was some skinny, blonde woman that stood in the kitchen calling him a bastard and yelling for him to get out. Whenever he tried to answer her, she just disappeared." Matt had already cleared half of the balls off of the table before he looked up at Tara. "He's on some really strong drugs now and…"

Tara ran to the lady's room before Matt finished his sentence. She was going to be ill and it wasn't going to wait. He instinctively ran after her, although he didn't know what he was going to do if he caught up. If there was a second date, he would definitely choose a place that didn't sell beer.

***********

Tara emerged from the lady's room fifteen minutes later. Matt was waiting patiently for her at the bar keeping watch over her purse. She insisted that he take her home and didn't say another word on the long drive back to the farmhouse.

Once parked in front of the house, she didn't wait for him to open her door. He followed her up to the front porch in an attempt to say goodnight. She fumbled with her keys before successfully unlocking the door.

"I'm sorry the night didn't end on a nice note. I would still like to see you again...that is if it's all right with you," Matt said, trying to make amends.

"Maybe," she said under her breath. "Your brother's not crazy. He doesn't need medication—believe me."

Tara walked in to the house, closing the door behind her. Matt stood on the other side thinking through Tara's last statement. Drained from their rollercoaster date, he concluded she must be or had been on medication herself much like his brother. That would explain the change in moods. Satisfied with his quick evaluation, he decided one date would be more than enough. There were other prospects out there—he didn't need to waste his time with this one.

## 55

Tara woke to an argument over who got to eat the last of the *Captain Crunch* and *Sponge Bob* elating over his new spatula. She was on the couch, covered by an afghan and still wearing the floral sundress she had on from the night before. Joey announced that Aunt Tara looked like a raccoon. Ami, without taking her eyes off of the cartoon, told her brother not to be rude.

"Hey, sleepyhead. Late night?" Sadie said.

Tara covered her head and told Sadie to leave her alone. The noise from the kids, cartoons, and the bright morning sun had made her feel nauseous. She just wanted to lie in her own bed and sleep away the day, but was too scared to. What Matt had told her the night before not only frightened the hell out of her, but also made her physically ill. It was a clear confirmation that she and her sister were not imagining things. If the séance didn't solve anything, she would have no choice but to move out and leave Sadie with the mortgage to deal with on her own.

Sadie brought her a cup of coffee. The smell turned her nausea into the urge to vomit. She leaped off of the couch and ran in to Sadie's room, making it to the toilet just in time.

After spending ten minutes splashing water on her face, she emerged from the bathroom. Her head was pounding and her body ached. Sadie sat waiting on the edge of the bed. Tara tensed up knowing she was about to get barraged by an array of questions.

"Are you okay? I know, stupid question. Do you have a hangover?"

"No," Tara scowled. "I just don't feel good right now."

Not convinced her sister was telling the truth, Sadie continued with her questioning. "Was that guy a jerk to you? Did he try to take advantage?"

"Matt was nothing like that. He was really nice," she said, looking at the floor. "He probably won't be calling again, though."

"What happened? Did you get in a fight?"

"No. After dinner, which was great, we went over to that big pool hall off of Kellogg. I had a few beers and got a little loud and pushy..."

"Like you always do," Sadie finished Tara's sentence.

"If you're going to be condescending, then I'll just go take a shower and get the hell out of here!"

"I'm sorry. I'll shut up."

"Like I was saying...I got a little pushy and started asking questions about the house and why Matt's brother didn't bother working on the kitchen."

"Did he get mad at you for prying?"

"No, he told me why," she said, tearing up and covering her face.

"He got sick—right?" Sadie couldn't even think of what Matt might have said that would make Tara this upset.

"Matt told me things. Things he shouldn't have known about this house—like we have been experiencing."

"What have we been experiencing?" Sadie asked—then realized what Tara was talking about. "You mean what we saw upstairs?"

"Upstairs, the perfume smell, the woman in the kitchen. Everything! They put his poor brother in the hospital and then on medication because they thought he was losing his mind! Is that what's going on? Are we losing are minds?"

Sadie sat dumbfounded on the bed. She didn't know what to say. Her mind was numb. All of this time, she hadn't believed anyone about what they had seen nor heard in the old farmhouse. She wasn't even convinced that she had seen what she did. The séance was more like a placebo for her sub-conscious and Tara's wild imagination. Now it seemed all too real.

"Are we, Sadie? Because if that séance doesn't solve our problem, then I don't think I can live here anymore."

# 56

Arianna stood next to the time clock with her purse and keys in hand, waiting for the clock to click over to five. The bright, yellow apron she was forced to wear, with the *From the Earth Foods* logo on it, was draped neatly over her arm. The owner of the store peered from behind his desk and over his reading glasses, watching her every move. He never complained when a young, attractive girl was hired. Her long, blond hair fascinated him. He secretly hoped that she would come in to work with it down instead of tied back.

Still annoyed by his newest employee's actions, the owner cleared his throat and pointed to his watch. Arianna knew his policy about clock sitting or loitering in the store at the end of the shift—she just didn't care. All she had to do is walk by him time to time, playing with her hair, and all would be forgiven.

As soon as the big hand moved forward, she was clocked-out and out the door. The heavy weight of oppression that she felt every second while in the store was lifted.

The short five-minute drive down the street to her apartment seemed to take forever. Arianna hated to be late for anything, except work. Rounding the corner, her heart sank at the sight of Kate Seraphine waiting on the sidewalk. Her wavy, amber hair was pulled back exposing her typically tranquil face. A necklace of Celtic knotwork hung delicately around her slender neck. She rarely had a cross word to say, but Arianna felt apprehensive none the less. She knew her mentor took the business of contacting spirits seriously and didn't like to be rushed. They would need at least three hours to prepare and had no time to waste.

Arianna became more anxious when she didn't see Lindsey's escort parked in front of the apartment building. She had to work overtime to get her to agree to helping with the séance. After what she had experienced at the farmhouse, she had no intentions of ever going back.

"Hey, Sephers," Arianna greeted. "I left work as soon as I could. You haven't been waiting long, have you?"

"No. Just got here," she said. "I don't see Lindsey. Is she still able to make it?"

"I hope so," Arianna said, peering down the street in hopes of seeing her car. "Do you want to come inside and get started? I printed off the history I found on the house."

"Oh, no. I mustn't be influenced by anything associated with the house. I need to have a clear mind. With Lindsey, there will be five—three known and two unknown. All women?"

"Yes. Sadie and Tara are sisters."

"Good. It would have been nice to have a little more diversity, but I've found siblings are for the most part total opposites of one another. Having them both there should make up for having all the same sex."

Arianna breathed a sigh of relief as Lindsey's car appeared around the corner. Even with Sephers' help, she knew she didn't have the experience needed to successfully conduct the séance. She wouldn't be the medium tonight—that was Sephers' job. But in order to first make and then maintain contact, her mentor needed two experienced and spiritually strong people to help keep their clients emotions under control. Just a brief moment of hesitation on the part of either sister would result in the connection being broken and the possibility of losing the ability for making contact again. If their clients were truly in need of cleansing their home, everything had to be perfect, right up to the type of table they would use.

Both women turned as Lindsey's car squeaked to a stop. She emerged from the Escort with a large shoulder bag stuffed with what she needed for tonight and a change of clothes for tomorrow. She had planned on staying over at Arianna's house for the night. Séances had a way of zapping all of her energy and giving her a feeling of euphoria that at times could last for hours.

"You had me worried for a minute, girl," Arianna said. "I didn't think you were going to make it."

"Neither did I. My mother tried to change her mind at the last minute when she found out what I was doing tonight. She tried to tell me that I was doing the Devil's work and I would surely go to Hell if I died tonight. I just handed her the baby and diaper bag, and then calmly explained that I was going to Hell anyway, because of all the trouble I got into growing up."

Arianna laughed at her best friend's explanation. She had known Lindsey since the fourth grade and had been arrested twice with her—once for breaking and entering and once for possession of marijuana. Although both women had given up a life of drugs and crime, each of their families had a knack of reminding them of who they used to be with great malice toward their feelings.

Sephers was indifferent to their past. Though she had never even tried a cigarette, tasted liquor, or committed a crime, she held no judgment over Lindsey or Arianna. She had great respect for every person no matter what path he or she may have chosen. Her father had been a Methodist minister most of his life, teaching his daughter to never judge another—that was God's business.

"If you're both ready, we need to get started," Sephers said. "Our clients will most likely be nervous wrecks, so it's our business to make sure we are calm and in total control of our minds and bodies," she explained while leading the two women up the stairs to Arianna's apartment.

***********

The box of chocolate *MoonPies* on Arianna's kitchen counter drew a big smile from Sephers. Arianna knew they were her favorite and made a point to buy some as a thank you for conducting that night's séance.

The three women set right to work ensuring they had all of the materials necessary. Lindsey proceeded to light some incense while Sephers produced a single white feather from a black velvet bag, as well as hickory carved jewelry box containing cinnamon and frankincense, and a small crystal vile of holly water. She placed the items alongside two hollowed candles adorned with hardened drips of wax from several lightings.

"I have some newer candles, Sephers. Those look a little worn out," Arianna said.

"They'll do just fine for tonight," Sephers said. "They're like a couple of old friends. We need to create an environment of comfort. Newer objects, such as unlit candles or sticks of incense seem to create tension."

"What about the robes?" Lindsey asked. "Did you have some for Tara and Sadie?"

"Oh, that's right," Arianna said. "I have them hanging in my closet. I have mine plus three more just in case. I also have the tablecloth."

Sephers nodded in approval. She closed her eyes, exhaled, and opened a *MoonPie.* "Time to relax, ladies. We have a long night ahead of us."

Lindsey placed the lit incense in the pot of a house fern hanging in the corner of the small dining area. She, along with Arianna and Sephers, changed into their flowing, cotton white robes. The garments were void of any markings. Sephers had designed them herself to heighten the comfort level of the medium and spiritual advisors, as well as their clients. She even went as far as assuring they had all been washed in *Dreft laundry detergent* to avoid any unknown allergic reactions. Any distractions, including the discomfort of one's own clothing, must be eliminated—so no undergarments were allowed. All focus must be on the spirits they would be attempting to contact.

Arianna placed a CD she had burnt of ancient Celtic music into her boom box. The melodic tunes relaxed the mood further. The three women sat on the floor in a small circle, closed their eyes, and cleared their minds of all distractions. The recorded music was purposely two-hours long, acting as an alarm clock for the group so they wouldn't accidentally be late in leaving for the farmhouse.

## <u>57</u>

Tara and Sadie had just returned from their parents when Arianna's four-door Cutlass drove up the gravel drive a good half-hour early. Upon exiting the car, Sephers walked straight over to the barn without a glance toward the house, or a word spoken to either Lindsey or Arianna. Something disquieting called to her—a secret hidden deep within the shadows. She stopped short of the two large doors, taking heed not to make contact. Observing the secured pad lock, she laughed at the presumption that it would keep whatever dwelled within from leaving.

Sadie stepped out onto the porch to greet her guests. Lindsey cordially introduced Arianna and then pointed out Sephers. At first glance, Sephers appeared to be a child to Sadie. She was a small woman, barely over five-foot tall—her cotton robe rippling softly in the Kansas wind.

"She'll be over in just a moment," Arianna said. She does this with every house we visit. It's sort of a ritual."

Sadie felt oddly out of place with the two strikingly beautiful women standing before her. Their skin was perfect— their hair radiant. She became jealous of their little figures— she hadn't had a figure since high school. She didn't mind Lindsey when it had been just she and her daughter visiting, but now she had three attractive women to look dowdy next to.

She and Tara had always thought themselves as plain looking, but pretty none the less. They had been lectured early on by their mother that it wasn't looks men were after, but rather strong personalities, common sense, and the ability to cook decent meals.

"Men will grow weary of beauty when they find it doesn't pay out in the kitchen," Betty Jo often said. Neither Tara nor Sadie bought into her philosophy.

Tara stepped out onto the porch behind Sadie. Still feeling nauseous and scared, she stood with her arms crossed tight, letting Sadie do most of the talking. Arianna felt her discomfort. She calmly remained focused, knowing that any emotion, good or bad, could upset her to the point that she would be ineffective.

"Hey, Tara. How's it going?" Lindsey asked.

"Not good. What's with her?" she said, gesturing toward Sephers.

"She's performing some sort of ritual," Sadie said with a chuckle.

"She's just getting a good feel for her surroundings," Arianna said. "You're the one that I talked to on the phone. It's Tara, right?"

"Yeah."

Arianna had the feeling tonight would be more difficult than most. Both of her clients seemed uptight and untrusting. If she and Lindsey were unable to calm them down, Sephers would have no chance of making contact.

Sadie started to have second thoughts about letting the three women invade her home—especially the one by the barn. She didn't see the purpose of it all. If it wasn't for Tara's hysterics, she would have put the strange occurrence upstairs out of her mind and moved on with her life.

Tara invited Arianna and Lindsey inside, leaving Sadie no choice but to go along. Arianna told them not to worry about Sephers. She would find her own way in.

"How was your date?" Lindsey asked Tara, trying to break the tension.

"Don't ask," she semi-laughed.

"I think my sister is still suffering from a hangover—but you'll never get her to admit it," Sadie smiled.

Tara lightly backhanded Sadie in the arm. "Ha, ha!"

Sadie allowed Tara the honors of giving the tour of the downstairs' rooms. Upon entering the kitchen, Arianna felt herself pass through a thick wall of energy. An overwhelming feeling of grief flooded her body. She heard the faint sound of a woman crying—pleading for her life. The stains in the old, yellow tile floor popped out at her as if they were still fresh.

"Are you all right?" Lindsey asked.

"I'll tell you when we're finished. I can't..."

"I know. Sephers told me to keep a clear mind, too."

The tour continued upstairs'. Lindsey hesitated momentarily, and then followed up the wooden steps. The second floor was eerily quiet. A thin layer of dust had accumulated on the hardwood floor from lack of any substantial traffic. Each room also had a thin layer, giving the appearance of abandonment. This time Lindsey sensed something. She wasn't as accustomed to using her third eye as Arianna and Sephers were. She thought of herself as more of a tagalong then someone claiming to be clairvoyant—yet she knew she felt fear and someone very young.

"That's about it for the house, except for the attic and cellar," Tara said.

"Can we see both?" Arianna asked.

"There's really nothing in either space. The attics too small to be a useful place to store anything and the cellars' too damp," Sadie said. She'd already grown tired of the spiritual parade and was looking forward to their guests leaving.

"It will just take a moment," Lindsey smiled at Sadie.

Tara grabbed the rope hanging from the trap door and pulled forcefully exposing the dark hole in the ceiling and with it stale, cool air. Arianna took note of the attic's temperature. It should have been a lot warmer in the middle of June.

"The ladder unfolds," Sadie pointed out from a distance. Her accident was still fresh in her mind for her to get too close.

Lindsey climbed up the ladder, poking her head through the opening just long enough to acknowledge what she had suspected. Someone was hiding in the far corner of the attic—a young girl was with them.

"Anything?" Arianna asked.

"It's definitely an attic," Lindsey said, folding the ladder.

"I'll get it. The hinges were just fixed and it's pretty stiff," Tara said.

Sadie bounded down the stairs ahead of the other women. "I'll get the key for the cellar lock." She caught sight of Sephers through the living room window wandering around the backyard and thought she looked like an escapee from some insane asylum.

The lock to the cellar was rusted and difficult to open. Tara helped Sadie open the two large doors so Lindsey and Arianna could look inside. White paint chips and dirt fell onto the bare ground surrounding the base of the cellar entrance. The strong odor of mildew permeated their nostrils. Arianna assessed quickly that they needn't venture in— she had seen enough.

"I believe we're ready to set-up," Arianna said. "Are we missing anything, Lindsey?"

"Just Sephers. I'll let her know we're going inside."

Tara helped Sadie close and locked the cellar doors. They wiped the dirt from their hands onto their blue jeans and led the way back into the house. Waiting patiently for them was Sephers who was standing in the middle of the living room, surveying the area with closed eyes and out-stretched hands. She crouched down and removed the black velvet bag containing the single white feather from her woven, canvas satchel. She proceeded to draw a circle in the air around her and then placed the feather at her feet.

"What is she doing?" Tara asked out loud. Arianna touched her gently on the arm and whispered for Tara to be patient.

"The table needs to be placed exactly over the feather. Be certain not to touch the feather with the table or any part of your body. I will place it in its proper place when we are ready to begin."

"Would it be possible to remove the leaf from your kitchen table, Sadie? It's better to have a round table rather than an oval one, so we can all form a perfect circle," Lindsey said.

"I guess that will be all right. Let me de-crumb and de-peanut butter it. The kids just ate dinner and I haven't had the chance to clean it off."

Tara stood alone in the corner thinking the events taking place in front of her was nothing like she had imagined it would be. She knew Lindsey had always seemed a little off center—she just hadn't expected Arianna to be way out there, too. Then there was this Sephers person. Tara thought she looked just like an angel with her wavy hair, porcelain face, and flowing white gown—but acted like a total nutcase. If nothing convincing happened tonight, Sadie would be all over her, never letting her forget about it. Her thoughts switched to the apartments five-minutes from work, and what she would need to move in.

"Tara," Sadie snapped. "I've said your name three times already. I could use your help with this table."

Without another thought, Tara was in the kitchen wiping down the table and removing the leaf. Lindsey helped to carry the table out to the living room where Sephers was waiting. Arianna stayed back, not wanting to experience what she had in the kitchen again.

The three women lowered the table, placing it directly over where the feather had been laid. Sephers placed the feather back into the velvet bag, outreached her arms toward the ceiling, and spoke some words in Latin that Arianna didn't even understand.

"Your idea, not mine," Sadie whispered to Tara.

Sephers took a deep breath and made her way over to her two hosts. "Hello. I believe it's time that we were properly introduced. My name is Kate Seraphine." She held out her hand to Sadie who in turn reached-out with her own. She was unable to remove her gaze from Sephers' hazel green eyes.

"I will be the Spiritual Medium tonight, meaning I will be the one making contact as well as communicating with the spirits. You've already met Arianna, and of course are good friends with Lindsey. They will both be assisting us to ensure all goes as planned."

"Oh...um, I'm Sadie and this is my sister, Tara. It's very nice to meet you, Kate." Sadie couldn't believe how nervous she had just become.

"Kate's fine, if you wish. Most of my friends call me Sephers. I know all of this must look a little strange to you. There are certain things, however, that must be done if we are to have a successful contact this evening. Most important: we all need to be relaxed and have our minds clear and bodies comfortable. Arianna and Lindsey will help you both with the transition from the tension you're now feeling, to a place of peace and harmony within your mind and spirit. We brought along with us a garment for each of you to wear. They are identical to what we are already wearing—and if I must say, very comfortable."

"You don't mean I have to wear one of those nightgowns?" Tara said. Sadie jabbed her slightly with her elbow.

Lindsey gently took Tara by the arm and guided her into Sadie's bedroom, leaving Sadie alone with Arianna and Sephers.

Sadie thought she found an opening to explain how she really felt about it all. "I know you all mean well and believe wholeheartedly in this spooky stuff. I just don't want to mislead you in thinking that I do. I'm just going along with it for Tara's sake."

Sephers took Sadie's hands in hers. "We all have our own beliefs. Some are taught and some come naturally. As children, we are taught that the sky is blue and the grass is green—who are we to argue? My father instilled in me the glory that is God and the importance of salvation. I still to this day have a personal relationship with Jesus Christ. I know in my heart that he lives within me. I also know there are other forces in the universe and other worlds—planes of existence we can't begin to fathom. That doesn't mean they don't exist. Trust me when I say this to you: I will make contact with any spirits that dwell in this house. I will seek a resolution so you and your family can once again live comfortably in your home. All I need from you and Tara is to be trusting." She gently squeezed Sadie's hands. "Can you do this for me?"

Sadie shuddered. She felt an immense weight lifted just listening to Sephers speak. He voice was soothing with a hypnotic quality.

"Come on, Sadie." Arianna took her hand. "I'll help you get ready."

## 58

Tara felt embarrassed and exposed walking out of Sadie's bedroom wearing the white robe, even though she was completely covered from her neckline to her ankles. She just didn't understand why she couldn't wear her own clothes—she was comfortable already. None of it made sense. The séances she had seen on TV all had people wearing their street clothes.

Arianna sat with Sadie on the couch applying fragrant, lavender hand lotion. Sadie had her eyes closed and actually seemed relaxed. The CD of Celtic music was playing softly in the background.

"Come have a seat, Tara," Lindsey said, leading her by the hand to the far side of the couch.

"This seems more like a boutique than a séance," Tara said.

"Close your eyes and hold out your hands," Lindsey said softly.

The aroma of lavender seemed to encircle their heads—radiating through their bodies. Tara could feel each of her tense muscles relax as if a gentle wave was washing over her entire being. All of the negative thoughts in her head seemed to dissolve with each gentle stroke of Lindsey's hands on hers. She took a deep breath and surrendered.

Sephers, seeing Arianna and Lindsey had their clients under control, ceremoniously went about the business of setting up for the séance. The white linen tablecloth was unfolded and carefully placed over the kitchen table. The two candles were placed approximately one-foot apart. Between them, the hickory carved jewelry box, containing cinnamon and frankincense, sat with the lid closed.

Taking no chances of being disturbed by outside parties, she disconnected the downstairs telephone. Being thorough, she ventured into Sadie's bedroom in search of more phones. Finding the jack empty, she continued her search upstairs'.

Walking down the darkened hallway, Sephers felt an extreme change in air pressure. The feeling of being watched was overwhelming to her acute senses. Three emotions fought for attention—fear, sadness, and anger. The third was quickly turning into rage that was aimed directly at her. Not wanting to linger, she made her way into Tara's room and disconnected the final telephone from its jack. Usually prideful of her ability to deal with any situation with calm reserve, she felt for the first time a situation was slipping out of her control.

She exited Tara's room and proceeded down the steps with great haste. The slight odor of cookies baking caught her attention. The silhouette of a woman standing in the kitchen startled her. Sephers closed her eyes and breathed in slowly to clam her nerves. Upon opening them, the vision and odor were gone.

The music and scent of lavender helped to sooth her nerves, too. After turning all of the lights off, with the exception one small lamp by the television, she sat at the table, prepared the elements, and started the process of purging her mind of all personal and negative thoughts from what she had just experienced.

Unlike many of the spirits Sephers had made contact with in the past, the spiritual occupants of this house seemed to be crying out to her—asking for help—begging for protection. She tried to suppress their cries so not to be influenced by their emotions. A weak moment could leave her open for manipulation or worse—total possession.

The spirits she had just encountered didn't worry her—she would be able to cast them off without effort. What was dwelling in the barn was frightening—so much that she had trouble removing it from her thoughts. She knew for certain that it must be driven-out, but after what she had felt, she started having doubts about her abilities to safely do the job. This entity was different from any she had encountered before. It was full of hate and had the calculating mind of a predator.

## 59

Tara and Sadie were each led by the hand off of the couch. They felt the most relaxed that they had in years. Floating on air with each step, their minds were clear of all distractions. Every muscle in their bodies felt like gelatin.

Sephers waited patiently for Arianna and Lindsey to seat their hosts. When they had all taken their places, she lit the candles, opened the jewelry box containing cinnamon and frankincense, and placed the feather directly in front of her. She asked all four to close their eyes while she prayed to God for spiritual guidance and protection.

The holy water was sprinkled around the table and then on each spiritual adviser as well as their hosts. Both Tara and Sadie winced when the cool liquid made contact with their skin. Sephers asked all to join hands and to keep their eyes closed.

"Do not let go of one another's hand. To do so would break the circle and all connections with the spirit world," Sephers said. She had purposely sat Arianna in between the two sisters to encourage them both in case the spirits became active.

Tara started to tremble. The edges of her world turned gray and then began to spin slightly, making her feel as if she would pass-out. Lindsey squeezed her hand for encouragement, as did Arianna.

Aware that one of her hosts may not last, Sephers started the séance. "Spirits within the sound of my voice—spirits that dwell within this house—please make your presence known. We are here to offer hope. We are here to set you free from your earthly bonds."

No response.

Taking a deep breath, Sephers tried once more. "Spirits within the sound of my voice—spirits that dwell within this house—please make your presence known. We are here to offer hope. We are here to set you free from your earthly bonds."

After the second try without results, Sadie became disenchanted. The feeling of complete relaxation started to ebb away. Hearing Sephers calling for the spirits reinforced her feeling that the whole séance thing was corny and a waste of time.

Always patient, Sephers called to the spirits a third time and then a fourth. As if a window had been opened, a strong gust of wind blew through the room on the fifth invitation. Both Tara and Sadie gasped. The candles flickered as a warm, soft breeze encircled the table, caressing the cheek of each woman seated at the table. The room then filled with an overwhelming aroma of cookies baking. A feeling of love and warmth washed over them.

Sephers started to speak—her voice filled with joy. "Hello, Emma. It's very nice to make your acquaintance." She was grinning ear to ear.

The living room became filled with a dim glow. The warm air turned frigid and then warm again. If Sadie wasn't experiencing it first hand, she would have surely thought it was a trick.

"Emma. Who is here with you?" Sephers asked. The breeze picked up nearly blowing one of the candles out. Lindsey tensed up waiting for the answer. The breeze died down and Sephers asked once again. "Emma. Who is here with you?"

Sadie's pots and pans settled in their cupboard. The noise caused everyone at the table, except for Sephers, to flinch. A single door slammed upstairs and then a second. Two sets of running footsteps traveled from one side of the second floor to the other, and then descended down the steps leading to the living room.

"There they are," Sephers smiled. "Emma is a beautiful spirit who was equally beautiful in life. Are these two your boys?" Sephers paused, waiting for an answer. "Yes they are very rambunctious," she laughed. "Emma has apologized to both Sadie and Tara for her boy's behavior...and also to Lindsey, but they are claiming it wasn't them hiding in the closet." She paused again—seeming to go into a trance.

The fact that the spirit knew the events that had taken place earlier in the week threw Lindsey off guard. Visions that she had tried to suppress of that night in the hallway came rushing back to her. She knew for certain that it was not a boy peeking out at her, but indeed a small girl.

"The boys are saying that she's hiding because she's afraid," Sephers continued. "She's so sad..."

Arianna felt her, too. Tears trickled down her cheeks. She seemed to be calling for her mother.

"There's another soul with her, but he's well hidden. He's in the furthest, darkest corner of the house so they won't find him. I believe he's the girl's father....who are "they, Emma? Are you still with us?"

The air turned cold and then warm again. A single set of footsteps ascended the stairs. "She and her boys haven't seen anyone else. Only the girl and her father have. They're very frightened of who ever "they" are and seem to be reaching for Tara. They have an earthly and spiritual bond with her."

Tara tensed up, startled and then resentful of the implications that the spirits in question were her late daughter and husband. She tried to suppress the tears welling up in her eyes. The thought of them actually being alone—frightened and hiding in the darkness, troubled her deeply.

"Who's leaving, Emma?" Sephers asked the spirit. "She is telling me that someone in this house is upset...they want to leave because they are terrified of what they can't explain. They feel very guilty about their feelings, but feel they have no other choice." Sephers jerked and took a deep breath. "It's Tara...Emma wants me to tell you that she and her boys mean you no harm. Please don't be frightened—Sadie needs you more than she is able to admit."

Both Tara and Sadie's faces became flush from embarrassment. Tara wanted Sephers to move away from the subject. Sadie was stunned that all of this was actually taking place in her house.

"The girl is crying. Emma, are you still with us? All I can hear is the girl. She is telling me to be quiet. They can hear me talking...Emma doesn't know what the girl is talking about...be quiet, they can hear you...she's still crying..."

Once more, the air became frigid. The scent of cookies dissipated—with it the feeling of love and warmth. The color vanished from Sephers cheeks. She tightened her grip on Lindsey's and Sadie's hands and then relaxed again slumping forward. "She's gone, but not far. Emma's gone."

The air in the room became cold as a mid-January night. A fine mist from their breath rose above the table. The scent of jasmine drifted into the room. Gentle at first, it quickly became pungent.

Movement in the shadows caught Arianna's attention. Bare feet scuffed lightly along the hardwood floor. "Sephers, there's someone else in the room," she whispered.

A great weight of depression settled down upon the group, conjuring up visions of lost loves and broken promises in each of their minds. Tara had become so distraught, she was certain she could hear both Kayla and Kenny calling to her.

"Who has entered? Who is trying to make contact?" Sephers cried-out. "I am here to serve you. Please speak through me."

Sadie was now truly frightened. She too had heard Kayla's and Kenny's voices. The urge to let go—to break the circle—to run out of the house was great, but she knew that would be impossible with the grip Arianna and Sephers had on her.

"Please speak through me," Sephers cried-out again. "I am here to serve you."

A silhouette of a woman was huddled in the darkness of the foyer. She was rocking back and forth sobbing—calling for someone that was apparently lost.

"Norah?" Sephers called. "I'm here for you, Norah. Please speak through me."

Arianna held her breath at the sound of the spirit's name. It was the name in the newspaper articles. Norah was the woman found dead on the kitchen floor. A feeling of dread came over her, followed by complete helplessness.

The sobbing turned into outright cries of anger. Sephers face had become ashen. The spirits emotions had started to take hold. "Why do you mourn, Norah? Who is it that you mourn for?"

The spirit stood up as if responding to Sephers' questions, and faced the group at the table. She walked toward them and then stopped short of the kitchen entrance. Long, blonde hair hung in her face, cascading past her breasts and ending at her midriff. She was wearing a long, flannel nightgown that had a large, dark stain from her chest down to her feet.

"What are you doing here?" the spirit asked without the aid of Sephers. "Why are you here?" Her tone was cold and un-friendly.

Sephers face had grown pale and her lips blue. "Norah. You need to find peace. The person you are looking for has crossed over. They are waiting there for you there. You need to go to them now."

The spirit drew closer. Arianna opened her eyes. She had a clear view of her pale, sullen face—eyes full of rage. She knew it was time to end the séance—it was growing far too dangerous.

Sephers again attempted to speak with the spirit. "Norah. You need to find peace. The person you are looking for has crossed over. They are waiting there for you there. You need to go to them now."

The spirit of Norah Stouts wailed. "He's not there! He's not there! How could you do this to me, you bastard?"

An ear-piercing cry emitted from the spirit, reverberated through the room. Sephers eyes rolled back in her head as she slumped forward, seemingly unconscious. The spirit charged at the table extinguishing the candles and knocking all but Sephers onto the floor—breaking the circle.

"Tara?" Sadie called out. "Are you all right?"

"I think so."

Tara had landed on top of Lindsey and was awkwardly trying to get up. Lindsey lay unconscious.

"Sephers. Is it over? Did it work?" asked Arianna.

Sephers was still face down on the table. The feather had fallen at her feet.

Arianna felt something caressing her hair. Upon turning around, she found herself face to face with the spirit of Norah Stouts.

"I thought if we broke the circle the connection would be lost!" Sadie declared.

"Oh, my god...Sephers. What do I do?" Arianna cried out. Her voice was trembling. "Sephers?"

Norah caressed Arianna's face with her long, thin fingers, admiring the smoothness of her almost perfect skin. Jagged, sharp finger nails traced the outline of her cheeks down to her jaw line, scrapping their way to her equally smooth neck.

"Are you the one that stole him away?" Norah asked. Her gravelly voice made Arianna whimper with fear.

Mesmerized by her piercing blue eyes, Arianna stood trembling—unable to look away. A burning sensation just beneath her ribs spread slowly throughout her body. The pain was slight at first and then exploded with great intensity. "The bastard killed her!" she said before passing out from the pain.

The air rushed out of the room, sealing all five women in a vacuum. Sadie collapsed onto the floor and lay unconscious next to Lindsey. Sephers woke suddenly. She sat up, serene, chanting in tongues, and breathing normally as if she were in her own eco-chamber.

Tara witnessed the strange events as if she were peering through hazy glass. Feeling dizzy, she closed her eyes. An immense force pressed against her thin frame. The world rushed by, transporting her to a familiar place. She was back in her bedroom—back in her dream.

*A gentle gust of cold wind blew through her open window, carrying with it flurries of snow. The distant cry of a woman in mourning drifted through the dark winter night, growing louder and then softer with each variant breeze. A small hand touched Tara's arm. She knew instantly that it was Kayla. Her heart breaking, she began to weep.*

*"Mommy," the sweet child's voice called. "Make her stop, Mommy. He's going to hear her." The words echoed in Tara's ears.*

*"Make who stop, baby?"*

*"The lady, Mommy. The lady that's been calling my name and Daddy's. Please make her stop."*

*"Daddy's here?" Tara gasped. "Kenny?" she called, searching the room.*

*"Daddy ran away. He's afraid that he'll find him, too. He doesn't like that woman talking. Make her stop," she pleaded once more.*

*"Who's going to find him? I don't understand." Tara was becoming hysterical. "Kenny! Where you? I miss you so much."*

*"It's too late. He knows," Kayla cried.*

*"I don't understand. What are you afraid of?"*

*"Run, Mommy! Run!"*

*The two large doors flew open, banging against the side of the barn. Tara rushed to the window to see what had happened. A tall, dark figure walked across the driveway—the new fallen snow crunching beneath his boots. He looked up at Tara as if telling her that he knew she was there.*

The front door slamming shut startled Tara out of her dream. Bitter cold air blew through the room. Snow flakes formed a fragile wreath around Sephers' head. She was still chanting.

The overwhelming need to run and get out of the house pushed Tara off of the living room floor. The hollow sound of heavy boots walking up the front steps and onto the wooden porch stopped her in mid-stride. Her heart pounding, she stood frozen with fear in the middle of the foyer. She watched with great apprehension as the antique doorknob turned and the front door swung open.

Filling the doorway was the dark silhouette of a large man standing over six-feet in height. As he approached, his face and body came into focus. His jaw was square and solid—cleanly shaven with a pronounced clef. Deep-set, blue eyes were accented by a classic Roman nose. His dark, wavy hair was cropped short. On his overdeveloped right bicep he bore a single tattoo of the United States Marine Corps insignia. Tara couldn't help but to stare—not out of fear, but out of pure animal attraction. She wanted him more than anything she ever had in her twenty-eight-years of existence. All thoughts of her daughter and Kenny vanished from her mind.

As he passed by, she reached out—her hands passing through his body. "No!" she cried. "Don't go!"

The stranger approached Sephers. She was still chanting—her face had a look of euphoria. An aurora of amber surrounded her instantly with the gentle touch of his hand. She stood with outstretched arms, ready to receive him in her embrace. He wrapped his thick arms around her small, frail body—lifting her up and against his powerful chest. The moment their lips met, Sephers face became emblazoned with a bright, white light, which traveled over the entirety of her body. As the stranger's kiss became more passionate, so did his grip. Each one of her ribs was stressed to the point of snapping. Sephers could feel her body dying. She was powerless to break his spell. With each heavy breath, her heart slowed—body turned cold. Her arms fell limp and fingers turned blue from lack of blood flow.

The brightness of the room brought Arianna back to consciousness. She sat up and took notice of Sephers limp body in the stranger's arms. His face was familiar, but she couldn't place where she had seen it. As his grip tightened, the tattoo on his bicep became more evident. The Marine insignia with its eagle, globe, and anchor popped out at her. It was if a nightmare had come to life. Dead or in the flesh, Gary Stouts was standing in the middle of the living room squeezing the life out of Sephers.

"Let her go!" Arianna tried to yell, but the spit had gone from her throat. She swallowed hard and tried again. "Let her go! You're killing her!" This time she was loud enough for him to hear.

Gary turned his gaze from Sephers to Arianna. His brow furled at the realization that she knew who he was. Bluish veins in his arms and forehead bulged. His face turned a dark shade of green—his eyes narrowed, becoming solid black orbs. The bright light retracted inward, building into a tight ball of energy in the center of his body.

Released from his constrictive hold, Sephers struck her head on the table, and fell listlessly to the floor. Unable to come to her aid, Arianna stood paralyzed under the hypnotic control of the light. Her long hair stood on end—each strand pulled by the static charge building in the room. Her breathing became taxed until it stopped all together.

The walls of the house shook—the floor vibrated beneath their feet. The spirit of Norah Stouts rose up reaching toward the light. She cried out, pleading for her husband. Tara felt her essence brush past her. As the two spirits joined, the bright ball of energy exploded into and through Arianna, knocking her backward into the entertainment center. Each light in the house was instantly illuminated, and then extinguished just as quickly, plunging the women into total darkness. Tara could hear Sadie and Lindsey breathing but little else. Afraid to move, she called out to Arianna and Sephers for help.

Within seconds, the power was restored. The small light by the television came back on and the microwave beeped to life. Tara shook Sadie's shoulder in an attempt to wake her up and then did the same to Lindsey. Crawling over to Arianna and Sephers, she found both women bruised and bleeding but otherwise breathing. She got up on her feet and turned on every light in the first level of the house. Her next thought was to call 911. She pushed the talk button on the cordless phone, but received no dial tone.

"Damn it! What's wrong with the phone?" she yelled. "Sadie. I need your cell phone. Sadie! Wake up!"

Tara's shrill voice shocked Sadie back to consciousness. Disoriented, she laid on the floor trying to focus. All she could see was a bright blur of lights. "Tara? What the hell is going on? Where are the kids?"

"The house phone is dead. Where did you put your cell phone?"

A loud crash upstairs made both women jump. A woman's cry and the deep resonating voice of a man's laughter sent a chill up their spines. "What was that?" Sadie asked, her voice wavering.

"Oh, my God," Tara cried. She recognized both voices from her dreams. "Bastard..." she mouthed.

Before Sadie could ask her sister what she had just said, the clear, distinctive voice of a woman yelled the same word. Neither Tara nor Sadie could breath. The taste of fear overwhelmed their senses.

"We need to leave...we need to leave now!" Tara said.

The sound of her frantic voice woke both Arianna and Sephers.

"What's going on? What happened to my head? It's all wet and sticky." Arianna asked. She brought her hand close to her face, discovering it was covered with blood.

"Shit! You're bleeding," Sadie said.

Sephers sat up holding her own head in her hands. She had a deep cut just above her right eyebrow. She could still feel the spirit's lips on hers—the taste of blood lingered on her tongue. Her ribs ached from his constrictive grip. She could also still sense his presence. A feeling of panic deep within her soul that she had never experienced before urged her to leave. Gary hadn't forgotten about her and intended to finish what he had started.

"Are you all right?" Sadie asked.

Sephers turned toward her. Her eyes were moist and full of fear. She shook her head, feeling she had lost complete control over the situation. "We've got to get out of this house."

"Sadie! The phone! We need to call 911!"

The temperature in the room dropped once again. A hulking, dark figure appeared on the steps. Tara scooted back kicking Lindsay in the head and waking her up as well. Sadie turned to see what Tara was looking at. Gary Stouts was moving fast in their direction. Following close behind were over two-dozen murky figures extending their hands out to him.

Sephers could feel each one of their pained souls crying out—pleading for Gary to love them. It was too much for her to handle and once again she started to lose control. "Ladies, I believe now would be a good time to leave."

Arianna drug herself off of the floor and grabbed a hold of Sephers' hand. "Lindsey? Are you okay?"

"I think so. What's going on?"

"It's time to go. Someone help me with her!"

Sephers' eyes rolled back in her head and her body convulsed, causing Arianna to lose her grip. Before she hit the floor, Tara and Sadie caught her. Along with Arianna all three managed to drag her to the front door and out of the house.

Only Lindsey remained. Gary turned his gaze toward her and grinned. She knew better than to stick around and jumped to her feet, hobbling out the door as well. A cold rush of air forced its way past her—with it over a dozen screams of anguish.

Sitting on the walkway, staring blankly at the house, Sephers announced that the séance was officially over.

"No shit!" Lindsey said.

"Lindsey! Come on, babe. Gotta go! Help me get Sephers into the car… shit, the keys!"

Sadie realized she also had left her keys in the house. "I'll go in with you. I need mine, too."

Both women sprinted back into the house and re-emerged frightened and out of breath. "Is he still in there?" Tara asked wide eyed.

"No! It smells like goddamn chocolate chip cookies in there!"

Arianna jumped into her car and tore out of sight before Sadie could start her SUV. "Do you think we'll ever see them again?" Tara asked.

"I doubt it."

"Good, because I didn't pay 'em."

Sadie laughed and then cried. "I need to get my kids and then sell that stupid house!"

Tara sat in the passenger trembling. A flood of emotions washed over her as she envisioned Kayla and Kenny being frightened and alone. Deep inside she felt as if none of them were through with what ever had control of the house. Sadie felt it as well. She drove east as fast as she was able, hoping every thing was fine at their parent's house.

# 60

Betty Jo sat on the back porch with both of her Shiatsus, a full glass of rum and coke, and a cigarette. She loved the warm summer evenings in Kansas, especially when she was left alone to enjoy them. She had situated the three grandchildren in her bedroom watching a two-hour cartoon, and Stan planted in his chair watching baseball.

Far to the southeast, a distant thunderstorm was putting on a brilliant display of lightning. She turned her chair toward it and proceeded to enjoy the show. To her disgust, the phone started to ring, followed by Stan bellowing and complaining that it wasn't being picked-up soon enough to suit him. Before she could open the sliding-glass door, Ami appeared with the telephone in hand and a worried look on her face.

"Who's on the phone, Ami?"

Ami looked straight down at the floor as if she were embarrassed to say. "It's Daddy. He sounds really drunk, Grandma."

"Oh, dear," Betty Jo sighed, taking the phone out of her granddaughter's hand. "Jared. This is Betty Jo. What did you need?"

Slurring his words, Jared demanded that Ami was put back on the phone. "What happened to Ami? I was talking to Ami!"

"Maybe you should call back tomorrow when you're sober."

"Maybe you should mind your own damn business, you old bitch!"

Betty Jo's voiced quivered. "Don't you take that tone with me, Jared!"

Concerned the conversation was getting out of hand; Stan made his way into the kitchen and took the phone out of his wife's shaking hand. "Jared. This Is Stan Carter. Just what do you think you need?"

"All I want is to see my kids! That bitch daughter of yours is keeping them from me!"

"The name calling needs to stop, sir. It's not necessary. As far as seeing the children, even I know you have visitation scheduled for next weekend."

"Sadie won't even return my phone calls. I left her tons of messages tonight and she doesn't even have the decency to pick up the phone!" He was close to crying.

"She and Tara are busy tonight."

"Is she over there? Can I talk to her?"

"She's not here, Jared. Just leave it alone. You'll get to see the kids next weekend." The line went dead much to Stan's relief.

"If he calls again, Betty Jo, just hang up. The kids don't need to be burdened with that mess tonight."

Knowing her peaceful night was just a memory; Betty Jo called Erin and Joey into the kitchen for some ice cream. The ice cream was really for Ami in an attempt to get her father off of her mind. She prepared a generous portion of rocky road for each of them. A slave to his appetite, Stan joined them at the table. Betty Jo knew he couldn't resist and had a large bowl served up for him as well.

"Coffee?" he asked, pausing in between slurps.

"I've got half of a fresh pot," Betty Jo said as she poured him a cup.

"Thank you, Grandma!" Ami yelled. Erin and Joey copied their big sister.

"You're welcome!" Betty Jo yelled back, making them all laugh.

Betty Jo heard the noise first. To her maternal instincts it sounded like a child was crying. With all of the grandchildren accounted for, she dismissed it as just the TV in the master bedroom being left on.

The strange sound also caught Ami's attention. She sat wide-eyed with her spoon halfway to her mouth. "Grandma. Did you hear that?"

"It's just the TV, sweetie. Your movie must still be on," Betty Jo said while rinsing off the ice-cream scoop.

"Grandma! The cat won't leave me alone!" Erin said.

Stan yelled and stamped at the fat orange tabby, sending it scurrying outside with the dogs. "Damn animals!"

After taking one more bite of her ice cream, Ami excused herself and took the half-finished bowl over to the sink.

"Too much for you?" asked Betty Jo.

Ami nodded. "I'll turn off the TV, Grandma," she said, bounding out of the kitchen.

Approaching the hallway, the crying became clearer. She knew it couldn't be the movie. She had seen it too many times before and had almost every line memorized. It was hollow and lonely sounding, but also familiar. Although she should have been frightened, Ami felt oddly at peace.

The crying stopped, leaving a vacuum of silence in its place. Ami stood at the end of the long hallway peering down toward her grandparent's bedroom. The television was off and their room was dark. In the middle of the floor, halfway down the hall, something small and red lay on the carpet. Ami gasped and ran over to it. "What's this doing here?" It was her plastic ring—the very one Kayla had given her.

Joey cried out in protest because Erin had dipped her spoon into his bowl of ice cream. The squabble drew Ami's attention back toward the kitchen—the squeaky hinges of her grandparent's bedroom door brought it right back.

A large, dark figure moved past the doorway. Ami stood paralyzed with fear. Unable to scream or cry, she could only whimper. Then someone whispered in her ear. The voice of a small girl called her by name.

"Erin?" Ami answered back.

A smaller figure moved past her and joined the other. Goosebumps grew on Ami's arms as the temperature quickly dropped. The slight scent of cigarette smoke tickled her nose. Once more there was someone crying.

"Who's there?" she asked. Her lips were trembling. It was becoming increasingly hard to hold her bladder.

"Where's Mommy?" the small voiced asked, barely audible. "I want my Mommy," it cried.

Ami started to cry also—she knew who the voice belonged to—she knew for certain it was Kayla. "I want my Mommy, too," she wept.

Betty Jo heard Ami crying. Concerned, she hurried out of the kitchen, walking hurriedly through the living room. She found her oldest granddaughter standing in the middle of the dark hallway facing the bedroom. "Ami. What's wrong?"

Relieved by the sound of her grandmother's voice, Ami turned and ran to her sobbing. Her body was freezing cold in Betty Jo's arms. She was trembling from head to toe.

"What happened, Sweetheart?" Betty Jo felt as if her own heart was about to break.

Before Ami could answer, a familiar voice called from the end of the hallway. "Grandma?"

Betty Jo's stomach dropped. Standing before her was the granddaughter she had lost two-years prior. Her mind was racing, trying to find an answer to what was actually happening.

"Please help me. I'm so scared. He's going to find us. He knows where we are."

"Ami. Go and get your grandfather," Betty Jo pleaded. Ami refused, afraid to move from her grandmother's protective grasp.

Before Betty Jo could utter another word, the dark silhouette of a man emerged from the bedroom. He was hunched over with his arms wrapped tightly around himself. His face was blurred and partially covered with long, stringy hair. The aroma of stale cigarettes surrounded him—streamers of smoke arose from his tattered clothes. Horrified by the vision, Betty Jo could hardly breathe.

The argument between Erin and Joey turned into an all-out fight with Stan in the middle. He tried unsuccessfully to keep the two apart. Squeezing past her grandfather, Erin grabbed hold of Joey's arm and pinched hard. He immediately erupted into tears and took off running through the living room and toward the hallway.

The two dark figures moved forward, prompting Betty Jo to walk backward in an attempt to retain her distance. On her third step back her feet were tangled up with her grandson's. She and Ami fell, narrowly missing Joey, and landing hard onto the floor. A loud crack followed by a sharp pain radiated through Betty Jo's left hip. She screamed out in pain, prompting Stan to finally get out of his chair.

"What in the hell?" Stan said, seeing his wife lying helpless on the floor. "Get away from your grandmother, damn it all!"

Ami got back up looking back down the hallway. Stan turned on the light revealing nothing out of the ordinary. "Grandma...they're gone!"

"I think I broke my hip," Betty Jo said, wincing in pain.

"Go get the phone, Ami," Stan said. "Ami! Are you listening to me? I said run and get the phone. Your grandma's hurt!"

Before she could obey, Tara and Sadie came bounding through the front door. "Mom? Dad?"

"We're in the hallway!"

"Oh my God! Are you okay, Mom?" Sadie asked.

"No she's not! I need you to call 911," Stan said while on the verge of tears.

"I think I broke my hip."

Sadie ran and grabbed the phone out of the kitchen while Tara stayed with their parents. Stan was now on the floor with his wife holding her hand. Tears streamed down his bristly cheeks.

Movement in the darkened doorway of her parent's bedroom caught Tara's attention. "Is there someone else here, Dad?"

"No! Did Sadie call?"

"She's doing it right now..." Tara said while moving toward the bedroom. "Hello?"

"Please don't go in there, Aunt Tara," Ami said.

Tara hadn't noticed her huddled against the wall. The look on the child's face frightened her as much as all she had seen that evening. Instinctively, she knew she shouldn't get any closer to the bedroom than she had already gotten. Someone was waiting there for her.

"Ambulance is on its way," Sadie announced from the kitchen.

Sadie's voice echoed inside of Tara's head. Whoever was hiding in the dark had her complete attention. Faint at first, Tara swore she heard a child crying. As the crying grew louder, Tara knew it was Kayla. Her mournful cries tore through her heart. They were unmistakably her daughter's. This time, she knew it wasn't a dream. The reality of it all was more than her frayed emotions could handle. Overwhelmed with grief, she fell to her knees just as she entered the room. Through her tear blurred eyes she saw two figures—one big, one small—approaching. "Kenny? Kayla? Is that really you?"

"It's too late, Mommy. He found you."

"Oh, no..." Tara wept. "Kenny? What am I supposed to do? Kenny?"

Kenny's spirit backed away and then disappeared without uttering a word.

"Please don't go. I miss you so much." Tara's face was drenched with tears. The temperature in the room turned bitter cold. Her fingers and toes became numb in an instant. The feeling of complete helplessness was replaced by pure fear. "God...please help us," she prayed.

The small, shadowy figure of her daughter's spirit approached and knelt down inches from Tara's face. She stared directly into her mother's red and swollen eyes, uttering one final plea. "Run!"

Just as Sadie had returned to the hallway, the power went out plunging them all into total darkness. A frigid wind blew past Stan and Betty Jo, knocking Sadie into the corner of the wall and down to the floor. Joey ran and hid under the kitchen table along side Erin.

"Where are my children?" Sadie said in a fretful voice.

"I'm right here, Mommy," Ami said, huddling close by her grandparents.

"Where are Erin and Joey? Where are my babies?" she cried.

Erin cowered behind Joey—she didn't want to look at the stranger standing in the middle of the living-room. His distorted face and hulking body scared her. Joey wasn't frightened. He had seen the man before. He felt an odd attraction to him and a sense of calm in his presence.

The Spirit of Gary Stouts motioned for Joey to come to him. Joey obeyed, walking cautiously, but wearing a big grin. The air between them was icy cold. Joey shivered—his teeth chattered—his lips turned blue. Gary held out his massive hand, whispering to Joey that he had nothing to fear.

"No, Joey! Don't go near him!" Erin yelled. "Stay away from my brother!" she screamed. "Mommy!"

Joey didn't hear his sister. Gary's deep, resonating voice drowned her out. He was about to take his hand when Erin screamed again, drawing the attention of Gary. His face turned from a blurry, gray mass to stark green—every crease accentuated—his eyes, deep red and sunken in.

Joey froze at the hideous site towering above him. He wanted to run back under the table but was unable to move his legs.

"Run, Joey!" Erin cried. "Mommy!"

"Erin?" Sadie called. "Erin, where are you?"

"I think I see her under the table," Ami said. "I'll get her."

Tara also heard Erin's screams. Frantic, she crawled out of the bedroom. "We need to leave now! We need to get out of this house!" she yelled hysterically. "He followed us here. We need to leave now!"

"Are you sure? What are we going to do? Where's Joey?"

"Tara! For God's sake get a hold of yourself. Your mother's in a lot of pain. Why don't you do us all a big favor and go and wait outside for the ambulance.

"You don't understand," she said in a husky, quivering voice.

"I don't know what's gotten into you two, but it needs to stop now." His chest had started to tighten. "Tara! Do as you were told and help guide the paramedics when they finally arrive."

Tara didn't acknowledge her father's words. All she could hear was Kayla's voice telling her to run over and over in her head.

Peering into the living room, she saw Erin huddled beneath the table and Ami crawling to her. In the middle of the room, she saw Joey standing and looking up. Even in the dark, Tara could tell he was frightened. Something deep inside was pushing her to get to him any way possible.

Sadie finally realized what was taking place and jumped to her feet. "Stay away from my babies!" she screamed.

Her sister's voice woke Tara out of the trance like state, prompting her to move. Before she could reach the children, a bright burst of energy knocked her back to the floor. She felt as if a dozen people were sitting on top her—their weight forcing the breath from her lungs.

Seeing Tara lying helpless, Sadie ran full speed toward her children. As if panicked by her closing in on him, Gary hesitated, turning momentarily before transforming into a blinding orb of light and slamming directly into Joey. The force of impact sent the young child sailing through the air, throwing him hard against the sliding glass door.

Just as Sadie reached the girls, the electricity was restored. "Where's your brother?"

Tara was released and ran over to Joey, cradling him in her arms. "I've got him!"

"What in the hell are you two doing? I said to go outside and wait for the ambulance to arrive so they don't drive right by the goddamn house!" Stan yelled. He was completely oblivious to what had just occurred.

"Mommy?" Joey cried.

"I'm right here, buddy."

"Was that Daddy?" Ami asked. "Was he mad at us?"

"No. That was a stranger, sweetie. Your Daddy would never hurt you guys."

The faint wail of a siren was a welcoming sound to both Stan and Betty Jo. "Tara. Now would be a good time," Stan bellowed.

"You okay?" Tara asked Sadie. Sadie nodded and thanked her.

"Tara!" Stan sounded off once more.

Tara ran outside just as the ambulance was coming into view. A new sense of energy put a bounce in her step. She felt inherently different as if a tremendous weight had been lifted. The monster, who ever he was, was gone.

Sensing someone was standing beside her, Tara turned, but saw no one there. Instead she felt a tug and a squeeze on her hand. She had a sudden feeling of euphoria and then a release of anxiety. She knew instantly it was Kayla and Kenny. They had never left her and knew that they never would.

\*\*\*\*\*\*\*\*\*\*\*

With Tara and her parents gone on their way to the hospital, Sadie snuggled down on the couch with her children.

"Mommy?" Erin said.

"Yes, sweetie?"

"Is the bad person really gone?"

"Yes," she said and kissed Erin's forehead.

"What about Grandma? Is she going to be okay?" asked Ami.

"I hope so. Grandpa and Aunt Tara are going to make sure the doctors take good care of her."

"Why are you wearing that funny dress?" asked Erin.

"It is funny looking, isn't it?"

"Can we call Daddy?" Joey asked with a hoarse voice.

"Maybe tomorrow," Sadie said, stroking her son's hair.

She kissed each one of their heads and turned up a Sponge Bob cartoon they had all seen at least a dozen times, but still thought was as funny as the first time they had seen it.

# Epilogue

The first few weeks following the séance, neither Sadie nor Tara wanted to return to the farmhouse for any great length of time, so they found it convenient to help their parents with their everyday needs while Betty Jo recovered from her broken hip. With tensions growing thin in the heat of the summer, Sadie and the kids moved slowly back home one day at a time, eventually moving all the way back  just in time for the start of school. By the time Betty Jo was walking without the aid of a walker, a battle weary Tara had moved back in with Sadie as well.

Although the occasional door shutting by itself from time to time and the scent of cookies baking caused the two sisters to be a little jumpy, the recurring nightmares that had tormented Tara were completely gone, as were the visions of Gary and Norah Stouts. Before long, Tara and Sadie had both placed the past events away in the back of their minds. Only Kayla and Kenny remained in Tara's thoughts. She took great comfort in knowing they were both near.

The first of August saw the end of employment at Swift Jet for both Tara and Jared, and with it their income. The layoff was long in coming resulting in two-thirds of the workforce losing their jobs. Tara took full advantage of a federal retraining program by enrolling in nursing school.

Jared applied and landed a job working for a fast food restaurant in an attempt to lower his child support payments. The strategic move didn't work, resulting in his having to work two jobs instead of one. In addition to his long list of woes, his drinking problem had turned from occasional intoxication to full out alcoholism. He would often show up for visitations already drunk and would be asked to leave due to his out of control, belligerent mouth.

With Jared's visits becoming more and more infrequent, Sadie thought his absence would prove to be more positive for the kids than negative. The girls seemed to get along better, but Joey was a different story. He missed his father and was openly resentful when Jared didn't show up for his peewee football games. He increasingly took his pent up aggressions out on fellow teammates at practice and opposing players during the game, resulting in the coach requesting that he not return. His foul behavior spilled over to the classroom. The usual targets of his aggression were smaller boys and girls.

At home he developed a fixation for the barn. After several failed attempts at keeping him out, Sadie gave in and let him play in there with the understanding that it was to be kept clean and that the doors were shut each night to keep the feral cats out. Joey made it his own private getaway. Ami and Erin avoided their brother as often as possible and never once ventured over to or into the barn. He was mean and played too rough.

While sitting on the porch swing, enjoying the warm autumn day, Tara and Sadie heard a disturbing noise coming from the direction of the barn. Something was screaming. The cries echoed against the house, sending chills down both women's spine. As abruptly as the screaming had started, it stopped. Sadie dismissed the noise as just an animal caught by one the many cats in the area. After seeing Joey emerge from the barn with a smirk of satisfaction on his face, Tara wasn't convinced. There was an odd familiarity about her nephew's persona. She had become distrustful of the child—often catching him just staring at her as if working out some problem in his mind. He had been transformed from a loving little boy into a hellion that no one wanted to associate within just a few months.

Sadie had been quick to lay the blame of Joey's bad behavior on his father, claiming that he took right after Jared, but Tara knew better. Although Joey favored his father's looks, he didn't posses his outgoing personality. There was coldness about him.

Enjoying a rare day off from class, Tara decided to see just what Joey had been up to in the barn while Sadie and the kids were in school. She hadn't seen the inside since they had moved in, so nothing struck her as particularly odd or out of place, with one exception: the air didn't have the dusty, stale smell one would expect. Instead it smelled of fresh dirt.

In a far corner she found a clawed hammer, spade, flat screwdriver, and a spooled piece of rope, all neatly placed next to a pair of worn work gloves lying on a workbench. Finding the excessive cleanliness odd, she followed some footprints in the dirt floor from the workbench to various stalls and then out the side door.

Unable to fathom what her seven-year-old nephew had been up to past few months, she returned back to the house and ventured up to his bedroom. Unlike his sister's rooms, his was quite clean. Even his bed was made. Although faint, Tara thought she smelled the same odor of fresh dirt she had in the barn.

An all too familiar feeling of being watched prompted her to leave the room. She closed the door darkening the hallway and stirring her imagination. The entirety of the upstairs seemed to come to life, igniting a sense of dread that pushed Tara down the stairs and out the front door. Goosebumps covered the entirety of her body as she struggled to catch her breath. Out of the corner of her eye she thought she saw the large doors of the barn swinging slowly open.

Not wanting to acknowledge what was taking place around her, she braved running back into the house to grab her purse and keys. A visit to her parents was a long time overdue. Pulling out of the driveway, she made a promise to herself that the next time she had time alone she would definitely spend it with someone else.

\*\*\*\*\*\*\*\*\*\*

Watching the house come into view, Joey knew something was amiss. He impatiently waited for his mother to unlock the front door and ran inside ahead of his sisters, not stopping until he made it to his bedroom. The door was closed—something his mother had made strict rules against. He opened it carefully finding nothing had been disturbed. The barn flashed through his young mind prompting him to drop his book bag, bolt back down stairs, and run out the front door.

Finding the side door ajar caused his stomach to jump. Almost too afraid to enter, he first peeked inside. The barn was empty as far as he could tell. He headed straight for his work table to make sure it hadn't been disturbed. To his horror the dirt surrounding it was covered in adult size footprints. He followed them to each stall and corner of the old, wooden building. He checked the furthest stall last. He had been in there just the day before, but was unable to finish before his mother called him into the house for dinner.

To Joey's relief, the rotted plank of wood hadn't been disturbed. As if on a mission, he ran over to the side door and locked it to keep other trespassers from entering. He then took the work gloves off of the table, grabbed the spade and walked calmly back to the furthest stall. Once there, he removed the plank of wood revealing a blood encrusted, ball of fur and mutilated flesh. He stood confidently looking down at his latest accomplishment, knowing the ground beneath the barn held many secrets.

Late eighteenth century

An ominous darkness engulfed the Pine Barrens in the heart of southern New Jersey. Death had wrapped its cold fingers around the neck of a small village just a day's ride out of Philadelphia. With a dozen already slain, there was nowhere else to turn but to God. The Devil had come home and refused to leave.

Hand held lanterns cast an eerie glow. A low, booming voice recited Bible verse with the eloquence of a Sunday sermon. Mournful cries resonated throughout the surrounding woods—a disquieting song.

The Reverend Meeks walked backward through the dense undergrowth leading a dozen men bearing an eclectic array of farming tools and muskets. His voice unfaltering, he looked nervously about and to the men's worried faces.

The pungent odor of sulfur engulfed the small band, permeating their nostrils and burning their throats. A high pitched scream cut through the thick summer air causing one of the men to turn and run.

The group came to the edge of a clearing—a small cemetery lay at its center. Pausing, the reverend bowed in prayer and raised a wooden cross high above his head. The earth trembled beneath their feet, followed by a volatile wind that knocked all but the reverend to the ground. A large black shadow moved across the far end of the clearing and disappeared into the trees.

The reverend summoned a single man from the group handling a large brindle Mastiff. The men parted, allowing a wide berth for the massive dog. At the command of the reverend the animal was released. Growling low in its throat, it charged toward the trees where the dark shadow had entered. Crashing through the brush the mastiff emitted a bone chilling cry and then fell silent.

Holding up his hand, the reverend urged the men to be patient. Out of the darkness the Mastiff reappeared. Its muscular body stood rigid—its head lowered—eyes glazed and frothing at the mouth. It charged full out heading for the group and lunged at the reverend. Before the dog could reach him, a musket roared to life. The lead ball tore through the animal's body, dropping it to the ground.

Seeing the dog was still alive, the reverend called for two of the men bearing axes; instructing them to remove the head before the animal died. Even as the head fell free from the body, its powerful jaws snapped at the air.

"Into the bag while it still moves!" the reverend said, throwing a black velvet bag to the men. "Now into the ground before the demon breaks free! God have mercy on us all if it does!"

In the center of a circle of twelve headstones, the bag containing the still squirming head was thrown into a deep hole. A large, flat stone placed over top entombed whatever lay beneath it.

As the sun rose in the east, a serene peace fell over the woods. The reverend stood over the stone and said one final prayer. In the eyes of the villagers, he had restored hope to their lives—restored their faith in God. Only he knew the truth. The terror that had gripped the small village had been downcast, but not vanquished. Its essence still dwelled within the Barrens. The Reverend Meeks could feel it—hear it calling to him—a chorus of mournful cries as the wind traveled through the pines.